About the (

David Ahern grew up in a theatrical family in Ireland but ran away to Scotland to become a research psychologist and sensible person. He earned his doctorate but soon absconded to work in television. He became a writer, director and producer, creating international documentary series and winning numerous awards, none of which got him free into nightclubs.

Madame Tulip isn't David Ahern's first novel, but writing it was the most fun he's ever had with a computer. He lives in the beautiful West of Ireland with his wife, two cats and a vegetable garden of which he is inordinately proud.

To find out more about Madam Tulip and David Ahern, visit
www.davidahern.info

Madam Tulip

DAVID AHERN

MALIN PRESS
Ireland

MALIN PRESS

First published 2016
This paperback edition published 2016

A catalogue record for this book is available from the British Library

ISBN 978-0-9935448-0-4

Malin Press, Ireland

Malin Press is an imprint of Malin Film and Television Ltd
Registered in Ireland 309163

Acknowledgements

My special thanks to the wonderful people who generously read
and commented on an early draft:

Ces Cassidy (editor-in-chief), Aisling Chambers, Sheila Flitton,
Stephen Flitton, Anne Kent, Patricia Mahon, Breda McCormack,
the late Margaret Neylon, Iris Park, Wendy Smith.

Madam Tulip

Ask anyone about Madam Tulip's legendary talent with tarot and crystal ball or her astonishing knack for detecting crimes, and you'll be told her father is the seventh son of a seventh son. Everybody knows that in Ireland seventh sons of seventh sons have extraordinary powers and can do all kinds of mystical things. Some claim these gifted souls can find a parking space in Dublin City Centre—but at this, even the most spiritually inclined laugh out loud.

Thoughtful observers wonder why the daughter of a seventh son of a seventh son should have psychic powers at all. Hasn't the gift been male since time immemorial? But Tulip isn't in the least concerned. Times change even in the realms of the supernatural.

And a good thing too.

∼

1

When Madam Tulip grants a rare celebrity interview to the world's fascinated media, she sometimes mentions she was born in poverty. Insofar as Tulip was born at all, she is telling the truth. On the day Madam Tulip was conceived, her creator—Derry O'Donnell, MA (Theatre Arts) Trinity College Dublin, age twenty-seven—was broke. And she had been broke for five whole years.

Was it a coincidence that those years of destitution began the day Derry graduated? On paper, she was well suited to a showbiz career. She was reasonably good-looking, of medium height, had blond hair and green eyes, and a decent alto voice. She was American, and had been mostly brought up in the States, but she could play Irish and English parts too. When she graduated *summa cum laude*, she felt that if she paid her dues and learned all she could, she had every chance of success.

The truth was, Derry O'Donnell was fully qualified for unemployment in three different dialects.

She tried to be patient, and in time she did get some good roles. She toured Ireland and Britain with quality companies in solid productions of the classics. Mostly she played supporting roles, but was occasionally cast in the lead. A notable triumph was her Lady Macbeth in the Ballydoon Community Centre during the Ballydoon Anglers two-day fly-fishing competition. Unfortunately, they weighed the catch for the prize-giving onstage during the first interval, making for treacherous going in Act Two. Although Derry twisted her ankle, she didn't actually fall, so all's well that ends well.

But she was always, always broke. And her mother, who paid her rent while Derry supposedly developed her stage career, was losing patience. Derry knew, because on Friday at ten a.m. New York time her mother phoned to tell her.

Derry was sitting in her tiny Dublin apartment, sprawled on its miniature couch with her laptop on her knee, hopelessly searching the web for upcoming productions her agent might have missed and that might need any or all of her dialects.

'Darling!' said her mother.

'Mom!' said Derry. She was supposed to call her Vanessa, but *Mom* was tolerated as long as it wasn't in front of friends.

'Must rush,' said Vanessa. 'Bye, honey.'

'Mom!' said Derry. 'You only just called. Are you alright?'

'Oh,' said Vanessa. 'Dear me, I'm in such a state. I've got Edgar Booth opening tonight. I am *sooo* excited.'

'Wow,' said Derry, always happy to encourage her mother in her chosen career as art-gallery owner extraordinaire. 'Edgar Booth! Gee!'

Derry had only the vaguest idea who Edgar Booth was, except he was an artist, and her father Jacko, an internationally famous, if permanently broke, painter from the West of Ireland, called him 'that baldy gobshite charlatan from LA.' Derry guessed that meant E. Booth was hugely successful.

'The gallery is crawling with Secret Service people, and you know what *that* means!' said Vanessa, who might have squealed if she hadn't been an upstate New Yorker, polished, cosmopolitan and no squealer. Vanessa owned a stupendously upmarket Modern Art gallery on Fifth Avenue, others in London and Dublin, and was suspected of being filthy rich. The suspicion was mostly held by her ex-husband Jacko, who claimed that Vanessa had to be rich as she never had a problem choosing between making money and saving blind old ladies from being run over by taxis.

'We have to take stock,' said Vanessa. 'I'm talking about your future, dear.'

This was not the kind of cheery, hello-darling-daughter-apple-of-my-eye phone call that Derry had hoped for when she saw the Caller ID pop up on her phone.

'You've given it your best, sweetest. Time for real life, don't you think?'

No second sight was needed to see where this was going.

'And don't tell me your battery is running out or a low-flying airplane towing an advertising banner has interfered with the signal,' said Vanessa. 'All you have to say is, yes Vanessa darling, I'd be delighted to work for you so I can live like a normal human being.'

'Oh, come on Mom, what's normal?' said Derry, unwisely.

'*Normal.* Like everybody else, darling. Pedicures. A decent bag. Someone to go to the Oscars with who owns their own suit. And don't change the subject. Job. Say yes.'

Derry's response sounded something like 'Ummm' squeezed through a piping bag.

Vanessa grasped the situation at once. She had a keen ear for nuances, having listened to art buyers with vastly more money than taste agonise between the pricey picture with blue splashes and pink spots and the even pricier one with pink stripes and green wavy bits.

'A career in PR in New York, dear!' said Vanessa. She spoke slowly, implying that the career in question was not only desirable but might even be suitable for morons. 'Most girls would bite my arm off! What's wrong with you!'

Derry was enveloped by a gloom darker than the stairwell outside her door, whose bulbs hadn't been changed since the Titanic was news and the Irish ate potatoes rather than Croquette Perigourdine with truffles and nutmeg.

'Honest, Mom, things are looking up. Really,' she insisted. To her credit, Derry felt a teeny bit guilty. An unsympathetic observer might class her last statement as a blatant lie on a par with the time she had told a rival for the affections of a certain leading man that culottes really suited her. But what choice did Derry have but to play for time? Her mother had never understood her career path. More than once she had demanded to know how it was possible to be an artistic success, as Derry insisted she most certainly was, and a financial failure? To Vanessa that sounded suspiciously like Communism.

'I'm sorry,' said Vanessa. 'At least you should be able to pay your own rent by now. I mean, how old are you?'

Derry knew that whereas from most mothers the question about her age would be rhetorical, from Vanessa it was a genuine enquiry. Vanessa stuck unwaveringly to the principle that one should avoid at all costs allowing one's mind become cluttered with trivia.

'I am telling you it's over, darling,' Vanessa declared with a horrible finality. 'Last month's rent was the last. That gives you three weeks to think about things. I'm coming to Dublin Friday next. We can discuss it then. And darling . . .'

'Yes, Mom?' said Derry, appalled beyond words.

'This is not a negotiation, capisci?'

As Derry did the minuscule amount of housework her frugal lifestyle created, or as she called it 'moving the tat around,' she thought hard about her mother's ultimatum. She had tried to hold down regular jobs, but an actor had to be available for auditions at any time, so inevitably she got into trouble. Her most recent attempt ended when she was fired by a famously compassionate charity for the unemployed, accompanied by some unflattering descriptions of her timekeeping and aptitude. Derry had to admit they had a point, but found comments about her 1950s Audrey Hepburn rockabilly dress totally uncalled for.

She had finished the housework in under six minutes, not even a record. Her friend Bella was coming to have her cards read and hang out with a bottle of something, but not until seven. Derry had arranged her little table with the cards ready to show. She'd even put out her crystal ball, in case the cards were feeling neglected and refused to cooperate. All Derry had left to think about now was being broke.

The situation probably rated a stiff whiskey, but instead Derry made herself a nice cup of borage tea, a beverage she usually kept for before a performance or an audition. 'Borage for Courage,' the old saying went, and after a few sips of that musky yellow brew she felt not exactly cheerful but at least willing to look calamity in the eye. Or perhaps relax and read a magazine.

Derry sat on her little couch and turned the pages of a mag she'd picked up at the launderette. At once, her eye was drawn to a full-page article of startling relevance—*Tame your Vices, Save Money and Get Better Skin.* The piece was accompanied by a questionnaire:

Q: Do you own a car when you could cycle to work, get fit and save on gym fees?

A: No. Derry's ancient car had already been towed away as good only for recycling into manhole covers.

Q: Do you smoke, burning up cash and ruining your skin?

A: No. Gave up during a highly successful tour when the highly successful producer was arrested for highly successfully selling non-existent apartments in Bulgaria. No actors were paid for the last two weeks of the run, so all agreed to quit smoking together. Nobody could remember their lines.

Q: Do you binge on chocolate, cakes, etc?

A: No. That very morning Derry had considered buying a packet of cookies from the discount German supermarket only to reject them as an outrageous luxury at 24 cents. She had made a mental note to phone up a radio show to complain about the cost of living but then worried that other actors would bitch that she just wanted to get on air.

Q: How many units of alcohol do you drink per week?

A: Regrettably, hardly any. The only alcohol consumed by Derry in the last week was in the throat lozenge she took when she had a cold and was terrified she'd be called for an audition. She wasn't.

Q: Do you treat your partner to meals at posh restaurants you can't afford?

'Hah!' said Derry out loud. 'Ho-ho-ho!' she added. The first was at the part about the posh restaurants. The second at the hilarious idea she might have a partner. To meet men you had to have a social life. To have a social life you needed to go to clubs and bars and parties. And to do those things you need money for alcohol and cabs. Even if you settled for the weirdness of internet dating, that cost too.

After answering all the questions and adding up her score, Derry discovered that she was not eligible to *Tame her Vices, Save Money and Get Better Skin.* She was all out of vices.

'I'm too poor to be bad,' said Derry. She knew she was moaning, but what are friends for, especially actor friends, if not to listen to your despair? She was reading Bella's cards while they drank a bottle of wine so awful it made her wonder where she had left her lozenges.

Bella was also an actress, and being black she was even more unemployed than Derry. The market for black actresses in Ireland was limited to token roles on the national TV soap, one of each gender. Her prospects were further compromised by her being from Belfast. The northern capital is a famously tough city, and Bella had been known to suggest that if a director didn't like the way she was delivering her lines she had friends who could persuade him otherwise.

'You've gotta be *brutal*,' said Bella, imbuing the last word with a conviction that said she knew all about being that thing, and would knock it to the ground and kick it until it admitted as much. 'Count your strengths. You have to say No to Negativity!'

'No,' said Derry. 'I mean, Yes to No!'

'Strengths!' said Bella. She pronounced it 'strongths' but Derry knew what she meant.

'Okay,' said Derry, entering into the spirit of the thing. 'Let's see. Strength Number One . . .' She stopped right there. Did she have strengths? She got along with both her parents, a miracle that surely counted for something. She was an easy touch for a loan when she had the cash. Was that Strength Two or just stupid?

'That's definitely a strength,' said Bella. But she would say that. She still owed Derry twenty from the week before last, when she was desperate to see some singer she meant to shag if possible but didn't manage to, in spite of hanging around three hotels and buying drink for the wrong chauffeur. Now the singer was gone, unshagged, and so was Derry's twenty.

'But how,' asked Derry, 'is the ability to give away money good for making money?'

'I didn't say it was,' said Bella, tutting. 'We are enumerating. First, list those strengths.'

'Alright. Strength Number Three . . . erm . . . I'm kind to animals?'

'You don't even have a pet.'

'No. But if I had, I'd be kind to them. The kindest. Really I would.'

'We have to do better than that,' said Bella. 'And no need to stop the card-reading. I can think and be psychically open at the same time, if you please.'

'Sorry,' said Derry, dealing another spread. She stopped, surprised at what the cards said. No haziness or ambiguity there. 'I didn't know you were still seeing Joe,' she said accusingly. 'I thought he'd gone off with Mathew.'

'He did,' said Bella. She leaned forward and whispered, as if the future were listening. 'This is *a different Joe*. But well done.'

Derry frowned, 'Well what's with the secrets, Miss Secretive?'

Bella paused, looking almost sheepish. 'I was going to tell you, honest.' She put on what she believed to be her sweetest look, though it came out sweet in the way a bouncer at a biker's convention might look sweet. 'Really.'

Derry wondered whether revenge fortune telling was against whatever ethical code psychics were supposed to have. She decided to risk it. 'And by the way, this Joe is gay too.'

The effect on Bella was gratifying. 'For goodness' sake! Do they start that way or is it something I say?'

Before Derry could answer, Bella slapped her forehead, going 'Oh, oh, oh! That's it. Strength! Looking at us right there in the face. This! Cards! Psychic!'

'What *are* you talking about?' asked Derry. But as she realised what Bella meant, she too went, 'Oh.'

'Why not?' said Bella.

'I couldn't. It's just for fun,' said Derry. 'I've always done it. No one takes it seriously.'

'But why not ask for money?' said Bella. 'Not from friends, of course.'

'Of course,' agreed Derry. 'But I can't ask to be paid. I don't know what I'm doing!'

'Of course you do! You're a natural. You have the gift! And what makes you think all those psychics and fortune-tellers and mind-readers on TV shows know what they're doing? They don't. And they don't have half your talent. They act. Fortune-telling is a show like any other.'

'I suppose,' said Derry. 'But what if—?'

'No *what ifs*,' snapped Bella. 'You're great at this. You sometimes get it spot on!'

Derry shrugged modestly. It didn't do to big yourself up, she was sure. If anything was part of the psychics' code, she guessed it was stuff about being modest and self-effacing. 'Well, I suppose I do get it right a *little* more often than average, now you mention it. In fact—'

'But mostly,' Bella interrupted, 'you talk the biggest load of pure bullshit. You told me I'd meet a handsome man in uniform with flashing blue eyes and riding a white horse. Turned out to be a motorcycle cop chasing me for doing fifty in a thirty. And would he back off when I gave him the eyelashes and dental treatment?

Would he heck. He looked at the photo on my licence and said, 'How many years ago was *that* taken?'

'See!' said Derry. 'I get it wrong sometimes. If I took money, I'd feel such a fraud. Giving people false hope—'

'Oh bollox,' said Bella. 'You can be sympathetic, can't you? That's all people want, a chance to talk, tell you their troubles and hopes and dreams, all dressed up as questions. Will I be rich? Will I live to be a hundred? Will my husband die if I feed him loads of butter?'

'I suppose,' said Derry. 'I needn't charge too much, need I?'

'Wrong!' said Bella. 'The more you charge the better you'll make people feel. Ask anybody on Harley Street. That's psychology. That's why theatres charge fifty quid a ticket. Otherwise, people would *know* it was crap.'

'Can't hurt, I guess,' said Derry. 'I could try.'

'Of course it can't hurt. Treat it like a gig. Except you're the producer, the director, the writer and the actor. And the box office. And your own agent—no greedy parasite looking for 15% for doing sweet FA. We sort you with a costume, a bit of makeup, maybe a website.' Bella paused, pursed her lips and inspected Derry like she was a rabbit for sale in a pet shop. 'We need a name.'

'Isn't that going too far?'

'Since when were you in a play as Derry O'Donnell? You're a *character*. We're making you up,' said Bella, as if being this patient was something she only did for friends who were very stupid and to whom she owed money. 'It has to be 'Madame Something,' right? Okay, Madame . . . Madame Fortune!'

'Hundreds of psychics are called that.'

'Madame Alexander? Why is that familiar?'

'It's a kewpy doll,' said Derry. 'They'd sue me.'

The problem, Bella pointed out, was that Madame anything sounded like someone who made men dress up in diapers and crawl around the floor begging for forgiveness. 'Not a bad idea,' Bella added, her steel tooth glinting ominously. 'On reflection, you'd make a lot more than by telling fortunes.'

'No,' said Derry firmly.

'You need the money,' said Bella.

Pleasing images of generous amounts of cash on a hotel bed-room dressing-table briefly flashed through Derry's mind, until the rest of the picture followed.

'No!'

'Just a thought,' said Bella.

'The name can't be sexy,' said Derry. 'Fortune-tellers are always middle-aged. Comfortable. Like someone's mother. Sensible shoes. Chunky jewelry. What's the opposite of sexy?'

'Flowers?' suggested Bella.

'Hey, a flower—that's good. Madame Rose? Madame Violet? Why is that porny?'

'Madame Petunia?'

'No way! I'd feel like a character on Playschool. Madame Daff . . . naw.'

'Madame Iris, good. Madame Crocus . . . No. Madame Tulip. Hey! Madame Tulip!'

Derry thought for a moment. Madame Tulip? 'I like it. I really do.'

Madame Tulip. And they hadn't even emptied the bottle.

'With or without an "e"? Like *Madame* or *Madam*?' asked Derry.

Bella thought about that. 'Is she married to Monsieur Tulip?'

'Uh-uh.'

'No "e" then. Like Madam President.'

'Madam Tulip,' said Derry. The more she thought about her new name, the more she liked it. She smiled broadly and held out her hand to be shaken. 'Madam Tulip. Pleased to meet you.'

'Charmed, I'm sure,' said Bella, laughing. 'Right, gotta go. Joe is waiting to take me to dinner. He's loaded, the ignorant bastard. Tell you what, I'll be hung over tomorrow, so how about Sunday, two o'clock? I'll come here for you, and we'll get you sorted with a makeover. Wardrobe and props. Do it right.'

'Sorry, can't. Have to go to the races on Sunday. With my Dad. He's coming over from the West. I promised.'

'Monday? Afternoon? Here?' said Bella, flashing Derry a metal-toothed smile and throwing her leather jacket over her shoulder.

'Um, okay. Thanks,' said Derry.

'See ya, Tulip,' said Bella.

2

Most of Derry's meetings with her father seemed to be at race-tracks. This course was just outside the city, and Derry knew the place well. Early afternoon, and the long avenue leading to the stands was thronged. Cars nosed bumper to bumper into the parking areas. Chattering pedestrians overflowed the pavements. Derry wondered how many in that cheery crowd had been summoned by a father's pleading urgency. Few, she guessed, or they wouldn't look so carefree.

Either Jacko wanted to borrow money—unlikely as he knew Derry hadn't had an acting job in weeks—or he'd had one of his visions. These episodes of second sight often featured a horse thundering past the winning post, its name, colours and number tantalisingly obscure. Jacko would then plead with Derry to 'have a go' and see if she couldn't get a clearer picture.

The first time her father had pulled this particular stunt was barely a week after Derry had moved to Ireland to study.

'Dad, I thought you had second sight,' she'd protested. 'How come you lose money on half the horses you back?'

Derry knew this was a low blow. Questioning the second sight of a seventh son of a seventh son was like questioning a man's ability to fix a lawnmower. But she refused to feel guilty. He'd asked for it. A normal dad would have been buying ice creams and warning her off men who reminded him of himself.

'Like my father before me and his father before him, I share the gift,' Jacko said piously. 'Just as you are privileged to do,' he added, settling into the moral high ground like a comfy armchair with his name embroidered on the back. 'But sadly, the eyesight of the spirit grows hazy as the years go by. Consider yourself,' he announced, as if conferring on her an honorary degree, 'my spiritual contact lenses.' Jacko grinned that mad grin he had when he knew you were completely baffled.

As she trudged up the avenue, Derry promised herself that this time she would flatly refuse to comment on the horses running or the odds quoted. Nor, under any circumstances, would she tip a winner. Absolutely not.

Derry passed through the turnstiles, paid her entry fee and jostled her way to a corner of the stand particularly favoured by Jacko as it gave the punters a fine view of himself. She scanned the crowd, but her father was nowhere to be seen. She had just taken out her phone to call him, when he materialised behind her. She should have been used to the way he did that, but she was always startled.

'That's my girl,' he said, beaming and enveloping her in an enormous hug. 'Never lets me down.'

Jacko was a big man, six foot three in socks that never matched. He wore a flowing olive green coat down to his calves, and leather top boots, black with a striking brown cuff. A halo of white hair made him look more like an orchestral conductor than a painter. In a rave review, one art critic had described him as 'leonine'. Derry suspected Jacko had made his barber commit the piece to memory, as these days Jacko's glorious mane would make any self-respecting lion feel sadly inadequate.

At least, thought Derry, her father had stuck to gambling and had mostly sworn off women. Occasionally, some adoring graduate student less than half his age followed him around until he absentmindedly let her live with him for a month. But the affair always fizzled out as the acolyte went off to find someone else with sufficient name recognition for her Facebook page.

'I'd suggest a drink, but first to business,' said Jacko. Elbowing through the crowd, he led Derry straight to a bookie's stand. The blackboard listing the horses and the odds sheltered under a yellow umbrella. In front stood the bookmaker doing what bookies do, relieving people of wads of cash and smiling.

'Jacko!' said the bookie, his smile growing even wider.

'Paddy!' said Jacko, beaming right back, as if to say I can be even more pleased than you, see if I can't.

'Whaddlya have, sir?' said Paddy. 'Number Four movin' up sharpish, *Gentleman's Relish*. Three to two. Take a punt?'

'One moment, Paddy,' said Jacko. 'I have my excellent daughter here to advise. Pray allow me consult.'

'No bother at all, my friend. You take your time,' said Paddy, his grin broader than ever.

Derry had a nasty suspicion that that in the collective mind of the bookies' fraternity daughters dispensing tips were good business.

'What do you think?' said Jacko. 'Number Two or Number Four? I fancy Four meself—likes the dry going.'

'Meh,' said Derry, staring hopelessly at the list of ridiculous names. Could there really be a horse called *Hand Relief*? 'Honest, I haven't a clue.'

Jacko leaned closer, his expression serious. He whispered in Derry's ear. 'I need your help, dear child.' He looked around, as if being overheard might cause the police to hustle them out of the stadium for immediate interrogation. 'A little cash flow would do nicely. Do your best for your oul' fella, eh?'

'Oh, Dad,' said Derry, keenly aware that Paddy the Bookie was gazing at her fondly. A puzzling image of a champagne-fuelled party featuring three strangely underdressed women flashed through her mind. The picture was quickly followed by a brief glimpse of a yacht not quite as long as the average supermarket carpark.

'Dad, I can't be responsible. What if I get it wrong?'

Jacko gave her his most sincere look, the one he deployed when he knew one or both female members of his family were about to demand he not do something he had every intention of doing.

'Derry, you've always been my lucky charm.' He gazed at her, his eyes brimming with what might have been genuine emotion. 'I don't know how an old rogue like me could deserve a wonderful daughter like you.'

'Dad, stop it. I can't do this.'

'Of course you can do it,' said Jacko, indignantly. 'No bother to you. January!'

Derry couldn't remember much about January, except it was cold and she failed two auditions.

'We went to Galway,' said Jacko. 'You tipped me *Fantastic Fairy*. She won at 100-1.'

'Did I?' said Derry, whose memory of the day's events was hazy, possibly because Jacko had fed her three brandies before the race had even begun.

'You did!' insisted Jacko. 'I asked you to pick a horse. You didn't even look at the board. You said, "Fantastic, here am I freezing my ass off, and my father can't tell the difference between a daughter and a fairy godmother!" See? *Fantastic Fairy*. Perfect.'

Jacko regarded Derry with a look both proud and proprietorial, like the expression a victorious owner might wear as his champion horse parades triumphantly to the winner's enclosure.

'The facts speak for themselves,' said Jacko, resting his case.

Derry felt the resigned tiredness you feel when you see a long queue at the ATM and know that when you at last get to the machine it's going to smirk and suggest you take your business elsewhere.

'Maybe I did,' she said, weakly. 'Oh, alright. But—'

'No buts! Confidence! Panache!'

Panache wasn't easy with Paddy the Bookie smiling like a shark hosting a swimming gala, but Derry concentrated as best she could. Not sure what to concentrate on, she stared at the board with its baffling list of horses and odds, looking for inspiration. Nothing came. And now the sky was darkening. Why hadn't she thought of bringing an umbrella or a hat? She sighed.

'Looks like rain.'

'Hm,' said Jacko absently, his eyes fixed on the list of runners.

'Should have brought a brolly,' added Derry.

Jacko froze. He clutched Derry's elbow, pulling her to one side. 'What was that?' he whispered.

'I just said—'

'I know, I know! Oh, you're a darling!' Jacko was ecstatic. He reached in his coat for his wallet, waved it at the bookie and surged through the crowd. The queuing punters scowled, but Jacko didn't care. He left Derry standing, wondering what she'd said.

In under a minute, Jacko was back.

'You broth of a girl! I knew you wouldn't let me down,' he said. He folded the betting slip neatly, kissed it and slid the paper lovingly into his wallet. 'Two hundred quid at forty-to-one!' He beamed, his grizzled face a picture of relief. 'Thank goodness for that. Problem solved. I was running into a spot of bother. Can't rob Peter to pay Paul if Peter's already chasing you down the street shouting for the cops, can you?'

Jacko's pronouncement would have been puzzling if Derry had been trying to understand, but she was too busy being annoyed by his 'broth of a girl.' When Jacko came over all shamrock and leprechauns, he was invariably saying, 'I'm just a simple country-man from the bogs of the West, so don't imagine for a moment I've pulled the wool over your eyes.' Which he invariably had.

'"*Inside Out!*" Genius!' said Jacko.

Derry must have looked as baffled as she felt. Should she be worried about his mental state? Was this the early onset of senility? He hadn't even been to the bar.

'"*Looks like rain.*" Then the other thing —"*brolly something.*" And the wind blows, and the brolly blows inside out! "*Inside Out!*" Beautiful!'

Derry began to say she hadn't meant to pronounce on anything. She was only warming up to see if inspiration came. But Jacko was paying no attention.

'Forty to one!' Jacko repeated triumphantly. 'Money in the bank, begob!' He grabbed Derry by the elbow and dragged her away, waving cheerfully at Paddy the bookie. Paddy waved back, bestowing on Derry an especially fond smile.

'Drink!' announced Jacko.

In the heaving bar, Derry and Jacko stood propped against the wall, glasses in their hands. Jacko's eyes darted busily about. He was fully prepared to be irritated if he wasn't recognised, but a group near the bar raised their glasses and shouted, 'Jacko!' Confident that the risk of anonymity had safely passed, he turned his attention to Derry.

'Heard from your mother, at all, at all?' he said, wearing his Innocent Enquirer expression.

'She . . . called a couple of days ago,' said Derry. 'And . . . again yesterday.'

Derry decided not to mention her mother's ultimatum about her career, but late Saturday night Vanessa had called again. This time with a message for Jacko.

'Oh yes?' said Jacko, 'Enquiring after our well-being? Thought not.'

'Mom wanted to know why your number wouldn't work. I didn't know what to say. I lied and said you lost your phone and I didn't have the new number yet. I feel terrible.'

'Thanks, kid,' said Jacko, giving her a fond look. Derry found herself thinking of a stonemason chipping little bits off a big boulder, and apples falling close to the tree from whence they came.

'Stop that,' she said.

'Sorry,' said Jacko. 'But it's true. You know it is!' He grinned happily. 'D'ye know what? I love the way we share a sense of humour.'

'She wants you to call her,' said Derry, refusing to be schmoozed. 'You can't hide! She's your wife—was. She's my mother!'

'Fair enough,' said Jacko. 'Credit where credit's due. Motherhood is a wonderful, miraculous thing. Can't take that away from her.' He spoke in that balanced way that a mouse might speak, conceding that a cat's ginger fur was indeed attractive in a certain light, but politely declining to come out from under the sideboard. 'Happily,' added Jacko, 'she's *your* mother not mine. No reflection on you child, but the woman is a monster in human form.'

Derry couldn't help smiling. Jacko avoided Vanessa on the principle that she might reform him, and his creativity would evaporate in the cold light of clean living. But more than once, after too many drinks, he had admitted to Derry he still missed her mother. Every time he met Vanessa, if they weren't actively warring at the time, he flirted with his ex-wife outrageously. To Derry's amazement, Vanessa seemed to like it, once confiding that New York men were all very well but lacked that elemental something. It took years for Derry to work out that her parents still slept together when they failed to remember not to.

'Anything special happening at the galleries?' enquired Jacko. 'Any news from the Big Apple?' His casual tone implied he had no personal interest in the answer whatsoever, but Derry knew that, like most painters, Jacko saw competing artists as either beneath notice or deadly enemies.

'Mom did mention she had a seriously VIP guest to an opening on Friday,' answered Derry, carefully skirting the tricky subject of whose exhibition the VIP was attending. 'She said I might have found some of his Secret Service detail dishy.' Derry laughed a changing-the-subject kind of laugh.

'She's an awful name-dropper, your mother. Has she no shame?' said Jacko, scowling.

'She didn't name anybody!'

'Ha! No one said she wasn't clever. Only your mother could name drop *without mentioning the name*!'

Jacko prepared to sulk. A high profile opening in the New York gallery, and it wasn't his. His resolve weakened, then cracked. 'And who—?' he said, tailing off as if nobody could care less than he who it was had exhibitions attended by VIPs too important to name.

'Can't say I remember,' said Derry, innocently.

Father and daughter assessed each other's resolve like sumo wrestlers slapping their knees, rolling their shoulders and generally indicating that blinking first was not part of the plan. Jacko eyed Derry. Derry eyed right back. Jacko blinked.

'So how's the world of stage and screen?'

Sweet of him, thought Derry. For years Jacko had been asking that same question, always getting the same answer. *So-so. Got an audition for a great movie. Didn't get it.*

'Remember that play about the banker who goes on hunger strike? I got the part of the investigating reporter?'

'Sure,' said Jacko. 'Shame I missed it—I was in London. Sounded like a good story. As long as he died in the end, the thieving bastard.'

Derry frowned. 'Nah. Saved by the love of a good woman. Could be why it closed after a week.'

'Ah, don't worry,' said Jacko, genuinely sympathetic. 'Something will turn up. Don't you have the talent? And you're a grand little worker when they give you a chance. The rest is all luck.'

Sometimes, thought Derry, her father could be just a big old teddy bear. That is, when he wasn't being an unscrupulous, self-centred, hyperactive maniac.

'I've had an idea,' said Derry, brightening. As this was a little less than totally, absolutely 100% accurate, her conscience made her add, 'Or at least my friend Bella had an idea. I'm going to be a psychic!'

Jacko looked puzzled, then concerned.

'Em . . . you're already a psychic. You didn't resign, therefore you can't reapply. Why are we having this conversation?'

'Don't be silly,' said Derry. 'I don't mean a psychic as in anything real. And you know perfectly well I'm only a teeny-weeny bit psychic. If I was properly psychic I wouldn't be broke would I? I'd win the lottery.'

Jacko looked even more concerned. 'Less of the teeny-weeny! What about the brolly? Rain? *Inside Out*? Self-belief is important.' He glanced nervously at the giant TV screen high on the wall. Prancing horses were being led out for the 2.30. Prancing, except for *Inside Out* who slouched reluctantly as if he would much rather have a nice bag of oats and a lie-in with the Sunday papers.

'I am not,' said Derry, '*not* taking responsibility for your choice of nags. You picked him. I didn't say anything!'

Jacko looked so crestfallen she had to take pity. 'I'm sure it'll be alright. And if it's not we'll think of another horse, okay?'

Jacko wore the doleful face of a seventh son of a seventh son whose second sight was showing him €200 scattered to the winds over the green fields never to be seen again.

'Let me tell you about my idea,' said Derry. 'I tell fortunes. I dress up, read the cards, do some crystal ball. None of that cheap fairground scamminess. Classy. Good lighting. Proper makeup. Atmosphere. A show, right?'

Describing her scheme for the first time, Derry felt more enthusiastic by the minute. No more waiting for agents to call. Okay, she'd still be waiting for agents, but while she was waiting for auditions she'd be making some money and having fun.

Jacko sucked in his cheeks. He pursed his lips.

'I do it already for free,' added Derry. 'My friends like it. They even say it's useful. Well, sometimes useful.'

Jacko was unconvinced. He didn't say 'meh,' but he might have.

'I can make money. Quite a lot of money. I'll call myself Madam Tulip.'

Jacko's eyebrows slid skywards as scepticism was banished by opportunity. 'Madam Tulip, eh?' His gaze wandered lazily around the bar. 'A *lot* of money, you think?'

Jacko never finished whatever he was about to say. Suddenly transfixed by the TV screen above, his air of studied nonchalance vanished as fast as the drink he knocked back in one gulp.

'The 2.30! Can't miss the off!'

Jacko swept out of the bar, Derry trailing in his wake. His green coat flapped in the breeze like the cloak of an ancient bard striding forth to claim his purse of gold for a work of shameless but necessary flattery.

3

To reach Jacko's favoured vantage point in the stands, they had to pass an avenue kept clear of crowds by a series of low barriers. Security men in yellow jackets lined the route, which led from the private car park and helipad to the VIP Gallery. From the luxurious eyrie of the Gallery, the privileged could observe the day's racing in comfort for less than the price of a modest secondhand car.

'Ooh, look,' said Derry, who could never resist spotting a celebrity. She was also hoping to distract Jacko from the start of the fateful 2.30. 'Isn't that Marlene O'Mara?'

The supermodel in question was accompanied by a sleekly prosperous, perfectly tailored and perfectly handsome man of middle age. He had the look of a greyhound—alert, bursting with repressed energy, as if the rest of the world moved at too slow a pace for one such as he. Marlene was radiant but detached, ignoring the spectators, while he smiled and nodded sociably. Behind the pair strode a slight but athletic younger man in a chauffeur's uniform of peaked cap and black leather gloves. His eyes were hidden by the darkest of dark sunglasses.

Jacko, dragging Derry in his slipstream, elbowed his way through the crowd and leaned over the barrier.

'Doyle!' he boomed. The handsome man stopped. The chauffeur stepped towards Jacko in a surprisingly smooth catlike movement. He spread his arms as if to interpose his body between his master and anyone foolish enough to offer unwelcome attention.

'Jacko!' said Doyle, smiling broadly as though genuinely pleased to see him. To the chauffeur, he said, 'Alright, Paulo.' The chauffeur stepped back, gesturing impatiently to two security men who uncceremoniously pushed onlookers aside and lifted the barrier. Doyle opened his arms, enveloping Jacko in a bear hug. Mobile phone cameras flashed, on the principle that a celebrity was a celebrity even if you couldn't for the moment think who the person actually was.

Jacko acknowledged the buzz of interest with a friendly wave, followed by the semi-military salute he imagined attractively dashing. 'Marlene, my dear,' he said, revelling in the crowd's attention. 'You're looking stunning as always!'

Marlene smiled a distracted smile and breathed a little 'hi.'

'My daughter, Derry,' said Jacko, keen to make the most of the public formalities.

'Charmed,' said Doyle, giving a little bow as he walked.

'Hi,' said Marlene, pausing for the briefest moment before striding up the steps and through the entrance, trailing the rest behind. Derry might have been justifiably offended at the offhand greeting but recognised the signs of a woman bursting for a pee. That a supermodel needed to pee was a gratifying thought, even endearing, though Derry recognised it *was* odd to like somebody just because they had a bladder.

Waiting for the elevator in the opulent lobby, Derry found herself beside the impossibly gorgeous Marlene. The model was prodding the elevator button accusingly, like she thought the building was deliberately refusing to obey the simplest command and should explain itself at once.

Derry sighed. Her father was about to lose two hundred euro on a race, and although he wouldn't dream of blaming her, she felt responsible. And now she was condemned to spend the afternoon in the company of a supermodel. Next to Marlene, Derry felt like a hobbit—a hobbit overweight and round even by the famously relaxed standards of hobbits. She looked down at her shoes (charity shop) then at Marlene's (Jimmy Choos) and her soul shrank a little inside her.

The Gallery was a first-floor restaurant with a vast length of plate-glass window through which diners had a panoramic view of the last fence and the finishing post. Hanging from the ceiling were huge TVs so you could feel as keenly as possible the agony of losing large sums of money.

Their table was in a prime spot. Obsequious waiters hovered. Paulo the chauffeur remained standing, his back to a pillar, his arms folded, his face behind the sunglasses expressionless. On the table, flowers were artfully arranged and champagne sat chilling in a steaming bucket.

'Sit! Sit!' said Doyle, smiling expansively. 'Champagne for every-one, I think.'

Derry was seated with Doyle to one side and an empty place on the other. She guessed the vacant seat was for Marlene.

'Allow me,' said Doyle, smoothly taking the bottle from the wait-er and pouring for Derry as though she were his special guest.

'Why not?' said Derry. 'Thank you.'

Perhaps being waited on by a handsome zillionaire in a VIP suite wasn't the worst way a girl could spend a Sunday afternoon. But Derry knew drinking was a thoroughly bad idea. Champagne and the impending disaster of the 2.30 were unlikely to mix well. Then again, what else to do if your job meantime was making a super-model look even better?

'Don't mind if I do,' said Jacko, holding out his glass. 'Isn't she an angel? She's an actress, d'ye know. Talent by the bucketful, let me tell you.'

'Dad!' muttered Derry under her breath. Cringing and smiling at the same time was a contortion she had perfected in a lifetime as an O'Donnell.

Doyle raised his glass. 'To the Arts!'

Derry noticed he glanced over his shoulder. Was he irritated at his wife was taking so long at the ladies? You'd think a man married to a model would be used to lengthy waits.

Jacko's expansiveness had swollen to match his host's, and now he too proposed a toast. 'To Peter Doyle, patron of the arts, man of discernment, beacon of hope in a land of Philistines.' He emptied his glass in one go, sliding it out for a refill in a single smooth motion.

Doyle smiled, acknowledging Jacko's flattery with an urbane nod.

Jacko and Doyle were exchanging incomprehensible racing talk when Marlene eventually appeared.

'Hi!' she said, taking her seat beside Derry. 'Has anything happened? Has the race started? I don't know the first thing about horses, but I have to pretend.'

For the briefest moment, Derry saw Doyle's jaw clench. The polished smile returned.

'Champagne dear?' He nodded to the waiter. Doyle seemed unnaturally alert, tense like a man waiting for something unfortunate to happen. But all the while he kept up the flow of talk, dispensing witticisms at the expense of various owners and trainers he and Jacko knew, and reminiscing about famous races they had been lucky enough to witness.

Doyle is an actor, thought Derry. He's playing the rich and successful host, a man in control. He's having an off-day for some reason, but he doesn't forget his lines, and he stays in character no matter what. But why must he act if he really is those things?

Derry's reverie was interrupted by Marlene, who suddenly

seemed keen to chat. Was she making up for her earlier offhand manner? Marlene seemed happy to do all the talking, which was just as well. What do you say to an internationally famous super-model? Slept with any rock stars I know of? Eaten any good celery lately? How are your legs—still long?

'Did you ever see me feeling this relaxed at the off, Doyle?' said Jacko.

'Never,' said Doyle. 'I can't believe you haven't taken a punt. Or have you reformed altogether?'

Doyle's smile was the smile of a wealthy man being flattered by an amusing retainer. His eyes held a sardonic glint that said, *for the moment I like you—you should be happy.* Derry had the sudden, overwhelming feeling that Doyle might make people he didn't like very *unhappy*. Perhaps *very unhappy indeed.*

'I *am* relaxed,' Jacko was saying. 'As relaxed as a man in an alco-holic coma after a good funeral. As relaxed as the fella who's slipped the brown envelope to the judge and been told thank you kindly sir. I am relaxed because Derry has assured me that the winner of the 2.30—odds a princely 40-1—will be *Inside Out.*'

Doyle looked at Derry with renewed interest. Unfortunately, Derry thought, his interest was of the kind someone might show in the fate of a rabbit caught in the headlights of an oncoming truck. She wondered if keeping your eyes tightly shut with your hands over your ears while sitting at someone's table drinking his champagne would be bad manners.

'She has the gift,' Jacko continued. 'Ours is not to reason why, et cetera, et cetera.'

'Fascinating,' said Doyle. 'Are you saying that as well as her other talents, your delightful daughter can foretell winners? If you are,

I would have to ask whom she knows, in whose stable, and how much does she pay them.' He laughed, as if that information were something for which he too might be willing to pay.

Doyle turned, gesturing to Paulo to come close. Paulo approached and stood with head bent as though expecting a whispered order, but Doyle spoke loudly so all could hear. 'Paulo, a grand on *Inside Out*. Quickly now, they're lining up.'

Paulo stepped back, took out his phone and spoke rapidly as he retreated to his station by the pillar. Doyle leaned back in his chair, his head cocked on one side, contemplating Derry with no regard for her obvious discomfort. The feeling was like being observed patiently by a cobra—in this case a cobra who had all the time in the world, had nothing personal against you, but felt he was owed a little entertainment.

Above their heads, the giant TV showed the starting gates. The horses and their jockeys were restless and impatient. The commentator was speaking in a low voice, as if to speak loudly would disturb the horses. The restaurant fell silent.

'And . . . they're off!'

Derry didn't go so far as to close her eyes, but she didn't watch the screen either. She didn't have to. As far as the commentary was concerned, *Inside Out* might as well have been pulling a carriage of tourists round Dublin city centre. *Inside Out* was halfway down the field—three-quarters way down the field— forgotten.

Derry wasn't the only one not watching the race. She was uncomfortably aware that Doyle wasn't watching either. He was observing her, a small smile playing around the corner of his mouth.

'I guess you're not into racing,' Marlene said, her voice low.

'Um . . . No,' said Derry. 'Not really.'

'Me neither,' said Marlene, mouthing the words. She glanced

sideways at Doyle, although the chance of Doyle hearing anything above the shouts rising from the tables around was slim.

For a moment, Derry forgot to worry about the race. Why would Marlene not want her husband to hear something as innocuous as her not being into racing?

'My husband is a breeder; you probably know that,' Marlene was saying.

At this startling pronouncement, disturbing possibilities raced through Derry's mind. Her confusion only grew when, through the hubbub, she thought she heard Marlene add, 'He's a stud.'

'He owns a stud, you know,' repeated Marlene. 'Your father's been there. Peter has bought lots of pictures from him. You must come down for a visit. Peter sells horses all over Europe.'

'I'd love to visit, thank you,' said Derry, though being invited to the house of someone she had cost a thousand euro the first time they'd met didn't seem too likely.

The din in the Gallery was even louder than before. All the TV screens were blaring at once. Had Derry just heard the commentator mention *Inside Out*? Yes! And again! Now he was screaming hoarsely.

'And it's *Inside Out*, *Inside Out*, on the outside . . .'

Ah, thought Derry. So that's why he's called *Inside Out*! A mischievous owner wanted to make race commentators fluff their lines. Some playwrights did that. But then, all playwrights hate actors.

Now the commentator was howling, joined by almost everyone in the room.

'Oh, oh, oh, oh!' roared Jacko, his eyes locked on the screen.

Marlene was squealing and bobbing up and down in her seat. 'Here they come, here they come! Now!' She was pointing through the window to the charging mass of horseflesh tearing into view round the last bend.

Only Doyle was impassive, sipping from his glass, the picture of calm. While everyone else rose to their feet as one, craning to see the finish, Doyle sat coolly in his chair, as if a thousand euro mattered no more to him than the price of another bottle of champagne. He gave Derry a smile, raising his glass in a mock toast. The room erupted. The race was over. *Inside Out*, winner at 40-1.

Derry felt much as a highwayman on the scaffold might feel when the trapdoor opens beneath his feet, but miraculously the rope breaks and he is free. Jacko was hugging her and beaming, announcing to the whole room, 'She's done it again! What a gift!'

'I'm so happy for you,' said Marlene. 'That was amazing! How did you do that?'

'My dear girl, congratulations,' added Doyle, shaking Derry's hand. 'Very well done. I never would have picked that winner myself. Remarkable.' He turned to Jacko. 'And you say she can do this whenever she likes?'

'Indeed she can,' said Jacko. 'Drop of a hat. No bother on her.'

Derry was still stunned at winning. So great was her surprise, she was slow to protest. 'A fluke, honest,' she said, flustered.

'You mustn't be so modest,' said Doyle.

'That's the problem we women have,' said Marlene. 'We never take the credit.'

Few people surrounded by an admiring crowd congratulating them effusively would flatly contradict the opinions of their fans. Few people, and no actors.

'I guess I do seem to have a small knack,' said Derry, trying not to simper. She gave what she imagined to be a modest smile. She *was* pleased. In fact, very pleased. After all, she had helped her father out of a jam of some sort. And made Doyle forty thousand euro.

She was about to explain how important it was to properly focus when you tried to make a prediction, and how perhaps her training as an actress had helped her concentrate, when a disturbing thought struck her. Everyone knew racing was the sport of gangsters and crooked businessmen. What if word reached those gangsters, and they imagined she could do this all the time? They might kidnap her and make her predict winners until she failed, then exact some terrible retribution.

'Hit and miss. Totally,' she said, adding a laugh she hoped any experienced kidnapper would see at once was the laugh of a girl without psychic powers of any kind and far too annoying to risk being stuck with over a rainy weekend. 'I mean, how rich do *I* look?' she added. She laughed again, working on the annoying part.

Doyle considered her coolly. 'What is money compared to beauty?' he said, clicking his fingers to order another bottle of champagne. 'A libation to the other realm. Isn't that what we're supposed to offer?'

They drank a toast to *Inside Out*. Then they toasted Derry for tipping *Inside Out*. Again, Derry protested it was all luck.

'She's too modest altogether,' said Jacko. 'She tips a horse or two to please her old dad. But other things? Now that's a different story! Oh yes, let me tell you.' He sat back as if he wasn't going to tell anybody anything but could if he so chose.

'This is *sooo* interesting,' said Marlene. 'Really, what other things?'

'She sees the future,' said Jacko, matter-of-factly as if remarking on someone's ability to grow sweet peas. 'Reads the cards, the crystal ball, the lot.'

'Dad!' protested Derry.

'Did I ever tell you,' said Jacko, turning to Doyle, 'that I was the seventh son of a seventh son?'

Doyle looked politely interested. 'I believe you may have mentioned it.'

'Cards! Don't tell me you read the cards!' Marlene was enthralled.

'Only for friends,' said Derry, the spectre of kidnappings not quite banished. 'A bit of fun, that's all. No big deal. Honest.'

'Madam Tulip!' said Jacko, triumphantly. 'Famous psychic and soothsayer of old Ireland, daughter of a seventh son of a seventh—'

'Dad!'

'I am *so* interested in telepathy,' said Marlene. 'Don't you think it's mysterious? I'm fascinated by all that. I'm very spiritual.'

Derry was wondering whether she should try to explain that she wasn't a telepath, when she saw Doyle do something unexpected. He rolled his eyes, quickly disguising the lapse by looking at his watch.

Marlene pushed her empty champagne glass across to Doyle to be filled. He ignored it.

'I know!' Marlene was saying. 'You can come to our Charity Bash! That would be so cool. Everyone would love you. You could, like, do fortunes and everything!'

Derry hadn't a clue what Marlene was talking about, until she explained that she and her friends were running a celebrity charity auction at a stately-home hotel in the country.

'Madam Tulip, Celebrity Psychic,' said Jacko, appointing himself Derry's publicity agent.

'It's a weekend in a castle. On an island in a lake, and we dress up if we want,' said Marlene. 'We have an auction and buy crazy things! Last time we had like a huge funfair with throwing-rings to win teddy bears and strength machines for the men. *So* much fun. We made loads of money for charity.' She signalled to the waiter to fill her glass.

'And which charities were those dear? I've forgotten,' asked Doyle, smiling sweetly. His eyes were cold.

'Oh, lots,' said Marlene. 'Children.'

'Ah,' said Doyle. 'Of course. Children.'

Marlene turned to Derry, clasping her hand affectionately. 'You must come!' She took out her phone, insisting she and Derry swap numbers and giving Derry the contact of the event organiser.

'Call her first thing. Or maybe not first thing. After lunch, okay?'

Derry said she would make sure to call in the afternoon.

'You'll be my first psychic,' said Marlene, delighted, as though she meant to start a collection.

'So, when is the . . . er . . . event?' asked Derry.

'*The Celebrity Bash*,' said Marlene a little impatiently as if Derry needed to pay better attention. 'Next Friday evening. You could do some readings before dinner if you didn't mind. That would be fun. There'll be a cabaret and a burlesque after. Then the auction. You'd have a good room and all your expenses would be covered. And a fee, of course.'

The conjunction of the words *fee, celebrity* and *burlesque* were too much for Jacko to let pass. 'Sure couldn't I give a hand with the transport? Crystal balls and what have you—a terrible lot to carry around.'

'That is *so* good of you,' said Marlene, giving Jacko a look of practiced sincerity.

'Anything at all for the poor little childer,' said Jacko, his face expressing the limitless compassion of a candidate on the eve of a papal election. He sat back, his eyes on the TV screen above. 'Derry, my dear, did you have any thoughts about the four o'clock, at all, at all?'

'Oh, my goodness, is that the time?' said Derry. 'I've got to be at . . . I've got to be somewhere.' She stood, shaking hands all round.

Doyle stood, the essence of politeness and charm, 'Do telephone as my wife has suggested. I'll be at the event myself. I look forward to seeing you.' He didn't bow as he shook her hand, but somehow gave the impression he had.

'Dad, we could share a taxi,' said Derry. 'Beat the rush?'

The idea of leaving a racetrack early seemed to strike Jacko as admirably original but better suited for life in some parallel universe of which he was, fortunately, not an inhabitant.

'No, thanks,' he said. 'Don't you worry about me. Sure I have the car.'

Derry was certain that if he stayed his winnings would melt away within the hour. 'I forgot to say, Mom's coming to Ireland—she wants to talk business.' The ploy was cruel but for Jacko's own good. Up to now Derry had withheld this vital piece of intelligence as she didn't want to ruin her father's day too early in the afternoon.

Jacko's face grew pale. His eyes popped. He stammered something unintelligible. Derry ignored him, repeating her goodbyes. She assured Doyle that meeting had been a pleasure, and Marlene that she would see her next weekend.

Derry turned and made for the elevator. In seconds, Jacko was at her heels, his coat swirling distractedly, his hair more dishevelled than ever.

'Derry! Derry, we need to talk! No point wasting good money on cabs! Wait!'

～

Derry slid into Jacko's open-top sports car. 'Let me guess,' she said, 'an unscheduled overnight stay halfway to Dublin? You should carry a tent.'

Jacko revved the engine, spinning the tyres and showering pedestrians with dust.

'I will not dignify that remark with a response,' he said as they sped down the driveway to the main road.

Jacko's car, a red E-Type Jaguar of the 1960s was the love of his life. The outrageously expensive classic suited Jacko's image of himself as a swashbuckling, hedonistic, inspirational creative force, with a touch of the aristocrat and bags of taste. The trouble was, the car never, ever, reached its destination without a baffling interlude of peering under the bonnet, phone calls, tow trucks and often an overnight stay in the middle of nowhere.

'How did anybody drive these things before cell phones?' asked Derry, happy to rub it in.

'Mobiles, dear,' retorted Jacko. 'Here in civilisation, they're called mobiles.'

'I guess you could get a taxi to follow you around,' said Derry. She was enjoying herself hugely, but the all too rare experience of having her father at a disadvantage didn't last long. At the junction with the main road, one of Dublin's famously irritable motorcycle cops stopped the traffic and waved the red Jag through with a smile.

'There you have it, my girl,' said Jacko, complacently. 'Timeless automotive beauty softening the stony heart of a fascist bastard.' He grinned, waving at the policeman in the style of the Queen of England in her gilded carriage.

'So what does your mother want?' shouted Jacko, gunning the motor so the wind whistled through Derry's hair and the G-forces pinned her to her seat. She tried not to notice they were mostly on the wrong side of the road. A wailing of horns rose and fell in their wake.

'I don't like it,' shouted Jacko. 'Why now?'

'She said business,' Derry shouted back, stalling.

'The only business your mother knows is fleecing the creative classes. Leeches and vampires ask her opinion on technique.'

Though they'd been divorced for ten years, Vanessa still sold Jacko's paintings, taking the commission she believed she richly deserved. She said staying his agent was the only way she could reduce the alimony she had to pay him, and she refused point blank to let him out of his contract so he could sell his pictures elsewhere. Lately though, Jacko hadn't complained about that as much as he once had. Perhaps, Derry thought, he was mellowing with age, although that didn't seem terribly likely.

'Go on,' said Jacko. 'Level with your old Da. What does she want, the fiend?'

A well-developed instinct for self-preservation prompted Derry to wait for an empty stretch of road. 'She said something about'— she waited until Jacko had overtaken four trucks in a row—'limited edition prints.'

'What!' roared Jacko, sending the car careering across two lanes.

'Careful!' squealed Derry.

'She can't,' shouted Jacko. 'Not without my say-so, she can't. No way!'

Derry paused, picking her moment with care. 'She also said something about somebody selling fakes of your pictures. She wants you to do certificates of authenticity.'

This time, to Derry's astonishment, the expected outburst didn't happen.

'Tell her I'm flattered,' Jacko shouted back. 'Good luck to him if it's a he. If it's a she, send her to me and I'll give her a few pointers on technique.' He wiggled his eyebrows and gave a decent impersonation of a delighted leer.

'Mom wants to meet you at the studio,' roared Derry, completing the mission her mother had assigned her and silently swearing for the millionth time that never, ever again would she play go-between. Why couldn't you have ex-parents, like they had ex-spouses? It didn't seem fair.

'What a pity,' said Jacko. 'Shame I won't be around. Tell her I'm sailing to Greenland. It's a re-enactment. Did you know the ancient monks of Ireland discovered America?'

'I thought you were going to be my assistant at the charity auction!'

'Sorry, sweetheart,' shouted Jacko. 'The call of the sea. In me veins. Did I ever tell you your great-great-grandfather was a pirate in the Caribbean? They hung him, but not before he procreated successfully, thanks be to God.'

Derry closed her eyes. The one thing she never had to say to her parents was how they should take up a hobby and get out more.

4

Bella had arranged everything but refused to tell Derry what the plan was. 'You'll find out,' she said, with the same self-satisfied smirk she wore after scoring some unsuspecting hunk's phone number before he had been warned off by more far-sighted friends. Only as they turned in to the alleyway beside the Palace Theatre did Derry guess where they were going.

'Called in a favour,' said Bella, grinning. She rang the bell on a fading green door that looked like it hadn't been opened since the place was a music hall.

'Wow,' said Derry. 'Haven't been here since *A Midsummer Night's Dream*. Seems years ago.'

'Didn't know you were in that,' said Bella in the tones of feigned indifference actors use when they suspect a colleague of succeeding. She was only mollified when Derry admitted that the role in question was a lesser fairy (male) whose most challenging line was 'Hail, mortal!' Keen to make the most of any opportunity, Derry had put as much expression into those two precious words as she could get away with. She had been especially pleased at conveying precisely the true meaning of the line 'Hail, mortal.' Not one person she spoke to afterwards thought she meant bad weather was imminent. In this business you seized your triumphs where you could.

'I hear Carruthers was the director from hell,' said Bella, thumping the door and holding her thumb on the buzzer.

'He was,' said Derry. 'He didn't know that directors are supposed to make the actors cry, not the other way round. Nightmare.'

The door opened, creaking on its hinges. A wizened head emerged, scowling. The scowl saw Bella and grinned a toothless grin.

'Bella, me darlin',' it said, throwing open the door.

'Frankie!' said Bella. She gave him a gigantic hug.

'How's me favourite token minority?' said Frankie.

'And how's me favourite wannabe actor?' replied Bella.

Frankie looked at Derry, 'Don't you listen to her. If I wanted to live on the street I could pick up a cardboard box at the supermarket.'

'Here to see Lorna and Jasmine,' said Bella. 'They in?'

'Of course they're in,' said Frankie, 'How else would they pretend to work?'

Frankie led them down a dark maze of ancient corridors crammed with randomly stacked scenery. Cables hung like black tentacles from the walls. Chunks of plaster had fallen from the ceiling and been carefully brushed into neat piles.

'I'm surprised ye can't hear them bickerin' from here,' said Frankie. 'Never bloody stops. Give you a headache. Why don't they marry and be done with it? You know the way,' he added, and vanished into the gloom.

At the end of the corridor was a wide doorway and through that an open space with rails on all sides holding thousands of costumes hanging in plastic covers. The place reeked of moth repellent and nervous actors.

Lorna's face lit up when she saw them. Four foot ten and absurdly pretty, Derry wondered what Lorna's parents looked like to have produced a girl so impossibly cute. They probably lived in the woods and slept under toadstools.

'Derry! Bella! Darlings! Haven't seen you for aaages!' squealed Lorna, leading them to a dressing room. 'Take a pew and tell us all. Jasmine's on her way.'

Derry sat at the long dressing table with its rows of naked bulbs. Strange to be sitting in front of that vast mirror when you weren't about to go onstage. She felt the faint but unmistakeable stirrings of excitement all actors get in an empty theatre. A strange mix of nerves and exhilaration.

If Lorna looked like an elf, Jasmine looked like a troll—tall and round, with frizzy red hair sticking out in all directions. She augmented her natural attributes with a ring through her nose and tattoos on both forearms. Tartan trousers completed an effect that said, 'Hey, you! Who do you think you're looking at?' Jasmine would have been scary if not for the enormous smile she wore almost all the time.

Derry and Bella explained about Madam Tulip and the fortune-telling gig at the Celebrity Bash. The question was where to start.

'Can you guys make her look older?' asked Bella.

'That's why we're working in this dump darling and not in the Bahamas,' said Jasmine. 'If we could make her look younger that would be a different story.'

'Is older really necessary?' asked Derry. 'Can't psychics be young?'

Jasmine and Lorna shook their heads, crossed their arms, and sighed. Bella tapped her foot and whistled silently. All three looked as if they could spend the day varying the basic themes of arms, sighs, foot and whistle if Derry insisted, but they sincerely hoped not, as life was short.

'Alright!' said Derry. 'Whatever.'

'How old should we go? Old-ish? Old? King Tut's granny?' asked Jasmine.

'Not too old!' said Derry. 'Let's not get carried away.' She struggled for any argument that had nothing whatsoever to do with shameless vanity. 'I don't want to change the way I walk and talk. I mightn't be able to keep it up.' Feeling she was gaining traction, she made her pitch. 'Say fifty?'

'Do you get grey hair by fifty?' asked Bella. 'Dash of powder? Some streaks?'

'I guess you don't want to dye?' said Lorna.

Derry considered the point. Amazing how even sitting in a theatre doing something as trivial as makeup brought up the big issues. The arts were amazing. 'No,' she said. 'I don't suppose anybody does. But so many plays deal with themes of mortality and loss. As an actress you have to confront that.'

'Your hair,' said Jasmine, with the patient air of someone forced to talk to actors for too many years. She spoke extra slowly. 'Do you want to dye your hair for the show?'

'Ah,' said Derry. 'Wouldn't that be overdoing it? What if it rains?'

'Your department, I think, Jasmine dear,' said Lorna.

'I've got just the thing,' said Jasmine. Moving with a briskness that belied her gargantuan form, she darted out. Through the half-open door Derry saw her rifling in a tall stack of shallow drawers.

'Here we are!'

Jasmine was back, holding out what looked to Derry like an especially hairy cat. Black with streaks of grey, the object looked as though it had been sharing intimacies with a reluctant bag of flour.

'Turn around,' commanded Jasmine, 'and close your eyes!'

Derry did as she was ordered, swivelling round on the chair to face the dressing table mirror. 'No peeking,' warned Jasmine as her fingers did a complicated dance over Derry's head involving a self-adhering sports bandage, four clips, some hairpins, a kind of tight-fitting cap and, finally, the cat.

'Now!' Jasmine announced triumphantly, as if somebody were about to pop out of a cake.

Derry opened her eyes. She had expected to see an image of herself with a feline on her head. Instead, she saw an exotic woman with a medium-length coiffure elegantly streaked with grey. Derry had never had to wear a wig in a production, and she was astonished.

'Oh, wow! I look completely different!'

'Needs a little work, but it's going to be great,' said Jasmine. 'Lucky your own hair isn't long or we'd have had much more trouble. This you can easily do yourself. Right—makeup. Lorna, can you work a little of your magic here, sweetie pie?'

'Moustache,' said Lorna.

Derry's heart sank. Old. Grey streaks. Mustachios.

'Relax,' said Lorna. 'Not the sort you twiddle and put wax on the end, just a little shadow. Pay attention, you'll need to know how to do this.

'I do NOT want a moustache,' said Derry.

'Reality, darling,' said Lorna. 'Older women can be hairy.'

'I don't care!' said Derry. 'Next, you'll want me to wear wigs under my armpits!'

'Oh no, we won't, said Jasmine grinning, 'because you will always, and I mean always, wear sleeves at least to the elbows. Shoulders and arms would be a total giveaway. And you must always wear gloves. Fingerless if you like, but gloves.'

'That's *anno domini*,' said Lorna breezily as she instructed Derry in the art of aging herself with makeup in the least possible time and with minimum fuss.

'Right,' said Jasmine, her arms piled high with costumes. 'Stand to attention. Dressing time! And no looking.'

In quick succession, Derry was faced away from the mirror, half undressed, redressed, undressed again, stood up, sat down and twirled, until Jasmine and Lorna stood back and together said, 'Tadaah! Madam Tulip!'

Derry turned to the mirror. If it were possible not to recognise oneself she wouldn't have. The woman looking back at her had an unnaturally pale face that somehow looked chubbier than before. Her bosom was ample—achieved by a padded corset with beanbags the size of balloons in the cups. The bags felt squidgy but were thankfully warm and not heavy. Her dress was silk, calf-length—pale blue and beaded, with a high collar. A twenties-style cord was loosely tied about her waist. Around her neck hung multiple strings of heavy beads. To top off the ensemble, after several unfortunate attempts, they settled on a headdress—a delicate creation with three small blue feathers and two bigger yellow ones lying back over the hair.

'Distracts from the hairline,' said Jasmine. 'Try leaving it attached when you take the wig off. Remind me to give you a proper box to keep it all in.'

'Don't they look like birds?' said Derry.

'They are *not* birds,' said Jasmine. 'They are elegant flourishes.'

'Okay,' said Derry. 'Flourishes. I can go with that.'

'Now, wear these,' said Lorna, and onto Derry's nose she fitted a pair of glasses with exotic frames in mother-of-pearl. 'Clear glass, so you don't go arse over.'

Next came the gloves—black velvet, up past the elbows, fingers exposed so Madam Tulip could handle the cards.

Derry stood back, once again inspecting herself in the mirror. 'Amazing. Just incredible.'

'Awesome,' agreed Bella.

'And they think the artists are on the stage,' said Derry, meaning every word of it. Lorna and Jasmine took a modest bow.

'So how do we do this?' said Derry. 'Can I buy it? Doesn't everything belong to the theatre?'

'Sure,' said Jasmine, 'But wardrobe can do costume hire, and I'm Wardrobe. You can sign a chit. When you make your fortune, stick a few euro in the charity box. While we're at it, we'll rustle you up an embroidered tablecloth to put your crystal ball on.'

All Derry could do was mutter her thanks.

'Road test!' said Bella.

'Okay!' said Lorna.

'Take One!' said Jasmine.

'Um . . .' said Derry. But before she could protest, Bella grabbed her elbow and wheeled her out into the corridor.

Even though she was wearing her own shoes, walking in her new outfit was strange. Dignified and matronly seemed the right approach. Derry hardly noticed where they were going until they stopped outside a scruffy door. Oddly, it was marked 'Door,' but Derry saw that the other word, whatever it was, had dropped off.

'What are we doing?' whispered Derry.

'You're an actress, dammit, act!' said Bella. She knocked vigorously.

The door was flung open to reveal Frankie's outraged face.

'What the F—' Bella! What's happening? Please tell me the place is on fire.' His eyes widened as he caught sight of Derry. 'I don't believe we've been introduced.' His toothless grin morphed into a toothless leer.

'I want to introduce you to my friend Tulip,' said Bella. 'Just giving her a little tour.' She slapped herself on the forehead. 'Oh, I forgot I left something with Lorna. Back in a mo.' She was gone.

Frankie opened the door wide. 'Why don't you come in . . . Tulip,' he said in his most charming and seductive tones. True enough, if you closed your eyes so his features weren't the obstacle they clearly were and averted your face from his halitosis, you might indeed find Frankie's voice middling attractive.

'We could have a nice cup of tea,' crooned Frankie. 'Or would you like something stronger? I'm Frankie, by the way. That's why my friends call me Frankie.' He laughed uproariously, as though that were the funniest thing he had ever heard. 'Well, don't just stand there, come in.'

Before Derry knew what was happening, Frankie's hand was on her back propelling her into a tiny office. The desk was piled high with papers. A public address microphone, a small TV and an ancient switchboard were fixed haphazardly to the wall.

'Take a seat,' said Frankie. 'Please,' he added, indicating a battered red plastic chair as if it were the most delicate Regency.

Derry looked around frantically for a means of escape but saw none. She told herself to *get a grip*. She was an actress for goodness' sake, just as Bella had said. And she'd better get the hang of things. *Think of this as a dress rehearsal.*

'Why, thank you,' she said, perching on the plastic. Why her accent came out as Gone With The Wind when she looked more Gatsby, Derry had no idea. 'I'm sure you're far too busy to be entertaining me,' she added. She fluttered her eyelashes and bobbed, clutching her necklace to her throat in ladylike hesitation. She sat and crossed her legs, comfortable that in her long dress she was in no danger of inflaming Frankie's passions. But there she was wrong. Frankie paid no attention at all to Derry's legs. Or to the bosom that might have been expected to captivate a certain type of older gentleman with a maternal fixation.

Frankie dropped to his knees. He gazed up at Derry beseechingly. He took her hand in his. He stroked all the way up and down the long black glove. 'Oh,' he moaned, holding the gloved hand to his cheek. 'Oh!' The stroking grew more frantic. 'It's not often,' said Frankie, barely able to get the words out, 'that a man meets a *real* woman—' he gulped, his voice hoarse '—a *properly dressed* woman.'

Actors tend to disapprove of the stage direction 'Exit' on the principle that a few more lines would add to the depth of the scene, its emotional intensity and the chance of a nomination. But in this case, Derry concluded that exit was for once the appropriate course. She tried to retrieve her arm from Frankie's adoring grasp, but he seemed to be having a conversation with her glove he thought it rude of her to interrupt.

'They can keep their miniskirts showing their bottoms for all I care, the sluts,' breathed Frankie, 'but a real lady, now that's a different story. Let me get the door—'

Luckily, just at that moment, and before Frankie could get off his knees, that same door opened. Bella poked her head into the room. She stared at Freddie on his knees. 'Sorry to interrupt the prayer meeting, but we have to go now. Nice seeing you Frankie.'

Derry bolted for the safety of the door.

'No!' said Frankie, his expression stricken. 'We *must* meet again!'

'She'll phone you. Promise!' said Bella, slamming the door shut behind them.

'What do you mean I'll phone him?' protested Derry as she was hustled back up the corridor.

'What did you do to poor Frankie?' said Bella. 'And what are you complaining about? You're a hit! It works!' She recited as if reading a review, '*Madam Tulip's debut performance can only be described as*

48

a stunning success. What command of the stage! What presence! What conviction! What passion!

'What if that happens all the time?' said Derry. Normally, the prospect of kneeling men kissing her outstretched hand and professing eternal devotion would be perfectly acceptable, but not when the kneeler looked like Frankie.

'That's just him,' said Bella. 'They say his mother was a pantomime dame. Alright, let's get you back into civvies.'

Derry left the Palace Theatre with two bulging bags and a wig box. As she stepped into the glare of the street, she carefully placed the bags and her wig box against the wall. Fastidiously, smudge by smudge, she wiped off her moustache.

'There is,' she said to a puzzled passerby, 'a limit.'

Two minutes after Derry arrived back at her flat and one minute after she put the kettle on, the panic started. A dress rehearsal that fooled a randy old goat was all very well, but opening night was still to come.

Derry was on her second cup of borage before she had calmed down enough to think it through. She needed to phone Marlene's organiser person. She'd have to ask her about a fee, and Derry hated talking money. But first, she needed to work out what kind of show she was going to offer. She could do card readings, she was sure. Maybe a crystal ball would be better than cards? She'd have to think about that. What about sound effects, lights, props—all the things she'd been talking about with Bella?

She decided against sound effects and lights on the principle that anything electronic she touched instantly made strangled noises, told her that whatever happened had been 'exceptionally fatal,' and promptly cost her lots of money. But even if she had only her costume and props, how would she get to a gig in the middle of nowhere? A taxi would cost a fortune. Maybe Bella would run her down for a reasonable sum, plus debt cancellation?

First, she decided, phone Marlene's organiser. The phone was answered immediately, although Derry didn't catch the woman's name.

'Hello, I'm Derry O'Donnell. Madam Tulip,' said Derry. Introducing herself as Madam Tulip was strange. She expected any moment for the organiser to say she was an imposter and threaten to call the police. Instead, she didn't seem in the least surprised.

'Marlene spoke to me. She'd like you to do the event. Just don't take off too much. Not that anybody's a prude, if you know what I mean dear, but the hotel licence and so on. Don't want the paparazzi arranging a police raid at the first flash of a nipple, do we. Anyway, wardrobe malfunctions have been done to death, don't you think?'

It took a moment for Derry to grasp what the woman meant. Then she realised. Marlene had said there was to be a burlesque artist. 'No! I'm Derry . . . I'm Madam Tulip the fortune-teller.'

'Oh!' said the organiser. 'I see. Yes. She mentioned a Miss Violet or something. What do you do, exactly?'

'Um . . . fortunes, tarot cards, crystal ball,' said Derry, certain now the woman was going to say bad idea, forget it.

'I'll email you the contract. Fill in your details, address for the cheque, sign and return if you're happy, alright?'

'Oh,' said Derry. 'Yes. Thanks.' She remembered only just in time to mention the fee.

'Let me check,' said the organiser. 'Fifteen hundred alright?'

Derry felt faint. 'Euros?'

The organiser sounded put out. 'Well, we could pay in sterling if you wanted. We'd have to do a bank transfer, though.'

'No, no. Euros, fine. Thanks.'

Euros were almost the same as dollars, and fifteen hundred was three weeks' work for a theatre actress. Derry did some rapid sums. She could pay Bella fifty, say, for the ride down, plus debt cancellation. That left more than enough for a month's rent. All earned in a couple of days. For the first time in ages, Derry felt hope.

As she sipped her borage, she thought about this amazing piece of luck. She would have liked more details, but she hadn't dared quiz the organiser in case she changed her mind. Derry wondered—would taking a peek be so very bad?

Most people might imagine that a person with Derry's gift of second sight would always know what lay around the corner. But that wasn't true. Second sight was never foolproof and almost always confusing. Knowing your own future could easily backfire. If you saw a bad day coming you wouldn't get out of bed, which would make it either a good day (with no bad thing happening) or a bad one (because you hadn't done the stuff you were supposed to do while you were lying in bed). Altogether, the whole business was way too complicated.

But then again, Derry reasoned, curiosity about castles in lakes wasn't, in any normal sense, curiosity about one's own future, was it? Of course it wasn't. Not at all.

Derry sat back on her little couch and tried to clear her mind. She concentrated. *Nothing*. She imagined a castle on an island and limousines arriving to drop off their rich and famous owners. All that came were questions about how the limos got onto the island. Was there a drawbridge? A ferry? Derry shook herself. *Concentrate!*

There—the shimmering blue water of a lake. And in its uncannily still surface were reflected the turrets and battlements of a castle. The view shifted. This time the image of the water was close up, and Derry couldn't see the castle at all. Instead, her vision was filled with a huge floating lily pad. On the lily pad sat a tiny yellow frog, its black eyes glittering.

The frog croaked twice before hopping into the water with a plop. The lily pad dissolved. All around Derry was the familiar clutter of her little flat.

At that moment, her phone rang.

'Derry, it's Marlene.'

Derry was dismayed. 'Hi, Marlene.'

Obviously Marlene was calling to cancel the gig at the castle. So much for the cute frog. But Derry was wrong.

'Could you do a reading just for me?' said Marlene. 'I'll be in town this afternoon. I'll pay, of course. No fuss, just come as you are. Please say yes. It's important to me. There's something I need to know.'

5

Some hotels, when you walk into the lobby, have a way of making you feel like you've just dressed from the clothes bin at your local recycling centre. That was how Derry felt as she stood at the glistening reception desk of the plushest hotel in downtown Dublin.

'And . . . how can I help you,' said the over-groomed male receptionist, adding after an exquisitely timed delay, ' . . . Miss.'

The implication was clear—either Derry was looking for afternoon trade, in which case she was far too down-market for this hotel, or she was looking for a job washing dishes and had come to the wrong entrance.

Fortunately Derry had once played Lady Bracknell, a theatrical role much loved by actresses and the perfect training for slapping down the most condescending of upstart receptionists.

'I have an appointment with Marlene O'Mara, also known as Marlene Doyle, thank you,' she announced grandly.

At this, Mr. Upstart should have murmured obsequious apologies and hurried to phone the guest in question. Instead, he raised his left eyebrow in lazy disbelief. Was Derry really asking him to annoy his rich and famous client? Or was she going to do the sensible thing and leave *without* the assistance of the security staff. With a sniff, he busied himself with ignoring Derry altogether.

Luckily, Lady B. was only one of several roles Derry had played in which strong and assertive women administered withering put-downs to supercilious creeps. Derry knew she needed to deal a devastating blow that would keep this particular creep awake all night tossing and turning, wishing he hadn't been utterly baffled and defeated. Lady Macbeth? Cleopatra? Derry dismissed both as mild-mannered pushovers. Time to do *A Vanessa*.

Crooking her finger, Derry beckoned for Mr. Upstart to lean closer, as if she had a secret password to impart. He obliged in that automatic way people do when they are invited to share a confidence.

'Screw. You,' said Derry in her best Bronx. 'Pick up the goddam phone. Now!'

As if a hypnotist had clicked his fingers, instantly Mr. Upstart became Mr. Sheep. He paled. His hands trembled. He retreated as far back from the counter as he could without actually climbing into the hotel safe. But he made the call.

'I'm so sorry, Madame,' he said, his voice hoarse. 'Mrs. Doyle will see you now.' Mr. Upstart looked as if he had swallowed a trout.

'Hah!' thought Derry. *'Madame! Too right, my friend.'*

'Room three-twelve. The elevator is over there. Thank you,' said Mr. Upstart. Derry was gratified to observe a small bead of sweat form on his upper lip.

As she reached the elevator and pressed the button, something made Derry look back. Mr. Upstart was staring after her. He had a telephone to his ear—not the hotel telephone he had used to speak to Marlene, but a cellphone. As she caught his eye, he quickly slid the phone under the desk and made to look busy.

The lift bell rang. The doors opened, and Derry was whisked to the third floor.

The room into which Derry was invited by a beaming Marlene O'Mara was only a little smaller than Derry's whole apartment. In the centre was a gigantic double bed, its snowy acres obscured by dozens of oversize shopping bags emblazoned with the names of the most exclusive emporia in the city. But Derry had no time to wonder. She needed all her faculties to cope with the mwaahing and cheek-kissing. Marlene seemed keen that no petty distinction should be made between Derry and a long-lost sister.

Refusing the offer of champagne and a little foie gras from room service, Derry listened agog as Marlene explained how she always took a room in town for a day's shopping. These days your driver could no longer park outside the store, so what else could you do but get the store to send your purchases straight to the hotel?

'Why everyone doesn't do it, I honestly don't know,' Marlene continued. 'I mean, people complain about traffic congestion all the time when there's really no need.' She tilted her head to one side in a way Derry had to admit was charming, and smiled her perfect smile. 'And you can do your other business as well,' she added.

Derry couldn't help but notice that when Marlene mentioned other business her smile vanished. For something to say, Derry asked, 'Do you normally stay the night?'

'No,' said Marlene. 'Peter prefers if I come home. A couple of hours in the Merc. All do-able, really.'

Derry agreed it was indeed do-able. She didn't add *if you have a chauffeur and a limousine.*

The small talk over, they settled down to the promised reading.

In all the years that Derry had told fortunes for her friends, she had seen many different reactions. Some people were baffled. Others were impressed and a little in awe, usually when Derry was on particularly good form and the cards were feeling cooperative. But never had Derry seen the kind of nervous excitement Marlene showed now. And the reading hadn't even begun.

They were seated in comfortable leather chairs around a coffee table lit by a single lamp. Surprisingly, Marlene wanted Derry to read from the ordinary deck, not the tarot. No need for all that, she said. Let's keep it simple. Marlene's suggestion wasn't a request, and Derry realised she was now reading for a client, a paying customer rather than a friend.

The feeling was odd. As she took the cards from her bag and prepared herself, Derry wondered—could what she was doing be wrong? In the excitement of the scheme, she hadn't thought enough about that. Had her grandfather or great-grandfather ever taken money for using their gifts?

Hey, Granddads, she said to herself, cutting the deck. *Are you guys okay with this?*

Queen.

Derry smiled. *Okay.* She shuffled and cut again.

Two. Not a positive card, ever. She thought some more about her dilemma. Say she gave a quarter of what she made to a good charity? Again, she shuffled and cut.

Queen. *Alright!*

'Is everything okay?' asked Marlene. She was anxious, perhaps imagining the cards were being cut for her and Derry was hiding something.

'Nothing yet,' said Derry cheerfully. 'Just warming up the cards. They need to be . . . aligned. Why don't we begin with you asking a question? Shall we start?'

Usually, people took the most roundabout route possible to get to the question they most wanted to ask. But not Marlene. Marlene got straight down to business.

'I'm divorcing him,' she said.

'Oh,' said Derry.

'I need to know . . . if it will be alright.'

'Alright?'

'Will he make it hard for me? He doesn't know yet.'

Marlene's eyes left Derry in no doubt she thought the answer the most important thing in the world. Derry hesitated. What on earth could she say? She had to remind herself this was a card reading—so let the cards show whatever they were going to show. She gave Marlene the deck to cut then dealt a three-card spread. Nothing. Or nothing that made any sense.

'You'll need to be strong,' said Derry, reasoning that sensible advice would at least do no harm. She felt an immense surge of pity. Marlene had everything, and yet she was depending on a stranger to tell her if she were going to suffer dreadfully in a divorce. Of course she was. Didn't everybody?

Derry gathered up the cards and again gave Marlene the deck to cut. This time she dealt a nine-card spread, hoping for a story she could understand. But the cards were stubbornly opaque. Derry tried a trick she had used many times before, defocusing her eyes so the cards melted together in a hazy constellation, free from the rigid constraints of the square. It took a moment, but it happened.

In the centre of the spread, patches of colour coalesced. Fragments of light and shade flickered, shifting themselves one behind the other. As if floating beneath a pool of clear oil, by some kind of mutual attraction the elements slid together. The whole swirled ever more slowly, then settled, the scene filling the pool with depth and meaning.

A man, bare-chested, was seated on a kind of throne. He wore an elaborate headdress of gorgeous feathers, like an enormous shimmering green halo. On his lap was a disembodied head. Its features were unmistakable. The head belonged to Peter Doyle.

The shock made Derry sweep the cards towards her, covering them with her arm. Marlene couldn't have seen—of course she couldn't—but Derry's heart was pounding.

'Let's try another spread, shall we?' she said, working to keep her voice steady. She shuffled and offered the pack to be cut in a rapid, fluid movement before dealing yet again. This time, she would just read the cards. So much for openness.

The new pattern made sense from the start. An old-fashioned kind of sense. The kind that didn't involve horrible visions.

'Okay,' said Derry, hugely relieved. She described for Marlene what the cards said of her past, and the stress and confusion they told of her present. She had to concentrate hard, maintain a cool professional exterior. She struggled to put aside the ghastly memory of the man on the throne—the cradled, disembodied head—and see only the cards in front of her. Fortunately, the message was clear.

'I see . . . a lucky escape.'

'I knew it!' said Marlene, delighted. 'It *is* a lucky escape. Things were never right between us. I was young. He was sophisticated. Powerful. Like a king.'

Derry froze, then relaxed as she realised Marlene's words could have nothing to do with that dreadful vision. The man in the head-dress was somebody else—if he existed at all.

'I wanted to know was I doing the right thing,' said Marlene. 'You've put my mind at rest. It's going to work out, I know it is.' She smiled like a child assured that Father Christmas was real.

'You mustn't take the cards too literally,' said Derry. 'Sometimes they help with thinking things through, that's all.'

'You're special,' said Marlene simply.

'No,' said Derry. 'Really. Not at all.' If *special* meant more visions like the one she had just had, *special* she could live without.

'I knew you'd say that,' said Marlene. 'But that's not what your father thinks.' She leaned forward as though she were telling a secret, whispered, '*Inside Out!*' and giggled.

Marlene chattered happily as she saw Derry to the door, saying how she was so looking forward to another card reading at the Celebrity Bash. At the threshold, she thrust an envelope into Derry's hand. 'Thank you,' she said. 'I am grateful. I feel I have a friend.'

Derry didn't have to think about it. No need to ask the Granddads what *they* thought either.

'No,' she said. 'Honestly, no thanks. I'll be doing the charity gig for you anyway. Why don't you give it to the fund. From Madam Tulip.'

In the elevator, descending to the lobby, Derry was thankful to be alone. No matter how hard she tried to block it out, the dreadful vision kept coming back. She shook herself, wondering if she should again ask her father how he dealt with the bad ones, the upsetting ones. She had once before asked how he coped with their peculiar gift. But all he had said was, 'Everybody's different. You have to find your own way.' Then he smiled one of his manic smiles. 'Just don't walk into a lamppost. You *would* feel silly.'

At the memory, Derry grinned. Once more, the world seemed normal. Crazy, but normal.

The elevator doors opened with a barely perceptible *whoosh*. As she left the lobby, Derry glanced over to Reception, but Mr. Upstart was nowhere to be seen. She was about to leave through the revolving glass doors that led to the street when she paused to let an older couple go first. As she waited, she glanced around. To her surprise, sitting in an armchair near the ornate fireplace in the corner, his uniform hat on the seat beside him, was the chauffeur she remembered from the races. What was his name, Pablo? *Paulo!* He was startlingly handsome with piercing black eyes and glistening white teeth. Spanish? He was looking straight at her.

He smiled and blew a kiss.

6

Some moral dilemmas have no solution. Late Thursday night, Derry's mother phoned from the departure lounge at JFK Airport to say not to bother meeting her at Dublin. She'd be flying direct from there to Galway. Her plan was to catch Jacko at his studio before he got wind she was coming.

'I can count on you to stay schtum, can't I dear?' said Vanessa. What she meant was, 'I know your father wraps you around his little finger, but this time *I'm* in charge.'

So Derry had to promise not to tell. Then she remembered she had claimed not to have Jacko's phone number, so she had to promise she wouldn't tell even if she were able. By then she was so confused she forgot to mention the Celebrity Bash. Not that Vanessa was listening.

'Can you believe I had to board carrying *a yellow plastic bag?*' she said. 'You go to a world of trouble to accessorise, and they give you a refuse sack for your Chanel. Bad enough the cabin décor was created by some colour-blind kitchen installer from Akron. I hardly dared take a nap. I just *knew* when I opened my eyes it'd still be there.'

Much as Derry loved her mother, not having to meet her at the airport was good news. On the Friday morning she was able to concentrate on getting ready for her gig. Amazingly, Bella turned up on time and sat around more or less patiently while Derry went through her checklist.

The list was a lifesaver. Costume—check. Wig box—check. Corset and beanbags—check. Makeup kit—check. Fortune-telling kit of crystal ball, tarot cards, ordinary cards—check. Jewellery and shoes—

nearly forgotten! Embroidered tablecloth—check. Plus respectable daytime clothes and best dress for dinner. And a little stack of business cards, each boasting a red tulip and a crystal ball. 'Madam Tulip—fortune-teller.'

'You sure you don't need an assistant?' said Bella. 'I could carry the bags. Set up the crystal ball. Lay the table?'

'It's not a silver service,' said Derry. 'Honest, there's nothing to it.' Derry doubted that a leather-jacketed Bella would project the aura of mystery and other-worldliness required of a psychic's assistant. Bella might have suited a knife-throwing act. If Bella were throwing the knives.

'You'll be great!' said Bella as they motored at a leisurely forty miles an hour in the central lane of the motorway. Frustrated drivers honked their horns and flew past on the inside, the outside or both, like cats let out of a sack. If cats escaping from sacks made obscene gestures and mouthed the names of various parts of the human anatomy.

'What if the celebrities think I'm no good?' said Derry.

'Of course they won't,' said Bella, in the automatic way actors have when conversations begin with 'what if they think . . .'

'But they might!' said Derry, sticking to the age-old script.

'Rubbish,' said Bella. 'Your client's future is in your hands. Are they gonna tell you you're a fraud? Of course not!'

Derry tried to explain that predicting someone's future wasn't the same as causing that future, and anyway that was blackmail. 'I can't make up a future just because someone doesn't like me!'

Bella sighed. 'All that matters is that they *think* you can! Who's gonna be there anyway? Half-starved models, wannabe clothes designers, past-it film directors, some female singers trying to wear less than everybody else. All rubbish. Except Mojo, I don't have to say.'

Bella rolled her shoulders and swayed, dancing with the steering wheel and making the car lurch across two lanes. Brakes screeched and horns blared.

'What about Mojo?' asked Derry when the car's trajectory once more approximated a straight line and she could open her eyes. Mojo was an outlandishly gorgeous rapper from London, winner of numerous industry awards. He was also the star of TV ads for masculine cosmetics and a revolutionary vacuum cleaner also created especially for men, so presumably designed to withstand long periods of storage under the stairs.

'The Bash! He's gonna be there. Didn't you check his Twitter?'

Derry wasn't in the habit of checking pop stars' tweets, and certainly not a rapper, on the principle that checking a rapper's tweets would be like reading a railway timetable a hundred-and-forty characters at a time.

'*That man!*' breathed Bella. She spoke in the tones one might use to greet a vanilla ice cream with strawberry slices on an especially warm day in Death Valley. 'For *that man*, I would throw myself off a moving train, naked, at midnight, in Siberia.'

'He's only a singer!' protested Derry.

In Bella's view, the words 'only' and 'singer' didn't often figure together. 'He is,' said Bella, '*the* singer.'

'What about that singer last week you—?'

'Different genre altogether,' said Bella, airily. 'More Indy. Mojo is a poet.'

Derry was content to take Bella at her word. Unfortunately, Bella seemed to believe Derry's opinion was important. For the next hundred miles, at the top of her voice, Bella recited Mojo's entire canon, not forgetting the widely admired classic *Hand-Made-Shooze (Lick My)*.

Derry had never paid much attention to Mojo's music, but did enjoy a modest fix of poetry. She even had a passing interest in poetic technique, only natural for a performer in the dramatic arts. To her surprise, Mojo held her interest for two, possibly even three whole minutes. In the first dozen lines, she spotted numerous iambic pentameters, not to mention a spondee, a couple of pyrrhics and a dactyl. He had an especially strong facility for synonyms, achieving in a couple of verses thirteen different ways of referring to buttocks and seven ways of reminding his female listeners that they were of a canine persuasion.

Derry frowned.

'Bella, how can you sing this stuff?'

Derry would never describe herself as politically correct, on the principle of glass houses, stones and her own unfortunate inability to think before she spoke. But there was a limit.

'This is *Art*,' insisted Bella.

As Bella continued to recite the full and unabridged works of the awesome Mojo, Derry was forced to agree. Anything that bored you to the point of wishing for service station coffee just had to be Art.

～

'Wow!' said Derry.

'Class!' said Bella.

As the car crested a wooded hill, the sparkling expanse of a vast lake dotted with green islands appeared below. On the nearest island was a patchwork of parks and gardens and, at the end of a sweeping drive, a castle—not huge but impressive. A majestic stone stairway swept up to the frontage, while an elegant wing framed each side of the main building. Behind squatted a tower crowned with battlements.

As they descended the hill to the narrow stone causeway leading to the island, they had to stop and wait as a car was approaching. The powerful black limousine wafted past them without a glance from the driver. Derry and Bella tried to peer into the back, but the glass was heavily tinted and they could see nothing.

'Oh no!' said Bella, 'Do you think it's Mojo? What if he's leaving?'

If Derry hadn't been entranced by the vista of lake, causeway, and towering castle, she might have asked herself why Bella was so concerned. But she didn't.

As they approached the end of the long curving avenue, the castle loomed ahead like a mirage in a fairy tale. But fairy-tale castles weren't usually flanked by white marquees. Nor did they often boast a posse of tuxedoed security men talking into their sleeves while carrying unnecessary umbrellas.

In front of their car, a limousine swished to a halt by the magnificent stairs. The driver leapt out to open its doors, disgorging VIPs led away by security to a reserved entrance in one of the castle wings. The driver backed the limousine into a marquee, a security man directing him like he was parking a jet on a runway.

'Awesome!' whispered Bella, as if being overheard might lead to her being immediately expelled just when she had died and arrived in heaven. 'They've got special tents for the cars! I could live like this! Couldn't you live like this?'

They pulled up at the bottom of the steps. One of the security men came trotting down—an especially fit looking specimen with broad shoulders and chiselled jaw. He stuck his head in the open car window.

'Sorry ladies, special guests only. Would you mind parking round the back?'

Trouble, thought Derry. Big trouble. If Bella was being told *special* applied to other people and *round the back* was for her, this security man would need more than a brolly and a tuxedo if he were to emerge unscathed.

The man's face broke into a delighted smile. 'Bella ! Derry! Darlings! Go on dears; around the back and I'll catch you in two minutes. Wonderful to see you! Off you go now! Be with you in a mo.' He sprang lightly back up the stairway to his post by the door.

So astonished was Bella that she meekly obeyed, parking the car with a hundred other non-limousines in a vast car park round the back of the castle.

'What's Bruce doing here? I thought he did furniture removals. Wasn't he an instructor at some fitness centre?'

'He fixes my laptop—I thought he worked with computers,' said Derry. Bruce had often rescued her from technical disaster. A major plus was that she didn't have to feel pathetic. In a masterly demonstration of shameless sophistry, Derry persuaded herself that depending on a man to fix stuff was fine as long as the man was gay.

Neither felt the need to mention that Bruce was an actor. A person with so many occupations could hardly be anything else. What other profession demanded its practitioners make their living landscape gardening, waitressing, delivering singing telegrams and answering telephone sex lines?

Derry and Bruce had been classmates in theatre school. He was a fellow American, and Derry found it wonderfully relaxing to talk to somebody else who liked syrup on their pancakes. Over coffee between classes, Bruce had told her how he had joined the US Navy straight from school in Texas. He had so excelled he had been chosen to become a SEAL, a member of that select band of warriors renowned for dropping in unannounced while terrorists are watching television.

Derry had asked how on earth Bruce had morphed from military man in the US to drama student in Dublin. He explained how back then the Navy rule about being gay was Don't-Ask-Don't-Tell, but after he had won his tenth medal for doing something top secret involving hostages and skydiving, he thought telling would be alright. It wasn't, and they threw him out for being morally degenerate, albeit with an Honorable Discharge. 'I ask you darling,' he said. 'What did they think I was going to do? Make out with the lieutenant? His own mother would say he was ugly.'

Derry and Bella stepped out of the car to stretch their legs. They were wondering what to do next when Bruce came bounding round the corner. He skidded to a halt, showing no sign of being out of breath or otherwise inconvenienced.

'I am *so* sorry!' he said. 'But the front entrance is just for the VIPs. What are you guys doing here?'

'I'm doing a . . . show. At the Celebrity Bash,' said Derry, considering it wiser not to explain her new career as fortune-teller in the first thirty seconds of meeting anybody, even a fellow actor and friend.

'And I'm her assistant,' said Bella. 'Assisting.'

'What are *you* doing here?' said Derry and Bella together.

'I'm working for an agency. I'm sticking to weekend events in case I get a call.'

Derry and Bella fully understood the importance of being available when a call from your agent came. That marvellous event could happen day or night and could involve attending auditions at short notice. It hardly mattered that calls from your agent occurred somewhat less often than calls from world leaders asking for advice, and that shows running for more than a week before closing were rare unless they featured massed Irish dancers.

'Derry is doing a fortune-telling show—Madam Tulip,' said Bella. 'We need to bring in her stuff.'

'Wow, cool,' said Bruce. 'Don't worry about your things, I'm covered for ten minutes. I'll help you in. You staying over?'

'Yes,' said Derry.

'Yes. Er . . . Derry is,' said Bella.

'I don't have much to carry, just these,' said Derry, extracting her bags and the wig box from the back seat of the car.

'Awesome, you can tell my fortune,' said Bruce.

'Sure,' said Derry. 'As long as you don't take it too seriously.' The incident with Marlene was still fresh in her memory.

'I'm okay with that,' said Bruce. 'I went to a fortune-teller in Vegas. It was amazing. She had a booth and weird lights and a smoke machine and all. Won't you have a booth?'

'No,' said Derry. 'I'm hoping they'll give me a small room and I can draw the curtains.'

'Kinda unplugged,' said Bella.

'Hey, I've got just the thing,' said Bruce, 'Let me get something from the van. Back in a jiffy.' He trotted down the line of cars to a battered purple van squatting across two parking places.

Derry and Bella watched as Bruce administered a complex pattern of two thumps and a carefully modulated kick to the rear doors, which sprang open. He disappeared inside and emerged seconds later carrying an ornate old-fashioned table lamp and something glass and old-looking.

'Here we go,' said Bruce, flourishing the table lamp. 'Atmosphere. You just tilt it up a bit, get some shadows going. And check this.'

For an egg timer it was big, but this was no ordinary egg timer. The thing was obviously antique—two glass globes in a carved wooden frame. Sand ran between the halves when you turned the frame upside down.

'They call it an hourglass, but it times out after ten minutes,' said Bruce. 'You won't have to keep looking at your watch. Once the sand runs down, you're done. If the customer wants more, they pay more.

'Hey!' said Derry. 'Thanks! That's brilliant.'

'I was doing a removal for a guy who wanted his stable cleared out,' said Bruce. 'He said keep anything you fancy. I passed on the bondage stool, but these were kinda quaint. Come on, I'll take you inside.'

Picking up a bag under each arm, Bruce led the way to a discreet rear entrance, holding the door open for them in the most gentlemanly way. Derry sighed, American manners were so refreshing. Irish men were adorable, but they would be more inclined to slap you on the back chummily and hand you *their* bag to carry.

'I need to find whoever is running the Bash,' said Derry. 'I hope they remember I'm booked.'

'Of course they will,' said Bruce. 'These celebrity events are run like military operations. Man, I've seen looser arrangements for invading small countries.'

He was leading them up a back staircase painted in factory green and lit with fluorescents. Like the theatre, thought Derry. Nothing glamorous behind the scenes.

'The worst are the celebrity weddings,' said Bruce. 'At those we have to confiscate everybody's phone. The exclusive photo rights are always sold to some magazine. Can you imagine getting their phones off those people? It's like you're asking them for a kidney. Worse. They don't need their kidneys for tweeting.'

Through a passage and two doors, and they were in the main hotel lobby. The vaulted hall was magnificent, panelled in dark wood and dominated by a gigantic stone mantelpiece. The place was bustling with guests arriving for the weekend. Two receptionists manned the desk.

'This is the main lobby—the celebrity do is in the West Wing. We go through here,' said Bruce.' He led them to a double doorway guarded by two security men who gave him a cheery nod and let them pass.

Beyond the door was another hall, this one hung with portraits. A wide wooden staircase swept upwards, dividing in two at the first landing where one flight swept left and the other right. At the base of the stairs, tucked into the corner, was a reception desk boasting a computer, trays of paperwork, ID badges and tourist brochures, but no receptionist.

'Hang on,' said Bruce, 'Let's get the drill.' He put down Derry's bags and turned away, putting his cuff to his mouth and muttering into his radio. Derry carefully set the hourglass on the floor at her feet beside her precious wig box. Bella put the table lamp on the floor and idly perused the brochures.

Bruce had hardly finished speaking when a woman in a blue suit with padded shoulders and carrying a walkie-talkie bore down on them. She was smiling.

'So glad you could come. I'm Clodagh, your Organiser. Bruce says you're our fortune-teller. I believe we spoke on the phone?'

How odd, thought Derry. When the woman spoke, her lips didn't move. Her wide smile stayed fixed as if painted on her face. Her voice seemed to project from somewhere in the back of her throat, filter through her teeth and mysteriously emerge, as from a ventriloquist.

The Organiser consulted her clipboard. 'Room 204,' she said to Derry. She looked at Bella, her eyes flicking over Bella's leather jacket. The Organiser's mouth was still smiling, but her eyes were not. Her attention was fixed on the brightly painted logo on Bella's shoulder proclaiming '*Money is Murder!*' the legacy of a brief fling with an excitingly militant Scottish journalist. Bella had confided to Derry that although the hack in question had left her for an English heiress by way of taking class war into the enemy's camp, the memory of the thrilling way he denounced Rightist Deviationism still made her shiver.

The Organiser's eyes swivelled to the lamp on the floor by Bella's feet. Behind her permanent smile, Derry could see that complex calculations were whizzing around her brain. Like anyone working in hotels, she would be accustomed to celebrities leaving with furniture, fixtures or fittings. But Bella had not yet been inside a bedroom, and in any case no apartment in the castle contained anything as tasteful as Bruce's lamp, which boasted no knights, unicorns, harps, shamrocks or unlikely Latin proverbs.

The Organiser's brow furrowed. She fixed Bella with a look implying that the whims of satnavs brought all kinds of flotsam to the hotel's shores. Surely Bella was expected at a campsite somewhere? 'And who, may I ask . . . ?'

Derry was getting more and more worried with every passing moment. If Bella perceived some insult, she would at best quote the relevant legislation, an approach that somehow always ended up with the police being called. At worst she would prod a finger at the offender's chest, emphasising important constitutional and philosophical points, before pushing the unfortunate victim backwards into the nearest wall, table or orchestra pit. Fully aware of the danger in which the Organiser had unwittingly placed herself, and wanting at all costs not to be ejected from her first gig as Madam Tulip, Derry moved to intervene.

'This is Bella. My assistant,' she said. 'She won't be staying; she's helping me with my arrangements.' Derry smiled a smile at least as dazzling as the Organiser's.

'Oh,' said the Organiser. 'Well, she'll have to leave the reserved area as soon as you've settled in. Guests and authorised personnel only, I'm sure you understand.' She turned to Bruce. 'Can I ask you to see to that?'

'Sure,' said Bruce. 'No problem. She will be safely expelled.' He grinned. 'Sorry, Bella. Outer darkness for you, honey.'

To Derry's surprise, Bella didn't protest.

'Do you know where I'll be doing my show?' asked Derry, addressing her question to the Organiser. She was keen to get set up. She knew that only when her props were ready and she was in costume would she lose her nerves.

'I'll call you later on that,' said the Organiser. 'I've got your number. I need to sort our guests first, okay?' She handed Derry a plastic ID on a cord to hang round her neck. She turned to Bruce. 'Could you help them upstairs?'

'Sure will,' said Bruce, taking a bag in each hand and following Derry and Bella up the wide stairway, Derry with her wig box and egg timer and Bella carrying the lampshade. Just as they reached the middle landing and swung to the left to climb the next flight, Bella stopped dead.

'It's him!' Her voice was a cross between a squeal and a gasp.

Below was Mojo, standing at the desk, being greeted by the Organiser. Beside him was a woman, obviously his partner, and behind them two assistants talking into their phones. The security men guarding the doors to the main hotel lobby were now on full alert. Through the glass you could see a little scrum of faces pressed to the panes.

Mojo was just as good-looking in real life as he was on television, thought Derry. He was slight, shorter than he appeared on TV, and way too polite. His New York equivalent would be wearing six pounds of bullion and trail a posse of jail-tattooed hangers-on with bulges under their armpits. It occurred to Derry that if success in the States was what he wanted, Mojo had better spend less time at the beautician and more at the gym.

Mojo's partner was a strikingly beautiful young black woman in a white faux-fur cape, tight calf-length trousers and six-inch heels. She radiated cool detachment. While Mojo was listing requirements to the organiser, his companion stood watching with quiet amusement.

'I can't believe he's still with *her*!' said Bella in a stage whisper Derry feared could be heard in the marquees outside. Bella hurriedly explained that the woman with Mojo was Sonya Dee. Derry was often teased by her friends for being as ignorant of pop culture as a High Court judge, but even she knew that Sonya Dee really was a star. She was a wildly successful American R'n'B singer, whose pairing with Mojo was generally agreed to be a big mistake. Tabloid commentators asked was it wise for an artist as credible as Sonya to be seen with an English rapper who had yet to shoot anybody and had no designer clothes collection.

Sonya was absentmindedly picking a piece of fluff off the shoulder of Mojo's jacket when the security men briefly held open the doors. Three photographers pushed through the scrum of onlookers, their cameras already flashing. Calls for smiles and profiles, and the photographers were done, hustled away as Sonya's assistant shouted, 'Sonya needs some Sonya time, okay you guys? Thank you!'

The stellar couple had just turned back to face the Organiser at her desk when Bella thrust the lampshade she was carrying into Derry's arms—ignoring that Derry was already carrying her wig box and egg timer—and reached into her jacket pocket.

Bella's phone was almost to her face, her finger poised on the camera button, when in a single smooth movement Bruce whisked the offending article from her hand.

'Hey!' yelped Bella. 'I was only taking a pic!'

'We could be thrown out!' whispered Derry, appalled. 'What are you thinking of?'

'Not allowed, darling,' said Bruce, wagging his finger at Bella. 'Naughty, naughty!' He hustled them up the stairs out of sight. No one below seemed to have noticed.

Derry sat on the four-poster bed in a richly panelled room, its windows dressed with heavy drapes, the furnishings oversized and ugly. She'd seen Bella off with many thanks and an injunction to behave on the way out, although she was confident that with Bruce as an escort even Bella was unlikely to get into trouble. Bella had promised she would return to pick up Derry at three o'clock next afternoon, when the event would be winding down.

Even before she unpacked her own clothes, Derry opened her Madam Tulip bag and laid out her costume. On the dressing table she placed the box with her wig and her chunky jewellery. To get a feel for her show, she laid her embroidered cloth on the writing table by the window, arranging her crystal ball, her two packs of cards and Bruce's egg timer. On the sideboard behind her, beside the kettle and her supply of borage tea, she positioned the table lamp. From where she sat she could see her reflection in the wardrobe mirror and if she tilted the lampshade just so, she could create a terrific backlight. She pulled the drapes closed. Not bad, she thought. Not bad at all.

Derry peered into her crystal ball. Inside she could see the lamp and her face reflected, distorted but bright. She moved her head from side to side, watching the shifting image of the room as if from inside a goldfish bowl. Only curiosity had made her look; a fascination with the visual effect created by the crystal had never left her. But there, strangely off-centre, completely unexpected, something stirred.

Inside the ball, curving into its depths, the image perfectly sharp, was an unmistakable commotion. A horse race. The leaders were approaching a fence, taking the jump in a confusing melee. Right in the middle of the oddly silent chaos, Derry was shocked to see a horse suddenly fall. It wasn't the jockey's fault, a mount had veered in front of him. But down the rider went, his tumbling body disappearing under the vicious, slicing hooves.

Derry looked away, unable to bear the sight of the aftermath that must surely follow. Or perhaps somewhere deep inside she believed that if she didn't see, it couldn't happen.

7

At three o'clock, Derry still had no clue about the arrangements for Madam Tulip. The Organiser had said she'd call but hadn't yet done so. Derry's nerves about Madam Tulip's first real outing would have grown unbearable by now, except that Derry had discovered the Celebrity High Tea.

Amazing how excess is the best possible cure for nerves, Derry thought, as she took her place at one of the big circular tables in the dining room. On a pristine white tablecloth was an array of gleaming silverware. The china tea set was adorned with tiny roses, and nestling inside each cup was a little box containing a silk tea bag. Sandwiches delicately cut into neat triangles sat on silver pedestals, and cake-stands held clusters of cupcakes. Every diner had their personal patisserie—little pastries of every imaginable shape and colour, with no two alike. Most were adorned with icing butterflies, songbirds, peacocks or any creature generally agreed to be cute. Or almost any. Derry observed with interest that butterflies and swallows were okay, but not mice or kittens. Cupids were fine, but babies without wings were a definite no-no.

The room was filling fast, though nothing seemed coordinated. People looked for an empty place, took a seat, held out their champagne glass to be filled and began talking at the tops of their voices. For every celebrity in the place there were at least six non-celebrities, presumably people who had paid big bucks for their seats. The non-celebrity men were easily recognised—fat and wearing tailored business suits. The celebrity men were thin and wore brightly coloured clothes screaming 'look at me.' Non-celebrity wives were particularly easy to recognise. They were the ones pointing at the celebrities.

Derry was acutely aware that soon she would be working as Madam Tulip, so with a sigh she refused the champagne. But nothing in the theatrical rulebook said you couldn't eat a sandwich followed by two pastries and a cupcake before a show. All actors know that the nervous tension of a performance uses up calories like nothing else. Eating is positively mandatory.

Derry was just persuading herself that one more cake couldn't do any harm, when she felt a tap on her shoulder. The Organiser's smile was still in place as if she had forgotten where she'd left it.

'I'm sorry, Miss . . .'

'Derry,' said Derry.

The Organiser looked puzzled. 'I thought you were Madam . . . Violet?'

'Tulip,' said Derry. 'But I'm really Derry.'

'Oh,' said the Organiser. 'I'm sorry, Miss Derry. We can sort you out with a space now. I'm afraid I'm not sure what's needed for your . . . activities. Can you come with me?'

Reluctantly leaving Cake Heaven, Derry followed the Organiser. Behind, the noise level was rising to the peak of a late-season baseball game, and Derry realised she had no need to be nervous. By the time her clients came to have their fortunes told, they would have drunk at least four glasses of champagne, be giggling helplessly, would fail to follow anything she said and remember none of it in the morning.

The function space where the cabaret and auction were to be held was a grand room with a stage at one end, lots of tables and a bar to one side. Near the entrance was an alcove and off the alcove a small windowless room used for storing fold-up chairs and tables, but now almost empty. A single round table was set up in the middle with two chairs facing each other.

'Will this do?' asked the Organiser. Her tone said it had better do because she had no intention of finding anywhere else. 'We can put a notice outside saying Madam . . . whatever, and I'll leave you a Do Not Disturb sign. We've timetabled you for a two-hour session now, half an hour from seven-thirty and two hours from eleven tomorrow morning. No overrunning your time this evening, please. We need the guests focused on the auction.'

Derry was appalled. 'Can we break that into two sessions? What if I need to . . . you know.' She wondered was the word *pee* allowed in a castle full of millionaires and celebrities.

The Organiser was obviously irritated, as if fortune-tellers should come equipped with plumbing for all eventualities, like astronauts. 'If you must,' she said, frowning while at the same time, in some miracle of muscular control, continuing to smile. The effect was alarming, but Derry held her nerve.

'Must,' said Derry.

'I suppose,' conceded the Organiser reluctantly. 'Just be sure to write on the sign saying what time you'll be back. Do you have a pen?' The implication was clear—no mere entertainer could be expected to have anything as sensible as a writing implement.

'Of course,' said Derry, making no effort to avoid sounding smug.

'Well then,' said the Organiser, grudgingly conceding a draw.

'Anything else?' asked Derry sweetly.

On the table was a champagne bucket, wearing the forlorn look champagne buckets wear when dry and empty. The Organiser picked it up and held it aloft like an exhibit to a jury. 'This is for your tokens,' she said. 'The guests buy tokens. They use them to pay for the entertainments. You give the tokens to me at the end. That means you don't have to handle cash.' She fixed Derry with a look that said, *and if you think we don't trust you, of course we don't. What do you take us for?*

Derry inspected her surroundings. The room didn't look too promising. Bare white walls, a table, two chairs and an antitheft bucket. But if she set up another table behind her and put her lamp on that, and covered her own table with the embroidered table-cloth, the effect could be atmospheric enough. It might just pass. The door seemed sturdy, so noise shouldn't be a big problem.

'Could I have a bottle of water? And I'll set up another table behind if that's okay.'

'I'll get someone to bring some bottles. Could you be ready in, say, ten minutes?'

'Can you make that fifteen?' asked Derry. Getting into costume and doing her makeup would take longer than ten minutes. 'I've got to change. Fifteen minutes and the curtain goes up, I promise.'

The Organiser looked around anxiously. 'Nobody told me anything about curtains. I did say to Marlene that this was getting far too complicated—'

'No, no!' said Derry. 'Just a phrase. No curtains.'

'Oh,' said the Organiser. 'No curtains?'

'None,' said Derry. 'I'd better get ready. Fifteen minutes, that's all. I promise.'

The door opened. The face that peered around was Marlene's. Her smile lit up as she saw Derry.

'Derry, darling! I'm so glad!' Has Clodagh been looking after you? I came down to say Peter had to leave early. We only just got here, but at least him being away means I can do girly things! So I want to be your very first. Can I be that?'

Derry assured her that she was indeed being looked after. Madam Tulip would be ready to start soon. Perhaps thirty minutes? The Organiser opened her mouth to protest but thought better of it.

'Cool!' said Marlene. 'But me first, okay? Is that a deal?'

Derry promised that yes, of course, Marlene could be first to have her fortune told.

Marlene disappeared, followed by the Organiser, who gave Derry a poisonous look as she left. Derry shrugged.

Showtime.

Enter: Madam Tulip.

8

Twenty-eight minutes later, Madam Tulip sat at her table in her makeshift booth. The Do Not Disturb sign hung outside the closed door. The lamps were positioned and lit. On the tapestry cloth, she had carefully laid out the cards, the crystal ball and the antique egg-timer. On the floor behind, she had placed her bottle of water and her contributions bucket. On her knee was her bag containing phone and life-support systems, including a small mirror she always brought to shows.

She checked her appearance. Wig—perfect. Headdress with feathers—adjusted. Pale makeup—like she hadn't seen daylight in ten years. Glasses and jewellery—impressive. Gloves—above elbow. Fake bust and hips—plain weird.

Getting dressed and made up without help had been a panicky business. All the while, the clock had been ticking. Getting the wig to look right had been the hardest part, but she managed. She checked herself again in her little mirror and was satisfied. She remembered to switch off her phone and had just closed her bag and shoved it behind her against the wall when the door opened. Marlene's head appeared.

'Oh,' she said. 'I'm sorry.' She withdrew, closing the door.

It took a moment for Derry to grasp what had happened. 'No! No!' she shouted, rushing to the door and opening it wide. 'It's me!'

Marlene stared. 'Oh my goodness! I can't believe this! That is amazing! Oh, this is *so* cool!'

'You like?' said Derry, giving her a twirl.

It's a well-known fact that to make an actor happy, all an audience needs to do is squeal, hold its hands to its mouth, open its eyes wide and go 'Ooh!' The degree of gratification experienced by the actor is in no way related to the size of the audience. All performers know that a small audience can easily make up for its lack of numbers by the distinction or sophistication of its members. Derry's audience this time was not large, but she was comfortably aware it *was* made up of world-famous supermodels.

This, thought Derry, *is A Good Start.*

'Take a seat, please,' she said, closing the door behind Marlene and resuming her place at the table.

As Marlene seated herself, Derry marvelled again at her perfection. She wore an exquisite designer dress, her hair was a work of art and she carried an antique jade-beaded bag, black and glistening. Marlene put the bag on the table in front of her. Derry could see at once it was Art Deco and must have cost a fortune, but valuable or not it couldn't sit there. She asked Marlene to pop the bag on the floor at her feet. As Marlene reached down to do as she had been asked, Derry smelt whiskey on her breath.

Marlene opted for an ordinary card reading rather than the tarot, admitting that tarot gave her the creeps. She was laughing but seemed nervous. Derry turned the egg-timer.

The cards fell out cleanly enough, and Derry was able to keep the reading innocuous. The nine of spades suggested that perhaps Marlene had recently experienced health problems, but the ten of hearts said she would get better. Derry settled for dispensing advice and vague predictions that couldn't do any harm even if they didn't do much good. Perhaps some of Marlene's favourite foods were worth avoiding? Marlene frowned, pursing her lips. Belatedly, Derry saw the problem. A model had to forego most foods most of the time, and now here was a fortune-teller advising she give up more. Time to move on.

As she dealt another spread, Derry wasn't really focusing on the cards. She was mostly thinking about how to avoid the tricky subject of husbands. Marlene was planning a divorce, and the less said about it the better. How could Derry forget that awful vision she had seen the first time she had read for Marlene—the king with the head of Peter Doyle on his lap? Derry shivered, turned the last card and saw its meaning as clearly as if the spread had spoken out loud.

A lucky escape. Again. Just like the first time she had read for Marlene. How strange. An escape from what? Nothing in the cards volunteered an answer. At least, thought Derry, it *was* an escape. Surely, an escape was always good? Derry knew she should say nothing about what she had seen. What if the knowledge changed the way Marlene behaved? Instead of avoiding the danger, she might walk straight into it. The future seemed to have a way of getting its own back. Instead, she said, 'I see you are sometimes afraid, sometimes alone. The cards say do not be afraid. All will be well.'

'You are so right about being alone,' said Marlene, sadly. 'It's true. They say that in the modelling business you don't have friends, only stablemates. Like we're horses. Only we're not horses,' she said quietly. She brightened. 'Okay, so am I going to get one of the big three?'

Derry didn't know what Marlene meant, until she explained that she was close to being chosen as the face of one of the three big perfume houses, the ultimate success for a model.

This time, Derry dealt a smaller spread. Her hands flew across the table with fluid movements in the way she found hugely enjoyable. And now the cards were unambiguous. For Marlene, they said, better times were ahead. They didn't say if that meant Marlene would get the job she wanted. But if you were already a supermodel, *better* should be pretty good.

The egg timer trickled out its last grain of sand. 'That's all the cards have to say. For now,' said Madam Tulip.

'That,' said Marlene, 'was *awesome*.' Her face radiated sincerity. Derry found her intensity unnerving.

'The main thing is not to take it too seriously. It's fun, that's all.'

'I understand perfectly,' said Marlene. 'That's why, this time, I didn't ask you about . . . you know, Peter and me.'

Derry gave an understanding nod.

'He's had to go home suddenly. A sick horse or something. He said he'd try to get back, but maybe he won't. He often disappears like that. I don't mind. I'm doing what you said last time.'

Derry struggled to remember what it was she had said.

'You said I needed to be strong. So I am being strong. My lawyer says I'm to keep things normal until I'm ready to move out. Will you come to my little party?'

'Oh' said Derry, unprepared for an invitation. 'That's very nice of you, but—'

'Tomorrow, after this is over. We're only half an hour away. A few people are coming over. Stay the night. Make the weekend of it. You can tell our fortunes. Say you'll come?'

Marlene's eyes were pleading. Derry felt as if she were being asked by an especially adorable dog to take it for a walk. The thought of saying no made her feel horribly guilty, but she had no wish to spend another evening with the rich and famous, especially the soon-to-be-divorced rich and famous. Besides, she had no change of clothes other than those she meant to wear that night at dinner. 'I'd love to,' she said. 'But I'm being collected tomorrow.'

'Call it off? Please? I need someone I can trust.'

All Derry could think of saying was that she was sorry but she had to be someplace. She promised she'd think about it. She felt bad about not wanting to go, and told herself that sometimes you just needed to say no. The thought occurred to her that saying no was exactly what she hadn't done.

'Oh!' said Derry. 'I'm supposed to collect some tokens. For the reading.' She pulled out the charity bucket from beside her chair and put it on the table with a smile. 'Now dig deep, it's for charity!'

'I nearly forgot!' squealed Marlene, all the seriousness of her appeal gone. She reached down, fished up her bag from beside her chair, rooted around inside and took out a handful of tokens. 'Here you go,' she said. 'That was just wonderful. Thank you so much.'

At that moment, the door opened and a head appeared. The head belonged to Sonya Dee. Celebrities obviously didn't think 'Do Not Disturb' signs applied to them.

'Sonya!' said Marlene. 'I'm just finishing. You're going to love this. Madam Tulip is just the best!' She giggled, then she was gone, pulling the door closed behind her.

Sonya strode into the little room as though she were walking onto the stage of a concert hall packed with thousands of fans. She wore a gold minidress glinting with hundreds of square sequins. As Derry anxiously tidied her table and rearranged her timer and her cards, she was aware of Sonya standing, hands on hips, watching her with an amused expression.

Sonya took her seat, dropping her bag on the floor beside her. 'Hi, honey. Look I'm not into this crap, but I promised Marlene. So first off, why not tell me what question *I'm* going to ask *you*.' She sat back, crossing her legs and smiling a challenge.

And who do you think you are, Miss Attitude? thought Derry. Derry had spent years dealing with directors who thought that the best way to get a performance out of an actress was to be an offensive prat. And here was another rampant ego. Her rising irritation wasn't helped by sitting opposite a globally recognised sex symbol while wearing a padded corset, two beanbags and with unspecified birds perched on her head.

Be professional! she told herself brusquely. She took a deep breath and smiled. 'The future is included . . . *honey,*' she said. 'Reading minds is extra.'

Sonya burst out laughing. 'I like you! So what's the story? I ain't never had my future told before. You just make it a good one. It's gotta be better than the past, that's for sure.'

Derry relaxed. She had some idea what Sonya meant by her past. It was common knowledge that Sonya Dee had grown up in a poverty-stricken ghetto rife with gangs and drugs. As a child, half the time she didn't have enough to eat and the other half she was in care. Amazing how talent can sometimes survive just about anything. Or maybe she was just lucky.

'Why don't we try the crystal ball?' said Derry.

'Whatever you want, *Madam Toolip.* Should be the same future, whatever way you see it. Am I right?'

Sonya was no fool, thought Derry. The point was a good one. Wasn't there something in science about how you can't observe something without changing it? So what if you observe the future in two different ways—would you get two different futures? She had no idea. And she sure couldn't think who to ask.

'You know what I really want to know?' said Sonya. 'Same as anyone wants to know. Will I have children? How long will I live? I've already got a tall dark stranger. Sometimes he seems like a stranger anyways. Is he gonna stick around?'

'Why don't we see what we can see,' said Derry, turning over the egg-timer and passing her hands three times over the crystal ball. Why three? Nobody ever asked that question, so luckily Derry never had to answer it. Three times was just what you did. In the paranormal three is a good round number.

Would Sonya have children? As Derry gazed at Sonya's reflection deep inside the ball, she felt that indeed she would.

How long would she live? Of all the questions Derry didn't like to be asked, that was the big one. She was thankful that no answer came. Fortune telling was often like that. and not getting an answer could sometimes be the kindest thing. The future could be surprisingly caring that way.

Sonya was enjoying herself. She neatly summarised what Derry had told her: kids—probably; career—great; death—not saying. Then she asked out straight, 'Okay, Tell me about *him*. Is he gonna stay or should I start the auditions?'

At that moment, the egg timer ran out. Derry smiled. 'Another session? Costs more tokens.'

'Mmm. I don't think so. Maybe it's just me being tight. Or maybe I don't want to know.'

'Perhaps you should ask him,' said Derry.

Sonya thought about that. 'You know, maybe I should. Thanks, Madam Tulip. I've enjoyed this.'

'My pleasure,' said Derry. She put the charity bucket on the table. 'It's for charity, remember.'

Sonya smiled, reaching down by her feet for her bag. 'Oh,' she said. She pushed her chair back and bent over scrabbling around on the floor. 'Hey, look what I've found!'

She surfaced, beaming triumphantly. 'Nice compact,' she said. 'Yours?' In her hand was an Art Deco powder compact, gold in the shape of a clamshell.

'No,' said Derry. 'Not mine. Must be Marlene's. No one else has been here. I can get it back to her.'

'Oh, don't you worry. You know you've got a queue out there?' she said, pointing to the door. 'I'll see Marlene. If I don't see her, I'll leave it at reception. And just to prove I'm really not tight—here.' She put several tokens in the bucket.

'Thanks,' said Derry. 'Nice meeting you.'

'You too,' said Sonya. She eyed Derry's wig and gave an approving nod. 'Cool birds.'

~

In an hour and a half, Derry got through five full sessions, far more than she had ever done in one go even at parties for friends. Her last client before her break was, unusually, a man.

'My wife said I should give it a go,' he said, blushing like a schoolboy in a chemist shop trying to buy contraceptives.

In fact, what he wanted to know was whether a particular company share on the stock exchange would go up or down. Derry had an easy answer to that one. Given enough time, it would probably go up *and* down. The man was not amused, and Derry had to remind herself to stay in character. Madam Tulip was *not* the type to make silly jokes.

Just as Derry was about to suggest they avoid the specifics and go for more general enquiries, the door opened. Marlene wore an apologetic expression. She wondered if Derry had found her compact. Derry frowned at the interruption as not fair to the client, but the man didn't seem bothered and instead grinned idiotically at Marlene.

When Derry answered that she had indeed found her compact, Marlene's relief was obvious. But when she explained that Sonya had taken it away and meant to return it or leave it at reception,

Marlene's face fell, and she struggled to hide her annoyance. Her scowl said that losing her compact was all Derry's fault.

'Why not check at reception and give Sonya a call?' said Derry. Marlene closed the door without answering.

Strangely, Derry didn't feel angry at Marlene's attitude. But she *was* disappointed. And that was ridiculous. A celebrity was bad-mannered and selfish—big surprise.

By the time Derry could take a break her bottle of water was empty, but her bucket held a generous load of tokens. Some clients had even taken away her newly minted Madam Tulip business cards. Derry put Marlene's hissy fit out of her mind. But now her head ached, and she desperately needed the ladies and a coffee.

Outside her door, four women were sitting waiting for their turn. Derry apologised and asked them to come back in half an hour. On the reverse of the Do Not Disturb sign, she wrote 'Back at 5.20.'

9

When Derry had first passed through the hotel lobby in full costume as Madam Tulip, she had been so worried about how her first sessions would go that she hadn't noticed people's reactions. This time, on her way back, she was painfully aware of the stares. But soon she relaxed. People seemed to think she was just another eccentric celebrity. Some were obviously trying to work out who she might be. A British theatrical Dame? A famous novelist? Derry realised she was getting a taste of what life might be like for celebrities, with people staring and taking photos when all the celebrity wanted to do was buy washing powder. Then again, real celebrities might be vastly more upset if nobody stared.

As Derry ascended the broad stairway to her room, she found herself beginning to enjoy the attention. Why not? This was a plum role, and she had created it herself. Or nearly herself. She was thinking of how helpful and ingenious her friends had been, paying no particular attention to the people she passed, when she stopped short. Could it be?

Coming down the stairs towards her, wearing a beautifully cut suit and looking every inch the aristocrat, was a man she knew. Not just any man—a man with whom she had once been almost, very nearly, in love. What on earth was Constable Lawrence FitzAllen of the British Metropolitan Police doing, dressed like a millionaire, at a celebrity function in the middle of Ireland?

Derry had met Fitz at a police station in London while she was working on a production of *Shadow of A Gunman*. She was playing Minnie and doubling as stage manager, so part of her job was to bring the fake firearms to the police station for safe keeping every night after the show. Taxiing to the local station house, lugging a sports bag clanking with what felt like lead drainpipes would normally have been the worst job of the night. But Derry's sense of martyred irritation vanished when she saw the officer approaching from behind the reception desk to help her with her bag.

If one of the guns had gone off with an almighty bang and everyone—the desk sergeant, two vagrants, a drunken driver and a man loudly complaining that he had lost his dog in a pub—had all thrown themselves to the floor, Derry wouldn't have noticed a thing. Neither, it seemed, would Constable FitzAllen.

Derry could barely remember the rest of that week. The days were obscured in her mind by a cloud of shimmering gauze, enlivened by spangles and with tinselly bits slowly dropping from heaven. Or so it felt. Both she and Fitz worked nights, so the days were all theirs.

Fitz' upper-class English drawl, straight out of a BBC period drama, was outrageously seductive to Derry's American ears. The big surprise was that someone who looked and sounded as he did was an ordinary policeman rather than a stockbroker or Conservative politician. Just as confusing, the West End flat where they spent their delightful afternoons must have been worth a fortune, way beyond a policeman's means. The mystery was solved when Fitz shamefacedly admitted that his father owned the street. Dad was some kind of Lord or Sir, but in spite of his father's opposition Fitz had always wanted to be a policeman.

In those heady weeks in London, Derry didn't care whether Fitz was a policeman or the Prince of Wales. She had never met anybody like him, and he seemed to feel the same about her. As Derry's show moved on to the next leg of its tour, she and Fitz met in cheap hotels in various dismal Midland towns. But before the tour had finished, Fitz was promoted and sent to Dover, far to the South. When Derry's theatre company returned to Ireland, she returned with it.

More than once in the four years since, Derry had wondered if they should have abandoned their hard-won careers, the dreams of their lives, for love. Perhaps they should have. But they hadn't. Reluctantly, and with more than a few tears shed on each side, Derry and Fitz had agreed to call it a day. To make it easier on themselves, they decided not to stay in touch. Being friends would be too hard to bear. Derry had once or twice checked if he were on Facebook, but he wasn't. She wondered if he had checked on her. If he had, he would have learned nothing. Derry had no inclination to bare her soul online, even to friends

Now, here was Fitz in the flesh, adjusting his tie as he tripped lightly down the staircase in front of her.

'Fitz!'

Derry knew she was staring wide-eyed, but she couldn't help it. Fitz looked shocked. He was rooted to the spot, but recovered quickly and to Derry's dismay hurried down past her. 'I'm sorry,' he said quickly, 'you mistake me for someone else.'

Only then did it dawn on Derry that she was dressed as Madam Tulip. As far as Fitz was concerned, he had been accosted on the stairs by a mad woman wearing birds. She almost called after him, 'Fitz, it's me, Derry!' but instantly thought better of it. For a long moment, Derry stood watching Fitz' retreating form as he blended into the crowd in the lobby. He didn't look back. Derry was appalled to find her heart was fluttering.

~

'I'm sorry,' said Derry. 'Really, I am. She made me promise not to tell you she was coming.'

'You're forgiven, dear daughter,' said Jacko, magnanimously. 'You were caught in no-man's land between warring legions, if you'll forgive me mixing my military metaphors. Not your fault.'

Derry was hugely relieved. She hadn't realised how guilty she felt knowing her mother was on Jacko's trail and being unable to tell him.

'Thanks, Dad,' she said.

'Don't mention it,' said Jacko. 'You owe me.'

Derry spluttered. 'You said it wasn't my fault! How can I owe you if it's not my fault?'

'True for you,' said Jacko. 'There's divil a bit of fairness in this wicked old world of ours. I need your couch.'

'What?'

'Your couch, my dear. Not for long. Just 'till I can get someone to retrieve my wallet. Unless you can lend me a couple of hundred?'

Derry was about to ask what happened to his wallet, why he needed to sleep on her couch and whether her mother had in fact caught up with him, when she realised that none of those questions needed answering. Of course her mother had caught up with him. The wallet part would no doubt be explained by some impromptu evasive manoeuvre on Jacko's part and—if past episodes were any guide—involved windows, studio roofs, hiding under an upturned boat or some other uncomfortable but effective retreat, followed by a sprint to his car. But why the couch? Ah, thought Derry. No wallet = no hotel = sleep on daughter's couch.

She sighed. 'You'll need keys.'

'You're a darlin',' said Jacko.

'You'll do your own laundry,' Derry added quickly. 'And wash your dishes.'

'No need to take a hard line,' said Jacko, adopting the wounded tone of a man faced with a blatant injustice. 'What is it with young people today? Why am I surprised? What else can you expect from a generation whose idols are geeky billionaires in pressed jeans.'

'Dad,' said Derry. 'You're ranting. Stop it!'

'Oh alright, but what's the matter with a little give-and-take? Play it by ear? See how it works out?'

'It is *not going to work out*,' said Derry, knowing of old never to offer Jacko a pain-free solution to a problem.

'Okay, okay,' said Jacko. 'Only a couple of nights, I promise. Keys?'

'Next door, number 11B. Her name's Patricia. I'll phone her, let her know you'll be picking them up,' said Derry. 'Where are you?'

'About an hour and a half from town.'

'Okay, I'll tell her. Text me when you're in?'

'I knew I could count on you,' said Jacko. 'How's the job going?'

'Fine,' said Derry. 'Okay.'

'Great. Well done. Bye now.' And he was gone.

Right away, Derry dialled her neighbour. Luckily Patricia expected to be home all evening and would give Jacko the spare keys. At least that was simple enough, thought Derry. Anything easy was a surprise.

Derry lay down on the bed and sighed. She had looked forward to spending the following night relaxing in her apartment, watching a box set of something silly and eating chocolates while thinking of the money she had made. Instead, she'd be tidying up after Jacko. Why hadn't she put her foot down, said he should simply talk to his ex? What could Vanessa do to him except nag? He only had to nod and say yes until she went away—surely he knew that? Derry decided that when she saw her father she would insist, *absolutely insist*, that he and Vanessa meet and thrash out the problem.

Derry had come back to her room to chill out, to recharge her batteries between clients. Instead, she found herself hopelessly wound up. She propped a pillow behind her head and tried to think calming thoughts. She closed her eyes, conjuring up the beauty of the castle as she had seen it first, nestling in its verdant island. She saw again the peaceful blue waters, the shining wavelets lapping on the shore. And something else.

At first she couldn't make out what she was seeing. A darkened room. Cramped. The walls were bare and the space empty except for a small iron bedstead. Someone was moving around inside, but she couldn't make out who. She heard sounds—echoing clangs, a hoarse, reverberating shout. She realised now why she could see so little of the happenings inside that room. She was looking through a peephole.

Derry jumped, startled by her phone ringing. She fumbled for the handset and checked the caller ID.

'Bella!'

'Where are you?' said Bella. She sounded out of breath.

'In the hotel, of course, why?' said Derry.

'Where in the hotel? I need to see you!'

'My room. What's happening?' But Bella had hung up.

Derry stared at the blank screen. She couldn't get her thoughts straight. Her mind was still peering through that peephole, struggling to understand. She had a hollow feeling in the pit of her stomach.

'Open up, please, Derry! Open the damned door!' Bella was hammering furiously.

Derry jumped off the bed and wrenched the door open. Bella almost fell into the room. Derry dragged her inside and slammed the door shut. 'Sit! What's happened? What are you doing here?'

Bella sat on the chaise longue, unable to speak, holding her head in her hands.

'Now,' said Derry, her hands on Bella's shoulders. 'Tell me what's going on. Why are you here? Let me get you some water. You talk.'

'Something terrible has happened,' gasped Bella.

'Here, drink some water first.' Derry handed Bella the glass. She drank greedily.

'I knocked on his door—'

'Who's door? And what *are* you doing here?'

'Mojo!' said Bella, as if Derry should have known all along who she was talking about.

'But what are you—? Never mind. Tell me what happened.'

'I wanted a selfie with him, that's all. I knocked on his door. I got no answer. I thought maybe he was out, but I'd been watching from down the corridor and I never saw him leave. I saw *her* leave ages ago, so I waited.'

'Waited where?' said Derry.

'In a linen cupboard. I knocked again, and his door opened. I thought, oh wow, surely he'll let me get just one selfie. That's all I wanted, honest. The door opened. He was on his knees. He was gasping like he couldn't breathe. It was horrible! He fell down right there holding his chest. Oh my God!'

'What did you do?'

'I laid him down on the floor. I didn't know what you are supposed to do except put him on his side, so I did that. I closed the door and called reception, said get an ambulance. I told them whose room it was and that he was ill. A few minutes later the manager came up with a doctor, I think a guest. So I told them I was a friend and I'd just knocked on the door. And they said okay and asked me to leave. So I did.'

'At least you got the doctor fast. Maybe you saved him getting really bad, getting help like that?'

'I don't know,' said Bella. 'He looked terrible.'

Derry couldn't think of anything to say, except that maybe he got some kind of food poisoning or had an allergy.

'What if they ask questions?' said Bella. 'I'll get you in to trouble and you'll lose the gig over me. And Bruce, what if they blame him?'

Now Derry was even more confused. 'What do you mean get Bruce into trouble? Anyhow, what are you doing here? You were supposed to have left.'

'I wanted to see Mojo. It was the chance of a lifetime. When we came in, I saw ID badges sitting on the desk. When Bruce saw me out, I drove the car to the other end of the carpark and walked right back inside. I had my badge, and the security guys must have remembered we were with Bruce—they didn't even ask questions.' The laminated plastic ID badge was hanging round Bella's neck. She clutched it like a talisman.

'I need to get out of here,' said Bella, desperation in her voice. 'What if that Organiser woman sees me?'

'Shouldn't you stay around in case they need to talk to you?'

'What can I tell them? I saw him fall over, that's all.'

'I guess,' said Derry. 'Oh Bella, you shouldn't have.'

'I'm sorry,' said Bella. 'Really, I am.'

Derry thought hard. Bella was probably right. If she were identified as a gate-crasher after coming in with Derry and Bruce, they would all get into trouble.

'We need to get you past Clodagh. She's not always in the lobby, so all we need to do is wait until she's away somewhere and you can walk right out. I've got to do my next session in a few minutes, so I'll be going down. You stay here. I'll check the lobby is clear, and I'll phone you. Alright? Make yourself a cup of nice borage tea; I brought tea bags. They're on the sideboard by the kettle.'

Bella forgot to be distressed. 'You're joking,' she said. 'Remember you got me to try that once before? At your place? And when I went down to the car the clampers had got me. Do you remember what happened? I mean what's in that stuff?'

Derry did remember. Better not the borage.

'Drink,' said Bella and headed for the minibar.

'Go easy, will you,' said Derry. 'The charity is paying.'

'This *is* charity,' said Bella, downing a miniature brandy by the neck.

~

Derry sat at the table in her booth, crystal ball and cards in front of her. On the way downstairs she had looked to see if the Organiser was away from the reception desk. No luck, she was right there on station. Derry had phoned Bella and told her to wait until later; she'd check again after her session.

Now Derry had to put all such complications out of her mind. No thinking about rap stars, fathers or star-struck friends. No puzzling over ex-boyfriends who didn't want to be themselves. *Concentrate*, Derry told herself. Madam Tulip had her job to do.

The first client, an expensively dressed woman whose face was aglow with excitement, took her seat in a flurry of breathless conversation. Only a few minutes earlier, she had seen paramedics emerge from a service entrance pushing a trolley to a parked ambulance with its lights flashing. With several other people, she had rushed over to see what was happening. The others knew who it was—that singer Mojo, lying there, his eyes closed like he was dead. Sonya Dee had raced to the scene followed by a TV cameraman who carried on filming as she followed the stretcher, holding Mojo's hand.

'Could it have been a heart attack?' the woman wondered. 'I hope it's not food poisoning—I ate far too much at tea. But surely if it was the food we'd all be carted off in ambulances by now, so I imagine we're safe.'

After the woman had told her story, not much time was left for Derry to read her fortune, but she did her best to answer her most pressing enquiry. Yes, the handsome young lawyer handling the woman's divorce might indeed be susceptible to a more mature woman.

'And why not?' said the woman with a conspiratorial smile. 'Why shouldn't he fancy an older woman? I'm sure *you* get propositioned all the time!'

10

Bella had calmed down. She was sprawled on the chaise longue watching Formula One racing on the TV. The sound was like a hive of angry bees.

'They took Mojo away in an ambulance,' said Derry. 'Sonya went with him. Poor Sonya, she must be worried.' She didn't say 'she loves him,' although the words almost came to her lips. To reveal the confidence would have been an unforgivable betrayal.

'I suppose it'll be an experience to write a rap about,' said Bella. 'Not as good as getting shot, though.'

Derry agreed food poisoning didn't have the same cachet as gang warfare, but you couldn't expect to choose your disasters.

'Guess he was unlucky,' said Bella.

Did she mean unlucky to get ill or unlucky he'd failed to get shot? Derry was too tired to think about it. She sighed and eased off her wig. She shook her hair out, and for the first time all day she felt cool. Was it worth getting out of the costume and into civvies for an hour? She decided it was.

'What is it with Miss Clodagh Organiser?' said Bella, helping Derry out of her dress. 'Doesn't she eat? Doesn't she go to the loo? Maybe you could distract her—make a diversion, and I'll slip past. I've only to get to the main lobby, and I can walk straight out.'

This didn't sound too good to Derry. It was easy for Bella to say distract her, but Clodagh didn't seem the type to be distracted by anything short of an armed robbery.

'We have to be patient,' said Derry. 'The pre-dinner cabaret starts soon. She'll be harassing the acts before they go on. We'll get you out then, okay?'

Derry wasn't too worried about Bella's escape. She was sure everything would work out fine. Go down to the lobby. Wait for Clodagh to disappear, sneak Bella away. Done. Instead, she found herself far more concerned about her own appearance. On went her good dress. Hair and makeup repaired.

Why such trouble? Derry had no intention of asking herself. But somehow she felt it might be best to look as different from Madam Tulip as she possibly could.

$\sim$

Amazing what dressing up can do. Strolling downstairs to the lobby, Derry felt light-hearted despite Bella's situation. She had carried off her first sessions as Madam Tulip without disaster. Her clients seemed happy to throw their tokens into the champagne bucket and tell her how much they had enjoyed her readings. Now Derry felt she could relax and savour an event that normally she would only get to read about in a magazine or on a celebrity website.

As she reached the lobby, Derry heard music from the function room. The cabaret had begun, but the lobby was still busy. In the plush armchairs, beautifully dressed guests sat chattering. Relays of white-jacketed waiters and waitresses circulated with trays of champagne. On a long table by the wall were arrayed canapés under covers. All at once, Derry felt ravenous. She edged her way to the table and greedily devoured two tasty morsels before she remembered to feel guilty about Bella. But then she reflected that if the only pain Bella suffered for the trouble she had caused was a few hunger pangs, she was getting off lightly.

At the desk under the stairs, a receptionist was dealing with enquiries from guests. No sign of the Organiser. That, thought

Derry, was both good and bad. Good that Clodagh was elsewhere. Bad not to know exactly where she was. Derry joined the queue.

'I wonder is Clodagh around?'

'I'm sorry, she's not here, can I help?' said the receptionist.

'I'm afraid not,' said Derry. She smiled her most charming smile. 'I need to clarify a point about tomorrow's schedule. Do you know when she'll be back?'

'She's in a meeting at the moment, but she'll be back in'—the woman checked her watch—'ten minutes. Shall I give her a message?'

'No thanks,' said Derry. 'I'll catch her then.'

Ten minutes should be enough. She made a quick call to Bella, who soon appeared sashaying down the stairs as if she owned the place. Derry pretended to read a tourist brochure while nervously watching Bella's progress across the lobby. Her heart almost stopped when Bella casually detoured to raid the side table, collecting three canapés in a napkin. Derry dumped the brochure and made a bee-line for the culprit, grabbing Bella by the elbow and propelling her to the door.

'Yow!' said Bella, her mouth full of canapé.

'Byeee,' said Derry, firmly. 'Call you tomorrow, okay?'

The security men guarding the way through to the main hotel gave them a friendly smile, stood aside and even held the door open for Bella. Then she was gone, instantly transformed from imposter, security risk and stalker into a legitimate if unconventional citizen.

With Bella safely out of the way, Derry had no need to return to the reception desk. But somehow, she found herself doing just that.

'Excuse me.'

'Oh, hi,' said the receptionist with a friendly smile. 'Clodagh isn't back yet, I'm afraid.'

'That's fine, thanks. One other thing—can you tell me if a Mr. FitzAllen is staying in the hotel?

The receptionist tapped at her computer. Derry admired the ornate ceiling as if her enquiry were no more than idle curiosity about a guest with whom one might be distantly acquainted. A whim, no more.

'I'm sorry,' said the receptionist. 'Nobody of that name.' She smiled again.

If Derry were being honest, she would have answered—*Never mind. I haven't seen him for four years. He claims he isn't him, and he probably really isn't him. And if he is him, I haven't the faintest idea what I mean to do about it.*

Instead she said, 'Thanks,' and added a convincing smile of her own.

Derry was still standing at the desk when from behind she heard a familiar voice demanding the receptionist's immediate attention. The voice belonged to Peter Doyle.

'Excuse me, young lady.' Doyle didn't acknowledge Derry. He looked anxious.

'Yes?' said the receptionist. The smile was gone.

'I saw an ambulance arrive. Has someone been taken ill?'

'I'm afraid so. One of the guests. Hopefully not serious. A precaution.'

'And who, might I ask, was taken ill, please?' asked Doyle.

'I'm sorry,' said the receptionist. 'We can't divulge information about guests. Hotel policy.'

'I see. Thank you,' said Doyle. He turned away only to bump into Derry. 'Oh, I'm sorry. I didn't see you there.'

'I couldn't help hearing,' said Derry. 'You were asking about the ambulance. The singer Mojo was taken ill. Hopefully not serious. I imagine it'll be all over the papers tomorrow.'

'I see,' said Doyle, stepping back from the counter. 'Never good to see an ambulance, of course.' He seemed to relax. 'And how is your father keeping? Well, I hope. If you see him, tell him we should talk soon. I have a little project that might benefit from some of his works. Ask him to give me a call.'

'I will,' said Derry. 'I'm sure he'll be pleased.'

As they moved to one side away from the desk, Doyle brightened, as if suddenly struck by an idea. 'Why don't you come up to our suite and join us in a glass of champagne. I know Marlene is a great fan of yours. Perhaps you can pick some more winners for me.'

Extraordinary the way this man could turn on the charm like a tap, thought Derry. And effective charm too, nothing greasy about it. Real charisma.

'I'd love to,' she said. 'Champagne sounds tempting. But I'm afraid I have to start another session soon. Maybe I could give Marlene a ring tomorrow?'

Doyle looked put out but only for a fleeting moment. 'I'm sorry to hear that. But I appreciate your professionalism, I assure you. I'll leave you to get on with your work.'

'Oh, I almost forgot,' said Derry. 'Did Marlene get her compact?'

'I'm sorry?' said Doyle.

'Marlene mislaid her compact. I was wondering did she get it back. Sonya Dee found it. She was going to return it, but maybe with Mojo taken ill she never got a chance.'

'I'm afraid I have no idea,' said Doyle, slowly. 'I . . . haven't seen my wife all afternoon.'

His phone rang. 'Please, excuse me.'

'Of course,' said Derry.

As Doyle turned away to a quieter part of the lobby by the grand fireplace, speaking quietly, his chauffeur appeared at Derry's elbow.

'Hello, Miss O'Donnell.'

What was his name? Pablo? Paulo. His smile was startlingly white. Something in his tone said that calling her by her surname amused him.

'Charming to see you,' he said. 'As always.'

Derry couldn't help but be amused. Paulo was gorgeous, no doubt about it. And he had a wonderfully exotic way of speaking—perfect English with an American flavour, but accented so the most ordinary statement sounded fascinating, even exciting. So much for old flames, thought Derry, remembering that only a few minutes earlier the only man on her mind had been Fitz. Could she really be that fickle?

'Twice,' said Derry. 'If it was charming to see me—and thank you for saying so—it was charming twice.'

'Three times,' said Paulo, smiling even more broadly, his dark eyes glinting with an arrogance that Derry knew must be irresistible to women. She reminded herself that she had never subscribed to the nonsensical cliché that said the bastards were always the most attractive. Complete garbage. Of course.

'I was never good at math,' said Derry. She tried to ignore the voice in her head that said, *THAT was a simper. You know it was!*

'In Spain, we say that Irish women are the most beautiful. Even more beautiful than our own. I did not believe it. Until now.'

Derry felt no pressing urge to argue that she was only half-Irish. Somehow, the point seemed trivial. Hair-splitting. Not at all relevant.

'I will call you,' said Paulo.

Not *may I call you* or *do you mind if I call you*. Not even, *can I have your number*. The arrogant swine!

'Marlene has my number, perhaps you should ask her,' said Derry, smiling and turning away. *Deal with that!* A neat little problem for Mr. Paulo, asking his boss's wife for a girl's phone number. *If you have the nerve,* thought Derry, *I might even take the call.*

Doyle reappeared.

'I'm sorry,' he said, his face serious. 'I have been called away. With horses, always problems. We must have that glass of champagne some other time. My regards to your father. Paulo—follow me.' Curtly, without looking back, he walked away.

The chauffeur of a rich man might have been expected to jump to attention and follow his master meekly across the lobby. To Derry's surprise, Paulo did nothing of the kind. He put his hands in his pockets, walked backwards towards the door and, as he had done once before, blew Derry a kiss.

If Doyle noticed, he paid no attention.

11

Mojo was dead.

Derry had finished her pre-dinner session and was back in her room, costume off, glorious shower taken. She had her cosy bathrobe on and was just choosing between a nice cup of borage tea and something a little stronger, when her phone rang. Bruce.

'Where are you, honey?'

'In my room, why? Is anything wrong?'

For a moment, Derry had the dreadful thought that perhaps Bella had turned around and sneaked back into the hotel. A picture of the Organiser holding Bella by the scruff of her neck and summoning Derry to explain flashed through her mind. But whatever the problem was, Bruce wasn't saying over the phone. He'd be at her door in a couple of minutes.

'We have a situation,' said Bruce. He looked stern in a way that Derry hadn't seen before. Derry had only ever known Bruce as either cheerful and smiling or terrified before a stage performance. Strange that a man who had scuba-dived with explosives strapped to his chest turned into a quivering wreck at the prospect of an audience greater than two. But now, sitting in Derry's room, Bruce was all business.

Derry's first reaction to hearing about Mojo was *poor Sonya*. She should, she supposed, have been thinking of Mojo too. But Mojo seemed less real. Was that what happened when you read someone's cards? You felt close. Maybe not to everyone, but to some.

'This must be so upsetting for the staff,' said Derry.

'Not at all,' said Bruce, surprised. 'They get stiffs all the time. That's what service lifts are for.'

Derry wondered why, if it were all so routine, had Bruce needed to confide in her.

'The police called the hotel. Mojo died of some kind of drugs overdose. They think cocaine. The room is to be sealed until they can inspect it.'

'I suppose they have to investigate,' said Derry, not at all clear where this was going.

'The person who found him was Bella. Derry, what was she doing here?' Bruce's face was stern.

'Oh,' said Derry, feeling that lately her vocabulary had shrunk to that single word of one syllable, if it even counted as a word. Her brain was spinning.

'I had no idea she was going to come back. She said she wanted a selfie. She knocked on his door and found him sick. She called for help, then she went home.'

Derry knew she was compressing events more than a little and had failed to mention the time Bella had spent in her room before sneaking out of the hotel. But that was hardly relevant, was it?

'And how did she get back in?' asked Bruce. 'I showed her to her car.'

'Honestly,' said Derry. 'I didn't help her, not one bit. She'd managed to get a guest badge while we were checking in. I had nothing to do with it, I promise.'

Bruce looked at Derry steadily. Derry looked back, unflinching.

'Swear to die?' said Bruce.

'Swear to die.'

'They want to talk to Bella. She was the last person to speak to Mojo.'

'But all she did was find him and call reception. She said he passed out right after he opened the door.'

'She'll have to tell them that herself. Can you give me her phone number and address? I'll pass it on.'

Only then did Derry appreciate that Bruce was being kind. The Bella connection wasn't going to do him any good. He was supposed to have cleared her off the premises, and now he could be accused of failing to do the job properly. But not once had he said 'look at the trouble you got me into.' He really was a sweet man.

'Management thinks the cops will make a big song and dance act out of this business. They love to be in the papers.

'So what happens now?' asked Derry. 'Will the organisers call the whole thing off?'

'They'll try to keep the news quiet for a while, but these days what can you keep quiet? I guess death or not, everybody will want dinner. Afterwards, I don't know.'

Bruce was right about it being impossible to keep the news quiet. He was right too about people wanting food no matter what. As Derry dressed for dinner with none of the pleasure and excitement she had anticipated, her phone rang. Bella was back at her flat in Dublin.

'I can't believe it!' she said. 'It can't be true!'

Had she been crying? Bella? Surely not.

'What did you hear?' asked Derry. Even as she spoke, she wondered why she was being so cautious. Why not come right out and say it? Dead.

'It's all over Twitter. They say an overdose.'

'That's what I've heard,' said Derry. 'Bruce told me.'

'This is terrible,' said Bella. 'I can't believe it,' she repeated. Of course, what she meant was she *did* believe it, she just couldn't accept it. But death wasn't asking anybody's permission.

'Bruce says they want to talk to you,' said Derry. 'You were the last to see him conscious. Or nearly conscious.'

'Terrible,' said Bella yet again, as if she hadn't heard a word Derry had been saying.

'I gave Bruce your phone number and address. Is that alright?'

'Sure,' said Bella. Derry could tell she was barely listening.

'Bella, call me if you need to talk. Alright?'

'Sure,' said Bella. 'Yeah.'

What is it when someone dies? As Derry descended the staircase to the lobby, dressed for dinner, she felt as if she were walking down into some weirdly luxurious air-raid shelter. The muffled sound of her footsteps on the carpet seemed impossibly loud. The guests sat hunched in armchairs pulled close together as though huddling for protection against whatever misfortune was stalking the place. Two uniformed policemen stood by the door. Derry guessed that others were in Mojo's room. Would they be searching everything? Testing for drugs? She guessed they were.

Was it the presence of death or the presence of the police that encouraged two couples to check out? They stood at the reception desk with their bags, shuffling uneasily, but unable to get attention. Then Derry saw why. In front of them in the little queue, deeply engaged in conversation with the receptionist, was Fitz.

Derry's heart skipped a beat. Fitz, no doubt about it. She was now herself rather than in costume as Madam Tulip, but the impulse to rush over and make herself known lasted only a moment. What if he again denied who he was? She could hardly pick an argument with a man about his identity in front of everybody in a hotel lobby. And what if he *had* recognised her the last time but was pretending not to? What could be more humiliating than to approach him only for him to run again?

Derry tore her gaze from Fitz and carried on down the stairs. She turned into the wide corridor leading to the dining room and had just reached the open double doors when she felt a hand on her elbow.

'Derry, can I talk to you?' said Marlene, her voice low and urgent.

'Of course. I was so sorry to hear about Mojo.'

Marlene wasn't interested in Mojo, or Derry's sympathy. 'I want to ask you a big favour,' she said.

'Sure,' said Derry. 'Whatever I can do.'

'Will you do another reading for me? Like now?'

Marlene must have seen Derry's surprise and sensed her hesitation, but Derry was too tired to care. She'd finished her readings for the day. The sad business with Mojo had changed everything. And then there was Fitz. She was in no mood for a reading.

'I'm sorry, how about tomorrow? I'm doing a session in the morning. I start at eleven, you can have the first reading if you like.' To her shame, Derry realised that part of her reluctance was caused by the smells of food coming from the dining room. She hadn't noticed how hungry she was.

Marlene hesitated, biting her lip. 'Derry, I need to ask you stuff. Now. Please?'

Marlene wasn't saying *please* in the way a five-year-old might beg to be indulged. Her pleading was like an adult asking for something so important they put aside all their grown-up defences and were prepared to risk rejection. *Unlike me*, thought Derry, painfully aware she had just walked away from Fitz out of that very fear.

'Please,' said Marlene. Derry smelled the whiskey on her breath. 'Is there somewhere we can go?'

'Sure, yes. There's a private garden.'

'We could just talk,' said Derry. 'If you want a reading we can do that, but talk first?'

'Okay, said Marlene. 'Sure. I need to ask you some things.'

Marlene led Derry further down the corridor, turned right, and ushered her through a pair of French doors leading outside. Now they stood in a garden surrounded by high, grey stone walls covered in ivy. Paved paths wended their way around planted beds, antique stone statues on plinths and a trickling fountain. Sheltered from any breeze, night-scented stock and woodbine filled the garden with a heady perfume. The daylight was fading, but light from the castle windows threw a gentle glow, softening the shadows.

Marlene led Derry to an ancient stone bench, arms shaped like crouching lions. A surprising smell of aniseed enveloped them, and Derry realised that behind was an enormous bush of fennel whose feathery leaves brushed their shoulders.

'Before you say anything,' said Derry. 'I have a confession to make. You're going to find out anyway. The person who found Mojo is a friend of mine. She sneaked into the hotel without anybody noticing. She was a fan.'

'Oh, I know that,' said Marlene. 'Clodagh is making a big fuss, but so what?'

'If there's a problem, I'll vouch for my friend. She came with me. I feel responsible.'

Marlene shrugged, as if to say *whatever*.

'What did you want to speak to me about?' asked Derry.

Now Marlene had the chance to talk she didn't seem to know what to say or where to start.

'The first time you read for me? In town?'

Derry nodded. 'Sure, I remember.'

'A lucky escape,' said Marlene. 'You said I'd have a lucky escape.'

'So I did,' said Derry.

'Look,' said Marlene, struggling to find the right words. 'If I say . . . Whatever I tell you, it's just between the two of us, right?'

'Of course.'

'You sure?'

For the first time, Derry realised what being a household name must be like. Anything you confided could end up in the gossip columns next day. Even best friends might feed juicy titbits to journalists. You would never know who you could trust.

'It's like the confessional,' said Derry. 'I mean that.'

'It's hard for me,' said Marlene.

Derry could only feel sorry for her. A woman who seemed to have everything, yet the only person she could confide in was a fortune-teller, a stranger.

'You have to decide,' said Derry. 'I can only make the promise. You have to decide if you want to trust me. I can't help you with that.'

Maybe it was Derry's directness, or the way she made no effort to persuade that tipped the balance.

'You told me to be strong. So that's what I'm going to be,' said Marlene.

Derry didn't reply. Best let her talk.

'This business I'm in . . . there's a lot of pressure. It's hard work—people don't know how much hard work. The hours are crazy. You travel all the time. Nobody cares much about anybody. It's all about the clothes, and the clothes are about the money. That's why so many girls try to marry a footballer or a rock star. Get out of the business while they're ahead.' She hesitated. 'So we get bad habits. We party too much. Booze. A few lines to keep us going and keep the weight off. It's normal, you know?'

The life Marlene described was familiar from the magazines and gossip sites. Diets, booze and cocaine. An actor's life was so different, thought Derry. Most were too poor to be coke-heads. Alcohol was the actor's chosen method of self-harm. So much for the glamour of showbiz.

'They say that Mojo overdosed,' said Marlene. 'On Twitter they say bad coke.'

Derry shrugged. Who knew what the truth was?

'I think the coke was mine.'

It all came out—how Marlene had put her little wrap of coke into her gold compact, and how somehow during her fortune-telling session the wrap had fallen out of her bag and been found by Sonya.

'Marlene,' said Derry, after a moment's thought. 'Maybe Mojo had his own coke. And what makes you think it was bad? *Can* coke be bad? He could have had a heart problem, right?'

'No,' said Marlene. 'They cut coke with different stuff. Sometimes, it's bad. Not often, like smack, but sometimes.'

'What makes you think the stuff was yours?'

Marlene looked at Derry strangely, as if the answer should have been obvious to anybody. 'You did,' she said. 'You told me I'd have a lucky escape. That's what I had.'

Derry hardly knew what to say. Maybe Marlene was right. But maybe she wasn't. Coincidences happened. Derry had seen that message not once but twice. Her head hurt. Something nagged at her, something she needed to work out but couldn't seem to grasp.

'Peter was away. If I'd taken it, I would have been on my own, nobody to help,' said Marlene. 'I want to say thanks.'

Derry sighed. Even if Marlene had been lucky, Derry could hardly take the credit. Anyhow, Mojo was the one who had paid the price. Suddenly, the thought trying to form in Derry's mind crystalised.

'We don't know it was your stuff, right? But it might have been. And we don't know it was bad. But what if it was? Whoever you got it from is selling poison. You have to tell them to stop. Can you do that?'

Marlene looked away, and Derry realised that maybe what she was asking was ridiculous. Would a drug dealer to the famous care what happened to his customers? If he had heard of the tragedy, surely he'd have disappeared by now. Still, there was a chance he hadn't heard the news or had heard but didn't care.

'You have to report it. Before someone else gets hurt.'

Marlene shrugged. 'You said yourself it might not have been my coke,' she said, looking at her watch. 'And it might not have been bad anyway.'

So much for Marlene's touching faith in Derry's powers. One minute, Derry had somehow saved her life. The next, her predictions were take-it-or-leave-it. The narrow escape was a figure of speech, and coke was just a slimming aid.

'You can't take that risk,' said Derry. 'How can you?'

Marlene spoke slowly as though she were explaining to a child. 'You don't get it, do you,' she said. 'The police would leak the story to the press. The papers pay them, you know. I'd be finished.'

Rarely in her life had Derry felt so foolish, so pompous and self-righteous. Here she was, taking the moral high ground, preaching about how Marlene should sacrifice herself to save others. But it wasn't her, Derry, who would be losing a career it had taken years to build. It wasn't Derry's life that would be all over tomorrow morning's papers.

But surely, something had to be done by somebody?

'Can't you say you heard a rumour? Give the police the name of the dealer like you heard it from somebody else? You don't have to say the stuff was yours.'

'Not really,' said Marlene.

'Why?'

'Because Peter gave it to me.'

Derry felt dizzy. That the urbane and intelligent Peter Doyle would supply his wife with drugs was impossible to take in. Derry had seen rich men with actress girlfriends showing off with champagne and drugs at parties, but Doyle didn't seem anything like those men. He seemed far too controlled, too disciplined. Hard to imagine him even tolerating his wife doing such a damaging drug as cocaine. Derry would sooner believe he'd lock her up until she quit.

'You seem shocked,' said Marlene.

'I guess I'm . . . surprised,' said Derry.

'At me or at Peter? Nobody would be surprised at me.' She looked sad. 'Peter hates me doing it.'

'He doesn't, himself?'

'No. He won't tolerate any drugs around. He'll even fire his workers if he finds they do it. He's, like, way over the top.'

'Then why does he get it for you?'

'To keep me away from dealers. He says it's too dangerous for me.'

Yes, that made sense.

'I got some myself once. I thought he was going to kill me. I've never seen him so angry. So he gets it instead. It's not fair, I know. He has to do it when I ask, in case I go somewhere else.'

Now Derry saw another side to sweet, vulnerable Marlene. 'Anyhow,' Marlene continued with a smirk, 'like I said to him, he gets the benefit. What man doesn't like his woman a little out of it?'

Now Derry was indeed shocked. She felt somehow tainted just by hearing the words. It was all wrong. She felt a surge of sympathy for Doyle, certain that he wasn't the kind of man that would take pleasure in his wife's horrible addictions. Derry felt infinitely depressed. Then the thought occurred to her.

'Surely you've told him you lost it,' she said.

'No,' said Marlene. 'I haven't. He'd be so mad at me. Causing all this trouble.'

'You've got to tell him,' insisted Derry. She stopped as the realisation dawned. 'He already knows.'

'No. No, he doesn't,' said Marlene.

'Does he know you keep the stuff in your compact?'

'I don't know. Yes. Probably.'

'Then he knows you lost it.'

'How?' said Marlene. Derry could see the fear in her eyes.

'Because I told him,' said Derry. 'I met him at Reception and asked him if you got your compact back from Sonya. Didn't he say?'

Marlene looked thoughtful. 'No, he didn't say. He had to go back to the stud. A vet.'

'You'd better talk to him, tell him what happened . . . what might have happened. There's no time to waste.'

'Yes,' said Marlene. 'I guess.' She sounded stunned.

'If the stuff was yours,' said Derry slowly, 'will Sonya tell the police where she got it?'

'No. I don't think so. Why would she blame me? Maybe Mojo got it somewhere else. Everybody knows to say nothing. Promise me you won't tell it was mine?'

'Nobody's likely to ask me. Why would they?'

'Your friend, the one who found Mojo? The police will talk to her. You won't tell her? About the compact?'

'I haven't told anybody.'

It wasn't a promise, but it seemed to satisfy Marlene. 'Will you do a reading for me now?' she asked.

Derry didn't even have to think about that. This was no time for vaguely encouraging platitudes and certainly no time for genuine insights. Derry didn't want to see what the future might bring for Marlene or for Peter Doyle. What had Marlene said—the models were like horses? Derry remembered her vision of a horse race and the falling rider. A lucky escape? Not for Mojo it wasn't.

'I'm sorry,' said Derry. 'I don't think a reading would be the right thing. Not just now.'

'How can it not be?' said Marlene. 'Can't you see anything for me?'

'Sure I can,' said Derry. 'Stop taking that crap and you might have a happy life.'

Marlene went pale. She stood abruptly.

'Sorry,' said Derry. 'I'm being honest with you.'

Marlene hesitated. 'I know. Thanks. But it's not so simple.'

'Are you going in to dinner?'

Marlene grimaced. 'I guess I have to. Keep everybody jolly for the auction.' She looked down at her impossibly slim figure. 'Really, I shouldn't be doing dinners just now. Will you do me a reading tomorrow? I don't know about the party after . . . this.'

Derry had forgotten that Marlene had invited her to a house party. She guessed that tomorrow not too many people would be in a party mood. But with celebrities you never knew, did you? She was wondering how you point blank refused the person who was paying your wages and who was desperate for help, when she was saved from answering. Marlene's phone rang. She stared at the caller ID, looked up at Derry and said, 'It's him. Sorry.'

'I'll leave you to it,' said Derry, rising to leave.

'No, no. I have to go in anyway,' said Marlene. She took the call. 'Hi,' she said, disappearing through the French doors and into the castle.

Derry sat down. She tried to calm her mind by concentrating on the heady smell of the herbs around her, but the best she could achieve was a brooding sense of dread. Who needed to get mixed up with the famous and their vices? Even the second sight her father bragged about so cheerfully was a two-edged sword. She had always thought of her modest gift as a comfortable friend, part of her, like a favourite pair of shoes. But lately, since she had met Marlene, her visions had been dark, edged around with fear. For the first time in her life, Derry hoped she would have no more visions, no more troubling portents, no more sly peeks into a future that would be far better keeping its mouth shut and its secrets to itself.

All she wanted now was to sit in her cramped apartment drinking bad wine with Bella. *Keep your castles and media stars. Stuff your celebrities.*

Some tiny change, perhaps the subtle occlusion of light from the castle windows or the almost imperceptible click of a heel on the stone paving, made Derry look up.

'Hello, old thing.'

~

Why didn't Derry jump up in shock, clutching her necklace like some silent movie queen? Surely all the rules of human nature said that a woman in a half-lit, lonely garden surprised by a male voice should at least give a sharp intake of breath. But she didn't jump. And she didn't gasp. Perhaps she had heard too many surprising things in the last hours, had too many shocks. Or maybe some obscure and secret part of her brain knew who had spoken before the words had left his mouth. She didn't turn around.

'Hi, Fitz.'

'I can't stay long,' he said, his voice low. 'And I can't explain anything. I'm asking you a favour old girl. For old times' sake? If we meet in public, don't, please, whatever you do, let on that we know each other.'

'Did you recognise me?' said Derry. 'On the stairs?'

Fitz laughed. The sound brought the memories flooding back.

'No. No I didn't. Hadn't a clue. Being named nearly gave me a heart attack, I can tell you. I asked at reception, and they told me. Madam Tulip, eh? Sounds fun.' He smiled. 'I liked the birds.'

A movement over by the fountain caught Derry's eye. A woman was standing in the shadows. She was tall, with short red hair, and was dressed in elegant black. Her earrings glistened. She was watching not Fitz and Derry but the door through which they had entered. She made no move to approach.

'All I can say is that I'm . . . we're working. And being recognised would be very dangerous for me. For both of us.' He indicated the woman.

'Mojo?' asked Derry. Even before the question was out she had dismissed the idea. Fitz, whatever his job, could never have had time to get involved so quickly.

'No. Not relevant. Regrettable, of course. The locals will deal with that. They're enjoying themselves.' He looked deep into Derry's eyes. 'Will you do as I ask? Perhaps I'll be able to explain some time. When it's over.'

What was he saying? A half-promise that one day she might be granted the privilege of having his extraordinary request explained to her? And meantime, she and he were to act as if their time together had never happened? No, she wasn't happy about that. Not one bit. But what could she say?

'Ignore you? Sure. Delighted, in fact.'

Fitz was disconcerted, as she had meant him to be. Though it was a cheap shot and none too clever, Derry felt some small satisfaction.

'If you'll just give us a minute or two's head start, I'd be grateful old thing.' His voice had the abruptness that said, *fine, job done, cheerio*.

Derry nodded. 'Goodbye . . . old thing.'

Dinner that evening was the strangest meal Derry had ever eaten. The food was superb, exquisitely prepared and presented, but any idea that she was living the high life was quickly dispelled.

At Derry's table were a middle-aged couple who mentioned their yacht every five minutes, a creepy music promoter and his much younger boyfriend, and a national TV presenter with her meteorologist husband who kept interrupting anyone who spoke. Between mouthfuls, Derry had to answer endless questions about fortune telling. She responded with as much charm and grace as she could, understanding that this was all part of earning her generous cheque.

At the head of the room, at one of the larger tables, Marlene sat with the most instantly recognisable celebrities, the handful of A-listers. As the meal went on, Derry couldn't help noticing that even when she caught Marlene's eye, Marlene didn't acknowledged her presence in any way. Derry hadn't expected to be invited to the top table, but the lack of a greeting, even a wave, was odd after talking so intimately only half an hour before. Surely Marlene couldn't still be annoyed with her for refusing to give a reading when she had asked? Or was she ashamed of revealing so much about her life and her weaknesses? Perhaps that was it. The one sin for which people would never forgive you was knowing their faults. Derry was being punished because she was no longer signed up to the myth of Marlene the Supermodel.

Derry soon had reason to be grateful for not being invited to sit at Marlene's table. Fitz strolled into the dining room, arm around his red-haired companion. Without hesitation, they wended their way to Marlene's table, air-kissed like they were old friends, and were introduced all round. If Fitz had spotted Derry, three tables away, he gave no sign and made no eye contact.

Derry knew she had a simple choice. She could either stare at Fitz and his friend all night, like some kind of obsessive, or she could ignore them, put them out of her mind, and remember she was working. She quickly found the solution was to concentrate on astonishing the meteorologist and annoying his wife by asking so many questions about the weather he grew ever more opinionated, certain he had made a conquest.

The meal must have been good, but five minutes after she had finished a course, Derry found she couldn't remember what she had eaten. The posing celebrities in their designer clothes and their wealthy hangers-on were laughing more shrilly than ever, working hard to persuade themselves they were happy, that they'd live forever. They looked and sounded ridiculous.

Over dessert, Derry's fellow diners pressed her to keep them company at the charity auction. She could predict the winning bids they said, as if she were a performing dog happy to do party tricks all night for biscuits. Derry excused herself from the table as if meaning to return. She didn't go back.

12

Waking on Saturday morning in the enveloping luxury of a four-poster bed should have been delicious. Derry tried her best to be content as she threw open the heavy drapes and let the sunshine pour into the room. She was working, always a happy day for an actress. She was certain to get paid, which should have made her even happier. She was in a castle, preparing to go down to a five-star breakfast. But yesterday, in this very hotel, a man had taken his first step from this world into the next.

Whenever death comes close, Derry reflected, the world we call real seems so unreal you could put your hand through the wall. As it was, everything in the room looked fake. The heavy, overcooked furniture was somebody's idea of what furniture in a castle should look like. No prizes for guessing the oak came from an industrial-sized can of wood-stain. Even the castle was fake in a way. Manicured lawns and blooming flowerbeds, carpets and tourist brochures made you forget what the place was really about. Derry knew enough history to know that this brooding pile, with its walls four feet thick, had been built to oppress, and its builders were well-dressed thugs hiding behind fancy titles.

Derry shook herself. This wouldn't do; she had a show to perform. She had agreed that this morning she would give two hours of readings from eleven to one, and she meant to do exactly that. Her job was to tell fortunes as well and as honestly as she could. And make it fun too. In this mood, she'd be predicting—with perfect accuracy—that all her clients would sooner or later die.

Not a good recipe for a full bucket of tokens.

As she took her place in the dining room for breakfast, Derry was relieved to see nobody she recognised. Many seats were empty as if the guests had decided to forgo eating, in favour of some-place where pop stars didn't retch out their lives in their rooms and where policemen didn't come and go at will. The few guests who did venture in were eating hurriedly and saying little. The hush was eerie, broken only by the clink of cutlery and the dull rumble of an extractor fan.

Derry had a small table to herself in a corner, her back to the wall. Had she chosen that spot to make sure of seeing something she didn't want to see—Fitz entering the dining room with his red-haired partner in tow?

But Fitz and his redhead didn't come in to breakfast, at least not while Derry was in the dining room. And neither did Marlene.

At eleven sharp, Derry was in costume and at her post in her booth. This time no queue waited excitedly outside her door. Nor had Marlene shown up for the reading she had insisted on only last night. In the first half-hour only two customers came in, both kill-ing time waiting for partners to finish a round of golf before they could leave.

Afterwards Derry had nothing to do but check her phone for email and messages. She quickly wished she hadn't bothered. The first message was a voicemail from her mother demanding she get in touch at once if Jacko surfaced; the second was from Jacko him-self. His message was so garbled that after Derry had listened to the end she had to play it all over again. He seemed to be saying she was the Scarlet Pimpernel, so obscure were her movements, and would she please pick up some of those excellent bagels she knew how to get. A second message followed, even more cryptic, saying he was fading from the hunger, and if she didn't mind he'd eat whatever he could find in the fridge—the bagels could wait.

Derry felt a familiar despair. Who needed children to worry about when you had parents who thought a day without a crisis was a day wasted?

Next, she phoned Bella about her lift home. Bella sounded much more her old self, and Derry guessed the shock of Mojo's death had receded. In the end, Bella was only a fan and Mojo someone she imagined she knew. But Bella did have a problem coming to collect Derry as she'd promised; she'd been invited to call in to a city centre police station to make a statement about finding Mojo. The interview was for twelve o'clock. She didn't know how long the business was going to take, but she'd phone Derry when she knew. *Great*, thought Derry. Hardly any clients, a donations bucket practically empty, and now she was trapped until further notice.

Just as Bella rang off, Derry's phone rang. The number was unfamiliar.

'Hi, Derry here.'

'I'm sorry,' said the voice. 'I'm looking for . . . Madam Tulip?'

'Oh,' said Derry. 'That's me. I mean, speaking.' Strange to answer the phone as Madam Tulip.

'Sonya here. Sonya Dee?'

'Oh, hi Sonya,' said Derry. In her surprise at being called by Sonya, it was a moment before she remembered about Mojo. 'I'm sorry, so sorry.'

Sonya said nothing.

'Hello?'

'It's alright,' said Sonya. 'Thanks.'

'Can I help?' said Derry. 'Is there anything I can do?'

'Unless you can roll back time a couple of days, no.' She paused again. 'Getting my fortune told wasn't the best idea I ever had. But it's not your fault.'

The coke Mojo took must have been Marlene's. Otherwise why would Sonya regret having had her fortune told?

'You heard it was coke?' asked Sonya.

'Yes.'

'It was in Marlene's compact. That I found.'

'Marlene told me.'

'We weren't gonna bring anything through the airport. And . . . we were expecting something to be delivered, you know? But nothin' showed. Mojo must have seen me stash the compact in a drawer. Maybe thought I was holdin' out on him.'

'I guessed something like that.'

Sonya spoke quietly. 'They say he had some kind of heart attack. I don't know. Maybe the stuff was bad.' She paused again. 'If he'd have waited, maybe it would have been me that took it. Or both of us. I don't think I'd have minded that.'

Derry felt her heart was breaking. How Sonya was bearing this, she had no idea.

'Will you do me a favour?'

All Derry could think was *oh no, someone else famous asking me for a favour.* But how could you refuse a favour to a woman who had just lost everything that mattered to her?

'What can I do?'

'If Marlene is smart she won't have taken any more—if she's got more. Maybe I should have called last night. I want her to know I won't be mentioning where the stuff came from. Nobody can prove a thing.'

'Have you spoken to the police?'

'Sure. They asked me not to leave the country for a few days.'

'Can't you call Marlene? Tell her yourself?'

'I'd prefer not. They might check my phone records. Mightn't look good. They can do all kindsa stuff now. But I can phone my fortune-teller, can't I?'

If a friend had asked Derry's advice about something like this, she'd have said straight away—hand on heart—don't be stupid, stay away from those people. Just put the phone down. But Derry couldn't forget the memory of her session with Sonya and the sweet way Sonya had asked about her future with Mojo. The simple hope in her eyes.

'I'm not too comfortable with that,' said Derry.

Sonya waited.

'Alright.'

'Thanks. I mean that. God bless.'

What else to do but phone Marlene? Derry was half hoping Marlene wouldn't answer her phone, so she could tell herself she had tried. But Marlene did answer, and Derry duly delivered Sonya's message.

'I suppose they can't pin it on a dead man,' said Marlene.

Not for the first time, Derry found herself surprised by how astute Marlene could be. One minute she seemed to be a scatter-brained naïf living off her looks, next she was sharp as a trader at a car boot sale.

'Did you tell Doyle?' asked Derry.

'Like you said last night, I didn't have to. He'd worked it out.'

'Was he . . . upset?'

'Being a model has one advantage they don't tell you about in career guidance class.' She paused. 'Men don't dare hit you so it shows.'

Derry was puzzled. Then it dawned on her. Every part of a model would be seen as she was dressed for the catwalk or the shoot. Bruises could never be hidden.

She didn't know what to say. Hard to imagine Doyle being violent with a woman. But can you ever tell?

'A little shouting never hurt anybody,' said Marlene. 'Anyhow, I won't be around him for long. I'm sorry we won't be having that party this afternoon. Maybe some other time.'

'Sure thing,' said Derry. 'You have my number.'

Why didn't she end the call then? She felt herself blushing as she struggled for the words. 'I couldn't help noticing at dinner last night . . . you had a man, a couple, sitting with you. She had red hair.'

'Oh! Philip, yes. I forget her name. Isn't he gorgeous? He's English. The Honourable Philip Gilbey-Jones. What a charmer. He's something in horses, a friend of Peter's. Taken, worse luck. She's his fiancée.'

'I wondered. Thanks.'

'Hands off,' said Marlene. She giggled. 'He might be taken, but *I* saw him first.'

13

By twenty-past one, Derry was sitting in the hotel's main lobby, camped on a settee by the vast fireplace. Bruce's lamp and egg timer were parked on the coffee table. Her bags squatted on the floor at her feet. Passing guests gave her puzzled glances, and Derry realised she must look like she was setting up a bric-a-brac stall right there, an impression reinforced by the suit of armour standing against the wall behind.

Every couple of minutes, Derry phoned Bella but got no answer. She checked her texts and email. Nothing but the usual junk. How was she to get home? She could take a bus or a train from Limerick to Dublin, but she'd have to get to Limerick first, and that was miles away—the taxi ride would cost a fortune. Just as she had decided she couldn't sit there all afternoon and she'd better ask reception for some taxi numbers, Bruce strode through the lobby and out the main door.

Leaving her baggage by her seat, Derry followed Bruce outside. He stood at the top of the broad stone steps leading down to the avenue and the causeway beyond, looking alert and capable as he always seemed to do. At the bottom of the steps, a limousine was swallowing its compliment of celebrities or millionaires. The car pulled away, sweeping down the avenue as if relieved to be gone.

'Hi, Bruce,' said Derry, taking up station beside him.

'Hi, Derry,' said Bruce, showing no surprise, not even turning his head, as if he had known all along she was there. He was relaxed, but his gaze never left the lake and the rolling countryside as though the landscape might conceal any number of gatecrashers or terrorists. Standing shoulder to shoulder with Bruce, Derry found she too was scanning the scene vigilantly but without the faintest idea what she was looking for.

'I need to give you back your timer and lamp,' said Derry. 'Thanks, they were perfect.'

'No, no,' said Bruce. 'They're for you. Didn't I say? A little prezzie. Be good and we might club together and buy you a gypsy caravan for your birthday.'

Derry laughed. 'Sounds good to me, I've got my dad staying in my flat.'

'Put *him* in the caravan, darling. Give him a couple of pounds of carrots for the nag and send him packing. Tell him you've taken two lovers and you need the space.'

'Meantime, I've got to get home. Know anybody heading to Limerick I could cadge a lift from? I can get the bus from there. Bella was supposed to pick me up, but I can't get her on the phone.'

'Why didn't you say? Wait a half-hour and you can come with me,' said Bruce. 'Bella is probably shagging somebody we're supposed to have heard of but haven't. It *is* Saturday.'

Derry didn't explain that at this moment Bella was probably answering a long list of awkward questions in a police station.

Half an hour later, Derry and Bruce were crossing the narrow stone causeway in Bruce's van, leaving the castle and lake behind. As they crested the hill, Derry looked back. The scene had none of the magic of the day before when she had first seen it with Bella. The sun shone and the water glistened as then, but the steely blue of the sky reflected in the lake surface looked like a stage set, contrived for effect, hiding a tawdry reality.

Soon they were bouncing over undulating country roads at wildly illegal speeds. The miles flew by and, to Derry's immense relief, Bruce never once mentioned the business with Mojo and the unfortunate role played by Bella. Anyone else would have spent the journey dissecting the whole affair—speculating, blaming and tutting their way across the countryside. Not Bruce.

'I'm thinking of changing my agent,' he said. 'Did I tell you? I'm with Beryl Carter. You're not with her, are you?'

No, Derry wasn't with Beryl, though it was so long since she'd had an audition it was getting hard to persuade herself she had an agent at all. 'I'm with Pam.'

'Did I tell you I've an audition week after next? *Pillage*. It's another series about Vikings.'

'Really?' said Derry, with that tiny but definite sense of alarm actors always get when they hear of an audition they hadn't known about. Had Pam missed a trick? She was only speaking to her a week ago—why hadn't she mentioned Vikings?

'Didn't Pam say anything? I mean there's always buxom wenches in these shows, right?'

Derry wasn't sure she liked being a contender for the buxom wenches vacancy. On the other hand, why was she being excluded? Wasn't she buxom enough? Too buxom? Should she phone Pam? Derry realised glumly that her agent would certainly have known about a show that important.

'Do you think I'll have a chance?' continued Bruce. 'I hope they don't ask me to improvise, I hate that. Don't you hate that? Last audition I did, they wouldn't even let me *hold* the script. I said to them how I felt so much more confident if I knew it was in my hand. But they wouldn't let me. I don't know why it threw me so badly. I just knew I was going to be terrible. Do you get that?'

Derry was about to make the encouraging noises that you make in these conversations, sincere but semi-automatic, when her phone rang. The number was no one she knew.

'Hi,' said Derry.

'Is that Derry O'Donnell?'

'Speaking.'

'Peter Doyle here. Missed you at the castle this morning but wanted to run something by you, if you don't mind.'

'Sure,' said Derry. Only then did it occur to her that she was conversing with a man who supplied cocaine to his wife. A man who had, indirectly, caused the death of another human being.

'You may be aware that it's Marlene's birthday next weekend.'

'No. No I wasn't.'

'I thought perhaps, astrology and so on?'

'No.'

'She wanted to have a little garden party this afternoon. Obviously in the circumstances that isn't going to happen, but she was so looking forward to spending more time with you. Marlene is working weekends so can't have a proper birthday party for a month or so. I'm arranging a little surprise, a meal at a rather good restaurant near Limerick on Tuesday. A small number of guests, just a few close friends, but we'll have the restaurant to ourselves. I'm organising some surprise treats for her. What I'm proposing is that you come down to the stud and keep Marlene occupied with some fortune-telling while we get ready. How does that sound?

'Limerick?' said Derry. 'I . . . I'm not sure—'

'Don't worry about transport. I can send Paulo for you. You would, of course, earn a substantial fee. I was thinking say, twelve hundred?'

Derry was dumbstruck. Silly money. Again. Never had she imagined that fortune-telling could be this lucrative. But something deep inside recoiled at the prospect of seeing those people again. All she wanted to do was forget. Forget Doyle, Marlene, Mojo, Sonya and the rest of them. Forget Fitz. And with the thought of Fitz came the memory of his cryptic request to remain unrecognised, his strange friendship with Doyle and Marlene, his false name, his redheaded fiancée.

'I'm sorry,' said Derry. 'I'll have to check my diary. I'm on the road at the moment. I have a feeling I have something on. But I'll get back to you. Is that alright?'

'Ah,' said Doyle, as if the idea that an unemployed actress offered money could have a prior engagement was something no sane person could have considered. 'I hope you'll see your way to coming. Marlene would be so happy. And I do want to cheer her up. After what happened, you understand?'

Derry did understand. She understood far more than Doyle realised. Or did he know that Marlene had told her everything? Surely not. Derry remembered Doyle's chiselled, urbane features, the hard observant eyes, the sardonic smile. You wouldn't want Doyle to discover you knew his secrets. No. Not even one secret.

Derry told herself to relax. If Marlene had admitted to Doyle that she had confided in her fortune-teller, he would not be handing out friendly invitations and well-paid work. All the same, there was no guarantee Marlene wouldn't tell Doyle sometime. Then what?

'I'll phone you when I've checked my diary. Is that alright? Tomorrow?'

'Please,' said Doyle. 'Do that. I'd be very grateful. Thank you. And please, if you are by any chance speaking to Marlene, do remember it's a surprise, alright?'

Even as Doyle hung up, Derry was annoyed with herself. All she had to do was say no—instead she had hemmed and hawed and dragged out the whole business. She hadn't even needed time to think. No amount of cash could lure her anywhere near the marital train-wreck that was Marlene and Peter Doyle.

14

'Why not come in for a coffee,' said Derry, as Bruce manoeuvred the van into the only parking space left on her street.

'I'm off coffee just now,' said Bruce. 'My doctor told me it raises anxiety. I've got to think about my audition.'

'But that's ages away! I thought the effect of caffeine lasted, like, three or four hours?'

'But what if it doesn't? I can't take that chance. Maybe if I *think* it'll make me anxious, it *will*. Do you have a mineral water?'

'Sure,' said Derry. 'And what's the hurry? You're not expected home are you?'

'No, worse luck,' said Bruce. 'Is it Ireland or is it just me? No one seems into commitment. Do you find that?'

Oddly enough, Derry did find that, though in a very different market.

'Do you have any coins?' asked Bruce. 'For the meter?'

Derry jumped down onto the pavement, fished in her bag and fed the parking meter. 'That's an hour, we'll need to be careful after that. The wardens are everywhere.'

As she was handing the ticket to Bruce to place on the dash, her phone rang. She jumped back into her seat in the van to take the call. Another number she didn't recognise.

'Is that Derry O'Donnell?'

Of course it is, thought Derry, irritated. *You just phoned me.* But all she said was, 'Yes, speaking.'

'Esther Simmons here. Warberg and O'Malley, solicitors. I'm representing Bella Langdon. She's a friend of yours?'

'Is Bella alright?' said Derry.

'I'm not at liberty to discuss my client, but Bella has asked me to tell you that she will not be in a position to do whatever it was she was going to do. Give you a lift somewhere? I'm afraid I'm not sure of the details.'

'That's alright,' said Derry. 'How's Bella? What's happening?'

'I'm afraid Bella has been arrested. She has been formally charged with possessing Class A drugs. In her car. She is being held in custody. She wanted me to let you know.'

Derry's mind stopped working, like freezing water had been poured directly into her brain. Her voice was a croak. 'That's impossible. Not Bella. I don't believe it.'

The lawyer paid no attention to Derry's rambling protests, as if she had a filter in her phone that automatically cut out protestations of innocence from clients, relatives of clients, and friends and acquaintances of clients.

'She also had a large amount of cash.'

'Hah!' Derry laughed out loud at the idea of Bella with cash. 'Bella has to think three times about buying a moisturiser! This is crazy! Where is she? How long will they keep her?'

'She'll go before a judge on Monday. The judge will almost certainly remand her in custody pending investigation and a full trial. There's no way a dealer will be let back on the streets.'

'Dealer! She's not a dealer! I'm telling you this is crazy.'

'Of course,' said the lawyer. 'We live in a crazy world, I'm sure.'

'When can I see her? Can I visit? How is she?'

'No visits until after the hearing and remand. She says to tell you she's fine. She said—the lawyer paused like she was reading from a note—"Say No to Negativity." Did I get that right? I suppose that means she's fine. In my opinion she is the type who will adapt reasonably well. Although she isn't admitting it, I'm imagining this isn't her first experience of incarceration.'

'You're saying that because she's black!' shouted Derry, all the tension and anxiety of the last twenty-four hours feeding her outrage. 'And an actress!' she added, irrelevantly.

The lawyer seemed not at all put out by Derry's outburst, as though her protestations-of-innocence filter included a discrimination-and-victimisation setting as standard. 'My client has asked me to phone you if we have developments. Perhaps a text will suffice. That's all. Thank you.' She hung up.

'You look terrible,' said Bruce.

'Come up to the flat, please. It's about Bella.'

~

Derry was so stunned at the news about Bella that she didn't remember Jacko was staying in her apartment until she and Bruce reached the front door. She hoped her father was out somewhere, but when she used her keys she knew straight away he had to be in. Of the two locks on her apartment door, a Yale and a mortice, only the Yale was locked. If Jacko had left he would surely have locked the mortice too.

As Derry stepped into her little sitting room, Bruce a pace behind, she found she could observe her own reactions in a surprising way. Mostly she noticed the things she *wasn't* doing. For example, she was failing to throw a tantrum. She was also failing to scream, shout and hurl solid objects. Amazing, because she would have been justified in doing every one of those things.

Beneath a reeking cloud of cigar smoke, the place smelled like sock. The fug could hardly have been worse if, in some fiendish spirit of efficiency, those socks had been rolled into cigars and smoked. Derry peered into the gloom. The curtains were closed. The floor-space was almost entirely occupied by the open bed-settee. On the coffee-table and chair, both pushed casually aside, were dumped a sweater, a coat and a wide-brimmed hat. Discarded on the floor was a large black boot, its mate lost somewhere in the chaos. The sink was piled high with dirty dishes. The cupboard doors hung drunkenly open.

'Hmmmrph!' said Jacko. He lay flat on his back, his eyes closed, one hand behind his head. In his other hand he held a lighted cigar dangerously close to his open shirt and hairy chest. Clouds of smoke emitted through his nose.

Jacko opened one eye, inspected Bruce and grunted. 'Thought you must have gotten distracted.' The eye closed once more.

If Jacko's cigar had led directly to a trail of gunpowder, itself leading to a barrow piled high with dynamite, the explosion could hardly have been louder.

'*Put that thing out now!*' roared Derry.

Jacko pursed his lips. He opened both eyes. Bruce seemed to find a framed photograph of old Dublin hanging on the wall a fascinating historical document worthy of the closest study.

Jacko frowned. He raised his eyebrows. He opened his mouth as if to protest, then closed it again. He stubbed out his cigar on a prettily decorated plate strategically placed on the coffee-table.

Stomping is difficult when stomping-space is restricted by obstacles of all kinds, including recumbent fathers, boots and tables, but Derry made as good a job of stomping as anyone could. She thumped her way past the disarray, ostentatiously pushing aside the coffee-table and chair, careless of clothing spilling onto the floor. She threw the window open as wide as it could go without actually wrenching it off its hinges.

'Up!'

'What time is it?' grunted Jacko, as if rebuke were so foreign to the soul of an artist it was wholly invisible.

'Four,' said Derry. '*PM.*'

'Hmm,' said Jacko, his tone laden with doubt. The implication was that he had only Derry's word for it and meant to check with the appropriate authorities when convenient. 'And to what do I owe the pleasure?' he added, eying Bruce quizzically. Jacko sat up, groaned and felt his head. He held out a large hairy fist. 'Always delighted to meet a friend of Derry's.'

Bruce stepped forward to shake Jacko's hand. 'Pleased to meet you, sir.'

Whether it was being addressed as 'sir' or thoughts of the coffee that Derry would probably offer when her blood pressure returned to normal, Jacko brightened.

'Don't mind Derry,' he said, sitting up. 'It's the sin of Eve. D'ye know that Garden of Eden story is only half true. She wasn't tempting Adam at all with the apple. She was tidying up for the tenth time that day, and she picks up the apple and she says to Adam, "And what do you call this, you slob?" And by way of ironical comment he takes an old bite. And sure we all know what happened next. Adam is in the you-know-what and trying to explain to the Boss.'

'Uh, Bruce,' said Bruce.

'Delighted,' said Jacko. 'Jacko.'

Derry slammed shut the cupboard doors, picked up a boot and dumped it on Jacko's lap.

'Up,' she repeated, though this time more resigned than angry. What was the point?

Jacko scrunched his eyes against the light, groaned in a satisfied way signifying his hangover was for once worthwhile, and threw his legs over the side of the settee. He was still wearing his trousers and shirt; dressing required only that he hunt down his missing boot.

'We had a bit of a session at McDaniel's last night,' he said, directing his words at Bruce in confidential tones, as though what he were about to say was too indelicate for female ears. 'Six John Lee Hooker songs on the trot I sang, with barely a pause to sup me pint. Mighty!'

'Dad. Stand. Now,' said Derry.

Jacko stood obediently while Derry stripped the duvet off the couch, reassembled the bed as a settee and returned her tables and chairs to something like their previous positions. All the while, Jacko and Bruce watched companionably, leaning against the kitchen sink. Through a red mist, Derry heard Jacko enquire about Bruce's origins in the States and his current career as an aspiring actor, sympathise with him on the travails of the actor's life, then deliver a pep talk on the artist's need for resilience, persistence, courage and a host of virtues that didn't seem to include washing the pile of dishes he was leaning against as he spoke.

Bruce, however, was made of more sensitive materials. 'I'll do these,' he said, rolling up his sleeves and starting right away on the dishes, displaying a competence that went a long way towards soothing Derry's annoyance. She reminded herself that Jacko would only be around for a couple of days, and now she was home she could enforce some discipline. But how could a grown man turn a decently tidy flat into a student squat in barely twenty-four hours?

Jacko seemed unaware of his debt to Bruce. 'She has *you* well trained, boyo,' he said, grinning in a way that suggested Bruce was halfway to the altar already. He turned to Derry who was now drying the dishes handed to her by Bruce. 'You should get some rest,' he said, blissfully unaware of the provocation. 'I'll be honest, when

I heard you this morning, even the thought of bagels couldn't stop me turning over and going back to sleep. I never even heard you going out again.'

Some people when hung over couldn't recite their own names. With Jacko, a hangover opened wide the floodgates of speech. Derry let his ramblings wash over her as she wondered how to patch up the dispute between her parents and restore the peace.

'D'ye know,' Jacko was saying, 'just before you came in this morning, didn't I have an extraordinary dream? A waterfall, pure white, tumbling down from way up high into a deep dark chasm. And in the chasm, like in a whirlpool, was this tiny person going round and round. And I couldn't save them.' He paused. 'Wasn't that tragic? What day is today?'

Derry agreed that Jacko's dream had some qualities of tragedy, though she forbore from pointing out the obvious absence of hamartia, peripeteia and anagnorisis. Pathos, she'd concede.

'Saturday,' said Derry.

'Oh no!' said Jacko. 'I promised I'd go to Danny's opening. Five o'clock. Heaven help us, more drink. Do you mind if I use the bathroom?' Jacko lurched out, weaving a little.

Bruce was contentedly removing glasses from the cupboard and polishing them before replacing them neatly in rows.

'You've just met my father. Sorry,' said Derry.

'I like him,' said Bruce. 'He's an artist, right? Ain't y'all lucky to have a dad who isn't, like, a banker or a stockbroker?'

Derry wasn't at all sure that having a father a banker or even a stockbroker would be such a terrible fate. You could probably get used to country clubs, dinner parties and knowing roughly the bounds of what might happen next. She extracted a mineral water from the fridge and handed it to Bruce.

'Take a seat. Let me tell you about Bella.'

'Big trouble?'

Derry, made herself some borage tea while she told him what the lawyer had said. Bruce's sympathetic expression was comforting. Lately, Derry felt, she seemed to have been doing nothing but listening. It was good to talk.

'Sorry for asking this,' said Bruce, 'but I guess there's no chance that Bella . . . you know.'

'No! Not in a million years. There's been some huge mistake. It's crazy.'

'Okay,' said Bruce. 'I believe you. The question had to be asked, that's all.'

'I suppose it did,' admitted Derry. 'Even her lawyer seems to think she's a dealer. Poor Bella.'

'She can probably look after herself, if I'm guessing right.'

'I wonder,' said Derry. 'She's not as tough as she makes out.'

They sat in silence. Derry was overwhelmed by a sense of helplessness. She thought of Bella being locked up, thrown into a cell, alone. Only then did she remember—her dream, vision or whatever it was. An empty room. A spy-hole. She shivered. What use was second sight when you couldn't even save a friend? All her visions ever seemed to do was come back and taunt her, like a message from the other world saying we told you so. *Well, thanks a bunch.* Derry didn't even want to think of the Granddads. If they were here in the room right now, she wouldn't even want to talk to them. They could go spin their yarns and talk Grandad crap somewhere else.

'How come coke is everywhere you look these days?' said Bruce. 'Is it boredom or what? I mean, why do people bother? Why not take up, like, hang-gliding.'

Somehow Derry couldn't see Mojo or Marlene hang-gliding to

get their kicks, but she understood what Bruce meant. Then it struck her. Just as Bruce had said. Everywhere you looked, coke.

'Bruce, do you believe in coincidence?'

'Maybe,' said Bruce. 'I once sat waiting for an audition and a guy from my school came and sat beside me, waiting for the same audition.'

Derry, agreed this was indeed unlikely, especially in Dublin, Bruce being American.

'Weird thing was, I remembered him from school because he had the same name as me. Coincidence, huh?'

'Bruce,' said Derry quietly. 'If Bella didn't sell cocaine—and she didn't—somebody put it in her car. The lawyer said there was cash in the car too. Somebody planted it there. Bella was set up. She was framed.'

'Isn't that a little far-fetched?' said Bruce. 'Somebody has to really dislike you to do that kind of thing. I mean, *really* dislike. How much coke was there anyway? How much cash?'

Derry didn't know, the lawyer hadn't said.

'Whatever, if it was enough to get her arrested and kept in jail it was more than a ten-dollar wrap. But if you're right, somebody spent money to hurt your friend Bella. Did she piss someone off?'

'Please don't say anything about Bella or any of this to Dad, will you? Or anybody else. Promise?'

'Sure, baby,' said Bruce.

Derry was so engrossed in connecting the threads surfacing in her mind that she overlooked his calling her *baby*. Normally, any man who called Derry *baby* was mere seconds away from what her father metaphorically called a clip around the ear, though in practice this could take the form of a stiletto on the instep or a toe in the shin. On reflection, Bruce was gay, so maybe the same rules didn't apply.

Derry summarised for Bruce the story of Marlene's powder compact and the strange relationship between Doyle and Marlene, with him supplying her with coke to keep her away from dealers.

Bruce was appalled. 'I don't even know who to feel sorry for. Should I be sorry for anybody?'

'What if Doyle wanted to deflect attention from himself?' said Derry. 'What if he was looking for someone to blame? Bella found Mojo sick. She was maybe the last to talk to him. Doyle would know that.'

The implications were horrible. Would Doyle frame someone innocent and get them sent to prison? He might if the stakes were high enough. He had access to coke. But how could Doyle have known where Bella lived or what car she drove?

'Uh,' said Bruce. 'That's easy. You told me. Remember, after Mojo was taken away I asked y'all for Bella's contact details in case there were questions? I added her car registration. It's normal.' He shrugged. 'Did anybody else know about the compact? Sonya—she knew, right?'

Sonya knew. If Sonya told her story to the police, the tabloid journalists would scramble over each other to implicate Marlene in a scandal. The beautiful, delicate Marlene could end up in jail.

'He's protecting Marlene,' said Derry. 'He's afraid Sonya will talk. He's setting up Bella to take the blame or at least muddy the waters. It makes sense. He's tried for goodness knows how long to keep Marlene out of trouble, even supplying her himself. He's still trying to keep her out of trouble.'

As Derry thought about Doyle and his wealth, the influence he must have in business and maybe even politics, she felt more frightened than ever in her life. Frightened, above all, for Bella.

Yet, to her surprise Derry realised that she didn't hate Doyle. If he were responsible for what had happened to Bella, she should loathe him, but she didn't. He must love Marlene so much. She remembered Marlene's smug comment about coke and men, and almost pitied Doyle. How far might anyone go to save a flawed loved one from disaster and disgrace?

Derry fumbled in her bag for her phone and dialled. Bruce raised his eyebrows. 'Lawyer,' said Derry. Bruce nodded. But the lawyer wasn't answering. Was she busy, or was she just busy for friends of drug dealers? When voicemail kicked in, Derry cut the call. What was the point? How could she explain in a message? She'd sound like a fantasist peddling a conspiracy in which millionaires framed actresses as drug dealers. She sipped her tea but felt no better.

The door opened and Jacko peered round. 'Don't wait up. Could be a late one. I have the key.' He disappeared. Seconds later, his head reappeared. 'By the way, I hope young Brucey here is handy with the spanners.'

Jacko put on the stage whisper he used whenever he thought he was discussing biological realities in front of those he chivalrously termed *the ladies*. 'The flush,' he whispered. 'It's not working right. I'd fix it meself, but you know how I am with plumbing. Your neighbours downstairs would prefer if I left it to the professionals. See ye later!' His head vanished.

'That's all I need,' said Derry. 'Plumbing. And it's Saturday afternoon. You know what?'

'What?' said Bruce.

'I don't care. I don't give a damn.' Derry decided right there that the best solution to all her troubles was to sit where she was and carry on sitting until something made her not sit. What was the point doing anything else?

'Aw, don't you worry,' said Bruce smiling. 'I'll fix ya up.'

Derry was astonished. 'You can do plumbing?' Derry had never had a friend, boyfriend or otherwise, who could plumb. Not even actors, in her experience, could plumb. Many could do just about anything else, but something about plumbing seemed to defeat even the most manly males. In her admittedly finite experience, even men who wore hi-viz vests in their day job couldn't plumb.

'Sure,' said Bruce. 'Navy SEAL. We can plumb. Okay, mostly we kinda un-plumb, like plumbing in reverse, but hey it's all the same thing. I've just got to remember I'm not trying to sink it.' He laughed uproariously, slapping his knee and rocking back and forth. 'Let me take a look,' he said, drying his eyes.

Derry knew she should protest she couldn't possibly put him to all that trouble. But somehow she didn't. Bruce sprang up and strode purposefully to her little bathroom.

Derry stared into her tea, as if in the swirling yellow of the borage she would find inspiration, think of something simple that would solve everything. But no inspiration came. Poor Bella. What were the chances a black, out-of-work actress, caught with cocaine and cash could persuade a judge that someone had planted it in her car? Zero.

Derry had a sickening thought. Was this Doyle's idea of a birthday present for Marlene—a present she would never find out about? And if she did find out, would she feel sorry? Derry thought about the Marlene she knew, but couldn't decide whether she'd be appalled or shrug her elegant shoulders and turn away. Derry felt infinitely depressed. Not only about Marlene and Bella, but about everything and everyone.

'Uh, Houston,' said Bruce, 'we've got a problem.'

15

Bruce was standing in the doorway.

'Sorry?' said Derry.

'No bubbles, no troubles,' said Bruce. His expression was deeply serious.

'What are you talking about?'

'It's a saying we have.' He held up a white bundle, a towel from the bathroom wrapped around something. Slowly he unwrapped it, holding the towel open to show two transparent plastic bags. One was white, the size of a cigarette packet. The other was bulkier and darker-coloured.

As Bruce carefully laid out the towel and its contents on the coffee table in front of her, Derry thought she was going to faint. She didn't know what she was looking at, or her conscious mind didn't know. But her unconscious must have understood all too well, and her unconscious mind was saying *faint now, it's the only sensible thing to do.*

'Derry, are you alright?' Bruce grabbed her by the shoulders and shook. Derry tried to get a grip on herself.

'I'm okay. Thanks. I'm fine—honest.'

She reached out to one of the bags.

'No! Don't touch. Whatever you do, don't touch.'

She drew back her hand like she'd had an electric shock.

'Is that what I think?'

'Yes it is,' said Bruce. He used the edge of the towel to manoeuvre the smaller of the two bags so Derry could see its contents. Cash. The notes were blue-grey. She could clearly see the €20 symbol on the top right corner. The wedge was maybe half an inch thick.

'How much?' asked Derry, her voice hoarse.

'A grand? Two? Only time I ever saw a bundle like that was when I paid for my van.'

'Where was it?' said Derry. To find words she had to dig deep into herself, like they were buried and had to be dragged up into the open.

'In the toilet cistern. Whoever put it there messed up. They let it get in the way of the mechanism. Otherwise you wouldn't have noticed a thing. Until the raid.'

Derry thought her heart would stop.

'Raid?'

'Sure. Why else?'

Derry couldn't speak. Her breath came in trembling gasps.

'I guess we know now how Bella must have felt,' said Bruce.

Derry stared at the bundles sitting on her coffee table. 'What do I do?'

'I humbly suggest we dispose of the white bag at the double. Like, soon as.'

'How?' Derry felt as if everything she said came out of her mouth with *stupid* written all over it.

'Down the drain. Let it brighten the lives of the fishes in Dublin Bay. I guess they need cheering up some.' Bruce smiled, put his hands on her shoulders and squeezed. 'Don't worry. We found it before anyone else did. Be thankful. Now, let's get rid of this stuff, okay?'

Derry nodded.

'Scissors?'

'Drawer. By the sink.'

Bruce got up, rummaged in the drawer and came back with a scissors. With the edge of the towel, he nudged the cash onto the table, wrapped the towel round the bag of coke and disappeared into the bathroom. Derry could hear taps running. A few minutes later Bruce came back still carrying the towel. Wrapped in it was the sodden empty bag, a limp sheet of plastic.

'This needs to go too. You don't have a fire?'

No, Derry didn't have a fireplace. It had long ago been blocked up and was now host to a temperamental and underpowered electric heater.

'The plastic normally goes in that bin there,' said Derry, pointing to where the two recycling bins sat side by side.

'Seeing as how this hasn't exactly been used to wrap cheese, and probably has a chemical signature you can read from space, it might be better if we didn't have it lying around.' Bruce took the towel and its contents to the open window where he cut the bag into strips, shaking them out into the gentle breeze.

'Sorry to litter your fair city, but hey.' He came back to the table and sat, staring at the bag of cash. 'What about this?'

'Same,' said Derry.

'You sure?'

'Sure.'

'You got a shredder? Don't want to cause a riot in the street.'

But Derry hadn't got a shredder.

How do you get rid of money? Never in her life had Derry imagined she'd be asking herself that question. 'I know,' she said, jumping up and rooting in a kitchen cupboard. She pulled out a blender, plugged it into the socket and poured in a little water from the tap.

'I guess if it'll turn cabbage into a smoothie it can do it to twenties.'

'Hey, a cash smoothie,' said Bruce. 'Wow! Guess it's the most expensive drink you've ever made. Wear rubber gloves and wash them after, okay? Give me the bag.' Bruce took the plastic bag that had held the twenties and again leaned out the window, shredding the plastic until it was gone.

'The towel might be contaminated too,' said Bruce.

'Throw it in the washing machine, here.' Derry indicated the machine under the worktop. Bruce did as he was told, setting the controls and turning it on. The device whirred and slurped as the wash cycle started.

Derry should have found it strange, feeding so much cash one note at a time into a buzzing blender, but nothing could feel strange any more. It was like she had stepped into a world where normal rules no longer applied. At least all the activity had made a space for her brain to start working for the first time since Bruce had emerged from the bathroom with those loathsome packages.

'Bruce, shouldn't I search the place now? See if they've planted anything else?'

Bruce thought for a moment. 'Uh, I wouldn't worry about that. Honest. What more would they need to plant? Machine pistols? They already found a good place. It's not likely they'd tip you off by hiding stuff anywhere more obvious. Search if you like, but I bet that's it. Unless there's anything else here y'all don't want 'em to find. A little bit of smoke maybe?'

'No!' said Derry. 'Makes me throw up. I stick to wine, thank you very much. Makes for an adequate hangover all by itself.' She stopped, motionless, as the realisation struck home. 'Oh,' she said.

'I'm afraid so,' said Bruce.

'The police are still going to come, aren't they?'

'For sure.'

'When?'

'No way of telling. Whenever they get the tip-off. Or soon after. Best be prepared. Don't put the mortice on or they'll smash the door in.'

'Oh my God,' said Derry. She slumped into the chair. 'I don't believe this is happening.' She paused, like her brain was one step behind where it needed to be. 'Bruce,' how did they do this? How did they know I wasn't here? How did they get in?'

'Clodagh must have had your address. So you could get paid, right? Easy for Doyle to get. And he knew where you were last night,' said Bruce.

'But Dad . . . they didn't know Dad would be here.' She stopped. 'The bagels! All that garbage he was talking! He was so drunk he heard them come in, but he thought it was me in from the all-night bakery. He could have stopped them! And he just lay here snoring!'

'Maybe that wasn't so unlucky,' said Bruce, gently. 'He's a big guy, your dad, but big's not everything.'

Derry was appalled. Suddenly, she had a vision of what might have happened to her father if he had disturbed intruders expecting to find an empty apartment. She blanked the images out of her mind.

'Bruce, what I don't understand is how they managed to get into the apartment in the first place. There's an entryphone at the street door. I've a mortice and Yale on the apartment door. Okay, Dad left the mortice unlocked, but they wouldn't have known to expect that.'

Bruce shook his head. 'Not so hard. Entryphones are easy. Late at night? Wait for a drunken neighbour to reel home. Slipstream in behind them as they open the door. They won't ask questions. Or maybe earlier in the evening, jam the mechanism so it doesn't quite latch. Easy. An entryphone stops drunks relieving themselves in your stairway. Won't stop a pro.

'What about the mortice? How could they have known it would be off? What about the Yale?'

'A child could get past a Yale. And they wouldn't have cared about the mortice. If the locks were too much trouble they'd have used a jemmy and broken your door. Maybe they'd have taken your TV to make it look good. Nobody expects burglars to leave something behind.'

Derry sat, unable to speak as she imagined masked intruders right there in her flat, her father asleep on the couch unaware of the appalling danger he was in. She looked around the little apartment that had seemed such a cosy, safe home and shuddered. Nothing would ever feel the same.

'We need to talk through a couple of things,' said Bruce. 'Like what you should do when you get raided.'

What to do when you get raided. Like those government information ads, what to do in case of fire. What to do if you break down on the highway. What to do in the event of someone having a heart attack. Insane.

'Couldn't I just not be here?'

'You don't know when they'll come. But you can guess about four a.m. We'—he laughed, embarrassed—'I mean, *they* like to get the enemy at the lowest ebb of their body clocks.'

'I am not the enemy!'

'Sorry. You know what I mean. The main thing is, don't panic. When they shout 'open up' or whatever, just say yes, you're coming, hold on. And be quick about it. Keep a dressing gown near the bed or sleep in your clothes.'

'Sleep in my clothes!'

'They'll probably be armed—'

'Armed! You're crazy! What would they—?'

'As far as they're concerned, you're a coke dealer. You could have a Mac-10 in here. Don't take it personally, they're just doing their jobs.'

'Whose side are you on? And what's a Mac-10?'

Bruce ignored her questions. 'Put your hands up as soon as you open the door, and stand back. They'll scream at you, right in your face. *Lie on the floor! Lie on the floor!* That's to confuse you. And they'll look pretty scary—flak jackets and balaclavas probably, but don't panic. You just lie down and let them put the cuffs on.'

'Cuffs!' Derry's voice came out as a strangled squeal.

'The most important thing is not to do anything surprising, and do what you're told straight away—accidents happen. Remember, they won't find anything, so you can't be arrested. You'll eat a little carpet. No big deal.'

Was it Bruce's casual acceptance that tipped Derry's reaction from horror to outrage? Or was the borage tea kicking in at last? If the raid had happened at that moment, far from meekly obeying orders, Derry would have put her hands on her hips, like her granny used to do, and given the intruders an almighty dressing down. The least they could expect would be prods to their armoured chests and an invitation to take their fancy-dress and silly toys elsewhere.

'Oh what a relief! I'm on the floor handcuffed at four a.m. in my own apartment, but that's okay because they're not going to take me to jail. I do not believe this!'

'Don't blame me; I'm just the help, honey,' said Bruce.

'Sorry,' said Derry. True, he was only trying to be supportive. 'I'm listening. Go on.'

'They'll ask a lot of questions. You answer them truthfully. Except for what we just found, of course. They may take a couple of hours to get through the place. No offense,' Bruce added, looking around, 'but it's a little, uh, cluttered in here.'

'*Those are my things!*' said Derry, with as much calm as she could muster. The awful knowledge was sinking in. Strangers were going to rifle through everything she owned, prying into every corner of her life. Did they make jokes while they went through your belongings? Probably. Derry now knew that everything Bruce had described was going to happen. And there was nothing she could do to prevent it. She felt as though she were sitting in the middle of a road, paralysed, in the path of a giant roller. All she could do was watch disaster coming.

'Bruce, you should really go now.'

Bruce looked hurt. 'I thought you might want company, that's all. I'll go if you want.'

'Please don't be offended. I mean, if they raid and come crashing in here—if they have guns like you say—wouldn't it be dangerous for you? They won't bother about me, but you might worry them. You don't want to be handcuffed for nothing.'

Bruce laughed. 'Aw, don't worry about me. We had a thing in training called Hell Week. I won't even tell you what they did to us. Suffice it to say, our little mantra was, "Mind over Matter. If I don't *mind*, then it don't *matter*." Try it. It works.'

For the first time that afternoon, Derry smiled. 'Bruce, you're a star. And I would appreciate it if you'd stay around a bit. Okay?'

So Derry made toast, coffee and more tea for herself, and they sat at her little table trying not to talk about drugs or policemen. Bruce tried to cheer her up by telling her about his mostly disastrous history of auditions but ended up depressing himself as he thought about the one coming up on Monday week. Surely for a Viking, they'd be looking for an actor with a bushy moustache and long straggly hair, like a refugee from a heavy-metal band. What was his agent doing sending him for something he was going to flunk? Derry was as supportive as someone could be who was expecting her door to be kicked in at any moment.

'We had another saying in Navy SEALs,' said Bruce. 'The only easy day was yesterday.' He looked thoughtful. 'You know, we can't just sit here and wait for more bad things to happen. We need to do some thinking. First off, is there anyone you can call? You need the inside track on this.'

Derry picked up her phone, 'Let me try Bella's lawyer again.'

'No,' said Bruce urgently. 'Don't do that. You tell her about this, and you're telling her about a crime.'

'But I didn't do anything!'

'You were in possession of a Class A drug, doesn't matter whether it was yours or not. And she'd have to report it as a crime and advise you to give yourself up. Those are the rules.'

Derry put down her phone.

'Come on, think; there must be somebody,' Bruce insisted. 'Didn't you ever sleep with a cop? You know, nice uniform, all that?'

'Bruce! Anyhow, that's a gay thing.' She remembered an acquaintance of hers from an aerobics class who once confessed that she only ever slept with men who wore hi-viz vests for a living. Derry had wanted to ask whether they, you know, kept the hi-viz on, but never dared. 'Okay, maybe it's not a gay thing. But uniforms never did it for me. Honest.'

Bruce looked sceptical.

'They did not!'

'Never?'

Derry remembered Fitz. Why had she never really thought of him as a policeman? Maybe it was the upper-class accent that made you think he did it as a hobby. Nothing as plebeian as a job.

'There's Fitz, I guess, said Derry. 'But I'm not sure that would be a good idea.'

'Fitz?' asked Bruce.

Derry explained. 'He wouldn't say what he was doing, but he must be investigating Doyle. He's pretending to be a racing guy. Something about betting syndicates? Horse doping? I don't know.'

'But he was afraid you'd blow his cover?'

Derry nodded. 'He practically begged me to stay away from him.'

'You trust him?' asked Bruce.

At that, Derry had to think. Not so long ago she would have said yes without hesitation. She knew Fitz like few people had ever known him, she was sure of that. But now she didn't know who to trust.

'I'm not sure,' she said. 'Yes. I think I can trust him. I think.'

'Not a resounding endorsement there, honey. Do you trust the guy or don't you?'

Derry hesitated again, like she knew in her heart of hearts that whichever little word she chose, yes or no, would change forever her future. And Bella's too.

'Yes.'

'Okay,' said Bruce. 'Phone him.'

But Derry didn't have a phone number for Fitz. She almost laughed out loud. The one person who might help and she manages not to have his number. *Well done, Derry. What now? Look up the Yellow Pages under 'undercover policemen?'*

'The hotel might tell me.' She picked up her phone and dialled the number for Clodagh the Organiser.

'Hello, this is Derry O'Donnell speaking.'

'I'm sorry, who?'

This wasn't going to be easy. The Organiser didn't mean to release a guest's phone number to anybody. Her tone implied that if a long line of people were queuing up asking for phone numbers, Derry the fortune-teller, friend of Bella the troublemaker, would be far down the list, well behind tabloid journalists, bailiffs, autograph hunters, internet trolls and axe murderers. Derry's insistence that Fitz had given her his card, but she'd lost it, got her nowhere.

Who else could she phone? Marlene? She would conclude that Derry was pursuing Fitz, which would be okay, if embarrassing. But she might tell Doyle, and that would be disastrous. Disastrous for Fitz and for Derry.

'Bruce, what about your security guys? Would they have a guest list?'

'We didn't keep guest details, no need.' He paused. 'Hang on.' He pulled out his phone and dialled. Derry could hear the faint beeping of the ringtone. As his call was answered, Bruce gave Derry a mischievous wink.

'Guess who!' Bruce announced expansively, as if he had just walked into an especially lively party. Derry couldn't hear the response, but whoever Bruce was talking to obviously knew him very well indeed.

'I said I'd call!' protested Bruce. 'What do you take me for, a slutty slut who loves 'em and leaves 'em?' They laughed, as if to say, 'perish the thought.'

Derry had to sit and listen impatiently while the conversation went from flirty to cooing and back again. Then Bruce got to the point, or what Derry hoped was the point.

'Honey, this friend of mine . . . No a chick, she's a cutie, you'll love her . . . she's got the hots for this guy who was staying Friday night, at the celebrity do. No! Not me, I swear! Cross my heart! Really! Can you get his cellphone number for her? Mobile, yes that thing. Name of . . .' He turned to Derry mouthing, *'Name?'*

Derry whispered Fitz' fake name. 'Philip Gilbey-Jones.'

'You'll call me? Hey great. He's pretty cute you know, maybe she'll broaden his mind and we can all get to know him better.' He laughed and hung up, saying 'Cheery-poo!'

'You were only working there two days!' said Derry, unsure whether to be impressed or shocked.

'Don't be such a prude,' said Bruce, grinning. 'Life is short!'

'Will he call?'

'Of course he will.' He pouted lasciviously.

'Stop that!' said Derry. 'You're a shameless hussy.'

'Hmm, that's what my lieutenant used to say,' retorted Bruce, laughing uproariously as if he'd said that same thing on a hundred occasions and enjoyed it every time.

Bruce's phone rang. His face was suddenly serious.

'Hi baby,' he said, catching Derry's eye and miming scribbling with a pen. Derry grabbed a ballpoint and an old envelope lying on the kitchen worktop.

'Hey, thanks,' said Bruce into his phone. He scribbled a number. 'You're a star! I know, I know. I'll call you, okay. Yeah, promise, really. Okay. Bye.' He hung up and pushed the envelope across the table to Derry. 'That's your friend. I hope you're right about him.'

'Will you come along? If he agrees to see me?'

'I'm not too keen on these spooks, plainclothes types, whatever. In my humble experience they're mostly posers and incompetents. All hush-hush and we-know-more-than-you, and nowhere to be seen when the doo-doo starts to fly.'

'Will you?' asked Derry.

'Sure, babe,' said Bruce.

'I'll make another cup of tea,' said Derry.

'Jeez, how much of that stuff do you drink? What did you say it was?'

'Borage. There's an old saying, "Borage for courage." Roman soldiers used to drink it mixed with wine.'

'Don't know about the porridge—'

'Borage.'

'—but wine sounds good.' He sighed. 'No drinking on duty, though.'

Derry made her tea and sat sipping. She knew she was playing for time, avoiding having to ring Fitz. But the borage seemed to be working. 'Alright,' she said. 'Here goes.' She picked up her phone, slid the envelope towards her and dialled.

'Gilbey-Jones?'

'Fitz?'

The voice hesitated. 'Who is that?'

'Fitz, it's me. Derry. I wouldn't call you if it wasn't important.' Derry felt herself blush. The humiliation of Fitz thinking she was chasing him was unbearable.

Again a hesitation. 'Can you hold, please?' Derry heard murmuring as if Fitz had his hand over the phone and was moving elsewhere to take the call.

'Hello? I'm sorry. Really, you shouldn't have called me. How did you get . . . Never mind. I don't have long.'

'I have a problem. I need to see you.'

'I'm sorry, that's out of the question. Look Derry, I asked you to help me in this. I thought you might. For old times' sake.'

Derry couldn't help her voice rising an octave and knew she was sounding exactly like the stereotype of the besotted, neurotic female. She pulled herself together.

'This has nothing to do with old times. Listen to me. Please. It's about Doyle.' Derry let her words hang, hoping they would do her work for her.

'Ah,' said Fitz. 'Alright. I'm listening.'

'I don't know what you're doing, but I imagine it's to do with Doyle and his business. You don't have to say whether I'm right or wrong. Either that or you're just as bad as him, and I'm walking right into it here.'

'Steady on, old girl.'

He said it just like she remembered. Despite the crazy, unbelievable seriousness of the mess she was in, the old-fashioned English phrase made her smile. It was what he used to say whenever she suggested something outrageous, like swimming in the Serpentine on the way home from a party. *Steady on old girl, we're not in Malibu now.* Suddenly, all her doubts evaporated.

'Tell me you're still a policeman.'

'Of course,' said Fitz. 'The old man hasn't popped off yet. No intention of, by the looks.'

By *the old man*, he meant his father, the Baron or whatever he was.

'It's about Doyle,' repeated Derry. 'And it's about cocaine.'

Again a pause. 'I see.'

'I need to meet you.'

'Alright. Tomorrow?'

'No. This evening. Soon.'

A moment's silence.

'Okay. I'll come in a car. Wait for me on a quiet street. Seven p.m. What part of town are you in? I need to be able to see you easily and pull in without problems.'

Derry told him where she lived. 'You know the gate of the old Guinness Brewery?' she asked. 'Where the horses and carriages line up to take tourists on city jaunts?'

'I know it.'

'I'll stand just past the last carriage. You'll see me.'

'Sounds alright. Seven p.m. on the dot. Don't be late.'

Derry had to suppress her annoyance. Of course she wouldn't be late. That was men, always insisting on the last word even if you were only going to the convenience store for an ice-cream. 'I want to bring a friend.'

'Not a good idea, I'm afraid,' said Fitz. 'Not at all.'

'It's important. He knows about you.'

'I see,' said Fitz. Derry could hear the anger in his voice.

'You'll understand when I tell you what happened.'

'I repeat, not a good idea.'

What Derry didn't say, because she had hardly admitted it to herself, was that having Bruce with her made her feel safe. From whom? From Fitz? If she really trusted him, she'd feel no need for Bruce, would she? The thought was sobering.

'I need him there,' said Derry. 'If you want to hear about Doyle.'

'Who is this person?' asked Fitz.

'He's . . . he was military. You can trust him.'

Fitz didn't answer. Was this a technique policemen had for making you do what they wanted? Just wait and wait until you agreed with them?

'He's my boyfriend,' added Derry without thinking. Had she said that because she wanted Fitz to know she had support? Or for some other reason.

'I see,' said Fitz.

'Seven o'clock,' said Derry. 'At the end of the line of carriages. Okay?'

'Alright,' said Fitz.

The line went dead. Derry sat staring at her phone. The screen switched to black.

'Did I get that right?' asked Bruce.

'He'll meet us at seven.'

'I got that part. I'm not sure this is a good idea, hon,' said Bruce. The uncertainty in his voice caused a knot to form in Derry's stomach.

'Please Bruce, come with me. I don't know if I can trust him. I think I can. But how can I be sure?' Derry was pleading now.

'It's not that,' said Bruce.

'It's just a precaution.'

'Honest, it's not that, sweetie.'

'For goodness' sake! What can he do? If he has a car full of thugs they can hardly threaten both of us, not in the middle of the city traffic.'

'Uh, that's not it. I don't mind that.'

'Well what is it?'

Derry had never seen Bruce like this before. Hesitant, unsure of himself, nervous. Was all that stuff about the Navy a big bluff, a fantasy? You read about guys claiming to have all kinds of medals and turning out to have been in the Parks Department. Surely not Bruce—everything about him said tough guy. When he wasn't playing diva or competing for title of campest bodybuilder on the block.

'Did you have to say I was your boyfriend? Couldn't I have been just, like, a *friend*?'

'What difference does it make?' asked Derry, exasperated, though she did feel a twinge of guilt. He was right. Strictly, it hadn't been necessary to say he was her boyfriend.

'He'll know straight away!'

'How would he know?' asked Derry, amazed.

'It'll be obvious! I don't know what boyfriends do! I mean, how they talk and everything.'

'But you've had boyfriends!'

'Derry, a boy boyfriend is completely different from a girl boyfriend,' said Bruce, as if he was explaining to a particularly dense learner driver the difference between Keep Left and Turn Left.

Derry didn't know how to approach this. Was it politically incorrect to ask how he had managed in the Navy when he wasn't supposed to be gay?

'Didn't you have to, like, pretend to have girlfriends when you were in the Navy?'

Bruce thought about that. 'Not really. All you needed was a picture of some carnival queen on your locker. SEALs don't do brothels and all. We're too tired. SEALs sleep, mostly.' He finished with such a despairing tone that Derry realised he really was worried.

'It's just a role,' she said. 'Leading man.'

Bruce was too much the actor to fall for that. 'I *know* who's the leading man here. And honey, it's not me.'

Derry felt herself blushing. She cast about desperately for another angle. 'We can rehearse, if you like. Think of it as an audition.' She had hardly said it before she knew it was a mistake.

'Don't say that!'

'Okay! Not an audition, a small part. Stand up.' Bruce did as he was told. Derry navigated her way past the coffee table to stand beside him. 'Okay, we're waiting by the brewery wall. You're my boyfriend. Put your arm around me.'

Bruce looked horrified.

'Around my shoulders.' Bruce tentatively did as instructed but was a rigid as if Derry were a wooden self-assembly table trying to make friendly. 'Relax! We're friends, okay?'

'Alright,' said Bruce, doubtfully. 'But what do I say?'

'You don't have to say anything.'

'Uh, okay.' He hesitated. 'What if he asks me questions?'

'He won't ask you anything.'

'How old am I? Like, am I my age or do I have to play older?'

'It doesn't— Okay, you can be your real age. The same. Everything's the same.'

'Where do I live; do we live together or what?'

'No. No need. Everything is like it is. Except—you know.'

'Am I American?'

Derry lost it.

'Of course you're American! Bruce, pull yourself together! This is not the Royal Shakespeare Company! Just don't say darling so often. Boyfriends don't.'

'But lots of actors say darling.'

'But non-actors think actors are gay.'

'But I am gay.'

'But that's not why you say darling!'

Bruce practiced his deep breathing as he had been taught to do. 'Could we do just one more run-through? Maybe you could make me some of that porridge?'

16

At five minutes before seven, Derry and Bruce were standing with their backs to the towering wall of the oldest brewery in Dublin. The roadside was lined with vintage carriages, each harnessed to a patient horse. The jarveys sat relaxed, perched on their high seats, exchanging banter amongst themselves. A small knot of tourists was emerging from the brewery gates, the last of the day. Some, obviously keen on a city tour, stood looking enquiringly up at the drivers, only to be ignored. Soliciting fares was obviously beneath the dignity of any self-respecting Dublin cabman.

Two hours since Derry had phoned Fitz, and meanwhile she had cleaned and tidied every inch of her apartment. After an hour and a half of making the bed, hanging up clothes, sorting out the contents of drawers, throwing grubby bras into a refuse sack, dragging cobwebbed and dusty books out from under the bed and vacuuming the whole place, she pronounced herself satisfied. The apartment was gleaming, every surface pristine, every dish dried and put away. She had even dusted the lampshades. Derry was embarrassed to notice just how much more light the bulbs seemed to give out.

'They're not going to give you marks out of ten,' said Bruce. 'Jeez, I thought I was house-proud.'

'If I'm going to be lying on the floor for an hour with my face in the carpet, I want the carpet to be vacuumed. What if I sneeze and they shoot me? Anyway, I feel better now. And I didn't find any more packages. So that's something.'

But there had already been packages enough. As Derry leaned against the cold brewery wall, waiting in silence for Fitz, she was forced to face the truth. Somebody meant her harm. Watching the lazy line of carriages and the tourists with their backpacks and parkas, their smiling untroubled faces, Derry found it hard to believe in such malevolence. She might have dreamt everything, except there, right beside her, Bruce was leaning quietly against the wall. And creeping slowly past the carriages, was a gleaming black limousine.

As the car crept closer, its motor whispering, Derry stepped to the edge of the pavement. Bruce hovered, not too close, not too far. Through the car's tinted rear windows it was impossible to make out who sat in the back, but Derry could see the driver. She had red hair.

The car stopped. The rear passenger door swung open.

'Hop in,' said Fitz. 'Smartish, if you don't mind.'

The car was huge. A Bentley? A Rolls-Royce? A glass screen, its centre pane lowered, separated the driver from the spacious rear compartment. Fitz sat on a small jump seat facing backwards. No sooner had Derry and Bruce sunk into the enveloping leather than Fitz had pulled the door closed, and the car was gliding forward.

'Perhaps,' said Fitz, 'we should get the introductions over with?'

Derry's mouth was dry. She had to cough to clear her throat.

'Bruce, this is Fitz—an old friend.'

Fitz stiffened. Perhaps others wouldn't have noticed, so controlled was his usual demeanour, but Derry saw immediately. Was it because she had called Fitz an old friend? Or was it because he wanted to be known as Gilbey-Jones?

'Bruce, I hope you don't mind, but you wouldn't happen to have your passport about your person, would you?' said Fitz.

Derry was startled. What an extraordinary demand.

'Can't be too careful,' added Fitz, as though that were all the explanation anyone could want.

'Sorry, no,' said Bruce. 'I can give you the number.' He reeled off a long sequence of numbers. 'You want my Social Security?' He recited yet another list.

'Did you get those, Janice?' said Fitz to the driver.

Janice, thought Derry. *Well, hello.*

To Derry's infinite satisfaction, Janice leaned back, her head turned, and asked could Bruce run those numbers by her again. Somehow, Derry had expected her to remember everything first time. Suddenly, she felt a lot more friendly towards Miss Janice. *Okay*, she thought, *a little more friendly*, and internally smacked herself around the head for thinking such stupid, childish, girlie things in the middle of a real-life crisis. Not for the first time, Derry wondered whether she had been born missing some vital component. Surely other people didn't think stupid things at all the wrong times? She hoped not. Some of them were driving airplanes and operating on people's brains.

While the car was stopped at lights, Janice scribbled Bruce's numbers on a pad and was now driving with a phone to her ear, clearly unworried about penalty points.

'Meanwhile,' said Fitz, 'why not tell me why we are doing this?'

Derry told him about her friend Bella finding Mojo dead from cocaine, and how cocaine and cash had been planted in her car.

'And *did* Bella supply Mojo?'

'No!'

'And how sure are you about that?'

'A hundred percent sure. It's crazy!'

'Admirable loyalty. But one often wonders how well one really knows anybody.'

'I know Bella.'

'Okay,' said Fitz. 'For argument's sake, let's assume she did not supply Mr. Mojo and was simply an innocent autograph hunter.'

'Selfie,' said Derry.

'Quite,' said Fitz. 'How do you know she was framed?'

'Because I've been framed,' said Derry.

'I see,' said Fitz, in the way people do when they see nothing at all. Derry thought how rarely she had seen him surprised by anything. He was surprised now. 'Perhaps you'd better tell me about it.'

Derry explained how Jacko had unwittingly led them to the packages in her toilet cistern, and how she and Bruce had gotten rid of the contents.

'And how is Jacko?' said Fitz, smiling for the first time. Was Derry imagining a touch of nostalgia in his voice? Perhaps he was remembering the time Jacko had visited them in London and the uproarious partying that followed.

'The same,' said Derry, smiling back. She had the strangest sensation of the years slipping away. Then the illusion was gone, and Fitz was once more a stranger.

'Why call me?' he asked. 'Why not go to the police?'

'You are the police, aren't you?'

'Wrong country. Can't imagine the locals would appreciate my muscling in on their patch without a by-your-leave.'

'How can I go to the police? Look what happened to Bella!'

'I'm sorry to disappoint, Derry, I have no powers here.'

Derry noticed another first. He had called her by her name.

'I have no access to whatever investigation the police are carrying out into your friend. Have you searched your flat for anything else that might have been planted?'

Derry assured him she had searched, and anyhow Bruce reckoned the intruders wouldn't risk a second hiding place being discovered prematurely. Fitz looked over at Bruce, his expression thoughtful, but made no comment.

'You should be worrying about yourself, not Bella,' said Fitz, turning to Derry. 'She'll have a lawyer to worry about her, I imagine. Tell me—and I need an honest answer—do you have connections with any coke users or dealers. Any little recreational activities of which the authorities might take a jaundiced view?'

'No!'

'Any friends or acquaintances who are themselves, shall we say, liberal about these things?'

'I'm an actress, for goodness' sake,' said Derry. 'I know all sorts.'

'Quite,' said Fitz. 'These . . . artistic acquaintances of yours—don't call them, don't take their calls. Send no emails or texts. Alright?'

Even before Fitz had finished, Derry had composed the haughtiest reply she could muster at short notice. Something like, *and do I have your permission to take a call from my agent?* would do nicely. But before she could deliver her line, Janice's phone rang. She answered with a curt 'Yes?'

Janice turned around in her seat as she drove. 'Checks out with our friends,' she said. 'Navy SEAL. Honourable Discharge.'

'Good,' said Fitz, relaxing in his seat. He turned back to Derry. 'So who would want to frame you?'

'Peter Doyle. I'm sure of it. You're investigating him, aren't you?'

'What makes you think it's Doyle I'm investigating, if anyone?'

'I just know.'

'Ask a silly question,' said Fitz, sighing. 'If I'm to help you and your friend, you have to trust me. Please tell me why you think Doyle is involved in this.'

'He supplied the cocaine that Mojo took before he died.'

Fitz snorted impatiently. 'Oh come on! Why would a seriously rich man risk selling drugs to singers. I doubt he even knew this Mojo.'

'It was an accident,' said Derry. 'It wasn't meant for Mojo.'

Fitz no longer bothered to hide his irritation. 'And how do you know all this, might I ask?'

'Fortune-tellers know things,' said Derry. Her answer was sincere. If she had discovered anything new in her short career as Madam Tulip it was that people felt free to confide to their fortune-teller their most intimate secrets.

Fitz exploded. 'Oh for goodness' sake! You're not still on about that, surely. Please don't tell me I'm driving around Dublin at eight miles to the gallon because you've read the future in somebody's tea leaves.'

Now it was Derry's turn to be annoyed. She had learned as a young girl that if she wasn't to frighten her friends or risk seeming crazy, it was best to play down her premonitions and odd visions. Back when she and Fitz had been together, she had always made light of her gift.

'Don't you use that tone with me! It has nothing to do with tea leaves! I don't read tea leaves. Fortune-tellers get told things!'

'Well do tell *me*, pray! Or must I wait for the instalments?'

As the exchange with Fitz got more and more heated, Bruce edged sideways, peering out the car window as though a parade were passing by. Janice slumped in her seat so only the top of her head showed. Then Derry realised—she and Fitz were arguing exactly as they used to all those years ago. Like no time had passed and they were still curled up on the couch in his elegant London flat disagreeing about a movie.

Derry took a deep breath. Perhaps Fitz was right. She was expecting him to solve all her problems while she tried not to mention that Marlene was the key to everything. She told Fitz about Marlene getting her coke from Doyle and the coke ending up killing Mojo.

Fitz nodded thoughtfully as if digesting all that Derry had said and trying to reconcile it with whatever he already knew.

'Could be a motive there. All a bit elaborate, but perhaps there's something in it.'

'If the two lots of coke are the same, and Mojo's coke came from Doyle, then Bella's coke came from Doyle. Right?'

'To you, it might look that way. But to anyone else it could mean that Bella supplied Mojo.'

Derry fell silent. So much for logic.

'Fitz, what if the coke Mojo took was bad, would that be murder?'

He spoke carefully. 'No. Manslaughter, maybe. For murder, the act would need to be deliberate. You said it was an accident. Anyhow, you can't deliberately kill someone with cocaine. Or not undetectably, anyway.'

'Oh yes you can,' said Bruce.

'Excuse me?' said Fitz, slowly.

'I'm afraid y'all are just plain wrong there.'

Fitz' eyes flicked to Derry, as if to say, 'Who is this person?' He spoke as though the towering American sitting beside her were invisible. 'Routine tests will detect arsenic, strychnine and the like. Far too obvious. I repeat, you can't deliberately kill someone with cocaine without being detected.'

'Suit yourself,' said Bruce, and he shrugged.

This is ridiculous, thought Derry. She needed them to cooperate, and instead they were posturing. 'When will the tests on the coke be finished?'

Fitz collected himself. 'A few days for early results, longer for more complex toxicology, but I don't imagine they'll find anything. In fact, I'm certain of it. Whether the batch of drugs was the same in Mojo's case and your friend's, we'll just have to wait and see.' He looked at his watch. 'I'm sorry, I have to be somewhere. I'll drop you off near here.'

Derry looked out the window. They had crossed the River Liffey to the other side of the city. *Thanks Fitz,* she thought, but didn't protest. What would be the point?

'One question,' she said. 'If Doyle planted the coke in my flat, why has he invited me to a party on Tuesday? I should be in jail by then, shouldn't I?'

Fitz sat rigid in his seat. 'What party? In Limerick, by any chance?'

'Yes, how do you know?'

'Never mind,' said Fitz. 'Are you sure the invite wasn't from Marlene, not Doyle?'

'No,' said Derry. 'He called me.'

Fitz pondered that.

'You can't go, of course.'

'Why not?'

'Why?' asked Fitz, as if the reason were the most obvious thing in the world. He leaned forward, his mouth a tense thin line. 'Because you're *here*. Because you know *me*.'

'I see,' said Derry, uncomfortably aware that she was starting to talk like Fitz. Any minute she'd be saying, *if you don't mind* and *awfully sorry.*

'So it *is* Doyle you are investigating.'

'I did *not* say that,' said Fitz. 'What I *am* saying is that you must not go into a situation in which you could reveal information about me. For my sake and for yours.'

Why did Derry think his words sounded like a threat? Or had everything that had happened made her pathologically suspicious?

'And what about Bella?'

'Nothing to be done. Leave it to her lawyer. Promise me you'll stay out of this.'

The feeling in Derry's chest couldn't be mistaken for anything else. Incandescent rage. But she had no intention of showing it. She wouldn't give him the satisfaction.

'You have no right to ask me to promise anything.'

'Janice,' said Fitz. 'Here, please.'

The car glided to a halt on the outermost bridge over the Liffey. The traffic behind honked, outraged not only at the blatant disregard for the rules, but at the British registration plates grievously compounding the crime.

Fitz leaned across Derry and Bruce to swing open the door. They climbed out without a word.

'Please do as I say,' said Fitz. He pulled the door closed with a click. The car swept away, disappearing into the traffic.

How was it possible to feel fury and despair at the same time? Fitz was impossible—arrogant and bad-mannered in the way only the British upper classes knew. Being rude wasn't just a sign of displeasure, it was to show you were so far down the social scale you didn't even merit manners. Dumping Derry and Bruce on a bridge miles from Derry's apartment was only one exquisite detail in the put-down.

The evening was chilly and overcast, making the sluggish green water of the river look even more toxic than usual. The pavement was thronged with people moving purposefully. Maybe the walk home would do her good, Derry thought. Calm her nerves, put things in perspective. Or would she arrive home to find her door smashed and her apartment turned upside down by armed police?

'I thought I did okay,' said Bruce. 'Don't you? Took me a while to get into the whole boyfriend thing, but then I started to feel quite comfortable in my skin. Don't you like it when that happens?'

What on earth was Bruce talking about?

'He, like, totally believed in my character. I feel so relieved. We should celebrate.'

How could Derry explain that she felt not at all like celebrating? What was to celebrate? Her only chance of help turning out to be an arrogant pig? Bella in a prison cell?

Bruce was oblivious. 'Why not come to my place? I'll make us something to eat.'

'That's sweet of you, Bruce. But if the police come, I want to be there.'

'Uh, no you don't,' said Bruce, shaking his head.

'I do,' insisted Derry. 'What if Dad comes back early? Or if the cops come in the night and he's taken by surprise?'

Should she call Jacko? She checked the time on her phone. Whatever social event he was at, an exhibition opening or party, he'd be in no state to understand. How were you supposed to tell your father to expect to be woken by armed police wearing balaclavas and telling him to lie on the floor?

Derry still hadn't made up her mind to phone, when Bruce hailed a cab. 'Come on, sweetheart, we'll taxi you home. I need to pick up the van anyhow.'

Derry nodded. The way things were going, doing nothing at all just about qualified as a plan.

As the taxi driver pulled into Derry's street, Bruce and Derry were arguing about who should pay the fare. They failed to notice that the end of the road was partly blocked by a double-parked flatbed truck. The taxi driver swore loudly. He stopped the cab and turned to Derry and Bruce.

'If God had meant there to be clampers and a car pound would you ever tell me why he bothered his arse making Satan and the fires of Hell. Tell me that!'

He seemed to expect an answer, but before Derry could think of what to say the driver swore again. Sirens wailed and, to Derry's horror, into her street swept four white patrol cars, blue lights flashing. From the opposite side, three police motorcycles roared around the corner, taking up stations on each sidewalk.

'Jayzus!' said the taxi driver. He spoke now in a whisper, as if afraid he'd be overheard by forces of law and order known to be famously arbitrary and well beyond the comprehension of a mere citizen. 'Culchie gobshites! Somebody must have dropped a coin down a drain.'

The driver peered through his windscreen, his brow furrowed. Derry and Bruce had the cab door open, ready to step out onto the sidewalk. Down the street Derry could see clusters of passers-by stopping to gawp.

'I'll take what you've got,' said the taxi man, hurriedly. Derry pushed a ten-euro note into his hand as they climbed out. Bruce was offering another ten, but the driver didn't wait. He was accelerating away even before they had slammed the rear door closed.

Down the road, partly obscured by parked cars and the flatbed truck, Derry could see the police cars disgorging uniformed officers. She turned to Bruce. He put his arm around her shoulder and squeezed.

'Should I tell them it's me?' asked Derry quietly.

'Uh, I'd just let them get on with it,' said Bruce. 'When they've gone into the building, if there's a cop left in one of the cars, go up to him. Don't go near the guys on the bikes.'

'Why?' asked Derry absently, her gaze fixed on the policemen fanning out across the street.

'Haemorrhoids,' said Bruce. 'Motorcycle cops always got haemorrhoids. Makes 'em bad tempered.'

'I don't see any guns,' whispered Derry.

Bruce shrugged. 'Maybe you don't rate a SWAT team.'

'Should I feel insulted?'

Bruce was paying no attention. 'Well-oh-well!' he said. 'Looks like we got a real catty whampus, right here.' He was peering at the line of parked cars and the flatbed truck. 'Come on,' he said, tugging Derry's arm and pulling her up the street towards the crowd.

A swarm of policemen was converging on a man in a black-and-yellow peaked cap and fluorescent vest—a traffic warden. The warden was gesticulating furiously, pointing at a white car sandwiched between the pavement and the flatbed truck. The truck mounted a huge mechanical arm hovering menacingly over the car's roof and obviously meant for lifting captive cars onto the truck. Cables dangled, already attached to clamps, but nobody gave the order to lift. As Derry and Bruce sidled along the pavement, trying not to be noticed in the milling crowd, she could see why.

Sitting in the driver's seat was a fat, red-faced man with the bushiest sideburns Derry had ever seen. Oddly, despite the overcast day, he was wearing sunglasses. The man was thumping the steering wheel and shouting, and although you couldn't hear what he was saying, you could tell his rage was directed at the traffic warden. The warden was also shouting, but nobody had any trouble hearing him.

'I told him not to get in the car but he got in,' he ranted, pointing at the driver. 'The eejit!' He appealed to the crowd, keenly aware that his vocation was not the most popular and he'd have to work for his support. 'Now he won't get out!' he squealed. Seeing the crowd's sympathies were firmly with the imprisoned driver, the warden fine-tuned his pitch. 'I'm only an ordinary Joe doing me job!' he wailed, brushing away a tear. Whether the tear was imagined or real Derry couldn't tell, but the man obviously had talent.

The phalanx of policemen now fanned out around the offending car as though the driver inside were a terrorist or a wanted gangster. Meanwhile, the helmeted motorcyclists tried to disperse the watching crowd, shouting, 'Nothing to see here, nothing to see! Move on!'

No crowd of Dubliners promised the delightful spectacle of raised voices, shouted obscenities and discommoded policemen will willingly accept an instruction to disperse, especially if accompanied by the ludicrous statement that there is nothing to see. Plainly, there was lots to see. The mood was turning ugly.

So riveting was what promised to be a full-blown riot in her own street that Derry almost forgot to be relieved that Dublin's finest had not come for her.

The entrance to the apartment was intact. Nobody had used a battering ram. Derry had half expected to see her door splintered and hanging off by its hinges. She had left the mortice unlocked, as Bruce had suggested, but the Yale was secure. She opened the door tentatively and poked her head inside. Everything was quiet. All seemed normal. She and Bruce walked around the apartment checking every room—Derry anxious, Bruce alert and watchful. Nothing was amiss.

'Thanks,' said Derry. 'I appreciate everything you've done; I really do.'

'No problem,' said Bruce. 'We artists have to stick together. United in the face of a hostile world.'

'Indifferent world, more like.'

'Good to see you smiling, hon. Okay, gotta go.'

'Thanks again,' said Derry.

'Anything . . . comes up, call me right away. Okay?'

Derry knew what he meant by *comes up*.

'One more thing,' said Bruce. 'Don't take this wrong, it's just a thought. Your friend Fitz . . .'

'Yes?'

'He doesn't want you to go to Limerick or to meet Doyle, right?'

'Sure. He made that pretty clear.' Derry couldn't make out where Bruce was headed. 'I can understand why. I don't like it, but I can understand.'

'If you were in jail, you couldn't go.'

The realisation struck Derry like a bucket of ice-cold water in the face. She could hardly breathe.

Bruce put his hand on her shoulder. He looked worried, as if regretting his words. 'Doesn't mean he's a bad guy. Might even be for your own good.'

'That's crazy! Fitz wouldn't do that.' Her words trailed away to a whisper. What did she really know about Fitz and the man he was now? The Fitz of old could have been transformed long ago into somebody else—someone who thought differently, felt differently, believed in different things. Or perhaps he hadn't needed to change. He had always been proud of his realism, his lack of sentimentality.

Derry could easily picture him saying with complete conviction that everything he had done was for the best. He might see the inconvenience to Derry of being taken out of circulation for a while as a small price to pay.

'Think about it,' said Bruce. He turned and trotted down the stairs, his feet echoing in the passageway.

'Hi, Dad.' Derry was leaning out her window holding her phone to her ear as she watched the rumpus continuing on the street below. The tow truck had lifted the offending car into the air and was swivelling its mechanical arm to drop it onto the flatbed. The angry driver with the sideburns was nowhere to be seen.

'Dad?' Between the noise from the street and the noise on the other end of her phone, where Jacko was obviously at a party, Derry could hardly hear what he was saying. He seemed to be suggesting she should come and join them and bring her fancy man.

'He is not my fancy man!' Derry shouted into the phone, making a knot of onlookers on the street crane their heads upwards. Now she could just make out the man with sideburns, or at least she inferred that it was he, underneath a scrummage of blue uniforms in a thrashing heap in the middle of the road.

'Sorry, Dad, I can't. Thanks for the invite. Lots to do. Look, will you do me a favour? Will you phone me before you come into the flat tonight? Just two rings will do. I want to be sure it's you at the door, that's all; we had a disturbance earlier. Will you do that for me? Doesn't matter if it's late. Okay, love you too.'

She hung up. Down below, the scrummage had disentangled itself to reveal Mr. Sideburns being led away in handcuffs and bundled headfirst, none too gently, into the back of a police car. Derry slammed the window shut. At least when Jacko came in at whatever hour of the morning, she wouldn't mistake him for a police raid. She could try to explain to him then what to expect if the raid did happen. How she was going to do that, she hadn't a clue.

Derry checked the time. Could it be only nine o'clock? Today felt like the longest day of her life. Only this morning she had been Madam Tulip in a castle. Now she was a suspected drug dealer, her friend was in jail and she had been invited to the house of the man who might well be the cause of it all. Oh, and she might have been framed by her ex-boyfriend.

Derry sank back on her couch and sighed. It could have been worse, she thought. She might have seen it coming.

17

Sunday morning, Derry woke at ten o'clock. At first she wasn't sure where she was, expecting to see above her head the ornate drapes of the castle's four-poster bed. Then it all came back. She groaned and rolled over, closing her eyes in the hope she would wake someplace else and on some other day.

She lay awake for several minutes, putting off getting up, before she realised that something that should have happened hadn't happened. No police raid. And something else, nagging at her consciousness, that she couldn't figure out. Her eye fell on her phone lying on the bedside locker. Jacko! He was supposed to have called when he got back from his party to warn her he was entering the apartment. But he hadn't called.

Derry frowned. She lurched out of bed with a groan, pulling on the dressing gown she had ready for her expected night-time encounter with the law. She threw open the sitting room door, taking no pains to be quiet. In fact, she was tempted to stamp her feet and whistle, maybe bang pots and pans. She had asked the simplest thing, a couple of rings on her phone to let her know he was back, and he was so debauched he couldn't even manage that.

'Oh!' said Derry to no one at all. No fug of cigar smoke. No reek of stale socks. The couch was still a couch, folded into its daytime disguise.

Derry shrugged, filled the coffee machine and switched it on. Where was Jacko? Probably being made breakfast by some hero-worshipping German graduate student besotted with the Celtic Twilight. *Good luck to her*, thought Derry, sourly.

Derry's habit—if she wasn't in a show, which was usually—was to have breakfast around ten o'clock, i.e. seven a.m. actors' time. Normally she turned on the radio and listened to the news, but today she changed station as soon as the bulletin began. She had enough bad news of her own, and she was afraid she might hear about Bella being arrested—*a twenty-seven-year-old woman was detained yesterday* . . . Derry shivered, reached for her phone and dialled Bella's lawyer. Voicemail. Of course, Sunday. She was probably lying in bed with the papers, wondering what to have for lunch. Meanwhile, Bella was sitting in a cold, bare cell, probably terrified. And Derry was waiting for the police to crash through her door.

Derry checked the time, a ludicrous gesture. What was she going to do, complain they were late? Anyway, did they even raid on Sundays? She guessed that might depend on whether they were paid triple time. Hadn't she read somewhere that budget cuts had meant police overtime was rationed? Poor them. Nobody paid actors double or triple time for working nights and weekends. But then, the most the actors' union could threaten was to shut down theatres, and hardly anybody would notice.

Thinking about acting galvanised Derry out of her torpor. Her costume! She hadn't even unpacked. In ten minutes, Derry was showered and dressed, with her Madam Tulip costume laid out neatly on the bed, inspected for rips and stains. Happily, she saw no marks or tears, and she wouldn't even need to dry-clean the dress— a sponge-down would do fine. Her wig and headdress were perfect. She folded the velvet tablecloth neatly and polished the glass of her antique egg timer to a glistening sheen.

What was it about acting, that even handling a costume was such a pleasure? Despite everything that had happened, Derry felt fortunate. Playing Madam Tulip wasn't quite Broadway, but it was a performance. And she had been playing a part, honing her skills, while most of her acting friends were sitting hopelessly waiting for the phone to ring. And who said she wouldn't still get roles in a proper theatre if she were lucky? Madam Tulip might give her the means to stick the course and not have to run away to New York to be a publicist and talk nonsense.

Just as Derry had finished replacing her costume and props in their proper boxes, bags and wrappers, her phone rang twice, then stopped. A few seconds later, the front door opened. In stepped Jacko, hesitant as though he had been called to the headmaster's study.

To be fair, thought Derry, as she surveyed the bedraggled bulk of her father, at least he had the decency to look embarrassed.

'Bagels,' said Jacko, proffering a crumpled bag.

'I've got the coffee on,' said Derry. What was the point saying anything more? She could hardly demand to know where he had slept; he wasn't a teenager, even if he acted like one. And she wasn't his mother, much as he often left her feeling like she had the job anyhow.

Jacko groaned, settling his frame on the couch. 'May the man who invented the bed-settee roast for all eternity. Worse, let him sleep on one of his own creations.' He slumped deeper into his seat, plonking his feet on the coffee table. Derry glared. He removed the offending appendages in a single smooth movement.

'Stop grumbling,' she said. 'The couch is what you get when you forget to leave a party. Or run away from home.'

Jacko inspected Derry's ceiling as if the broken moulding or the cheap paper lampshade would at any moment flood his mind with beauty.

Derry couldn't help it. 'You must be losing your touch,' she said slyly. 'Don't tell me she wasn't impressed.'

Jacko didn't rise to the bait. His tone was resigned, as befitted a misunderstood philosopher. 'Sure I couldn't get a word in edgeways! Why is it that the shorter the life the longer a person takes to tell it? No one under sixty should be allowed *have* a life-story. I could tell you mine in a dozen syllables. Paints pictures. Got married. Got unmarried. Paints pictures. Oh, and had wonderful daughter.'

'Flattery always welcome, however shameless,' said Derry. 'So what happened?'

'I don't know. She must have noticed me yawning at the part where she was wondering if life held any meaning.'

'There is no reason for you to be sleeping on couches,' said Derry. 'Anybody's couch.'

Just as she primed herself to bring up the business of his feud with Vanessa, her phone rang. The caller was her mother.

Derry prodded Jacko's outstretched leg with her toe, but to no effect. She waved and grimaced as if an insect were crawling up the back of her neck. He cocked his head to one side as if inspecting a curiosity, but seemed to accept her behaviour as an eccentricity unsurprising in a relative.

'Hi Mom,' said Derry, loudly.

To say that Jacko got up quickly would be like saying that a rabbit shooting out of a hole closely pursued by a terrier was merely 'leaving.' He stood rigid, panic etched into his features, his eyebrows locked in the 'up' position as though he expected a rabid pack of wild animals to stream into the room at any moment. Derry gestured furiously at the exit. In four mighty strides Jacko was out, closing the apartment door behind him with a surreptitious click.

'No, he's not here,' said Derry, truthful by the narrowest of margins.

'I am *not* going to tell you what your father has done,' said

Vanessa. She spoke in the quietest and most ominous tone Derry had heard from her mother since the Internal Revenue Service had presumed to query her accounts and she had reminded the officer concerned that her family included three senators, four congressmen and a private detective specialising in marital infidelity.

Derry considered what her mother had said. Two options presented themselves—the first was to enquire further, along the lines of 'please do tell.' Option Two was to decline graciously, saying something like 'maybe best not go into all that. He is my father, after all,' and laugh lightly.

Derry chose the second option. She executed the laugh pretty competently, all in all, even allowing for a light trill at the tail end. She waited.

'Oh,' said Vanessa. 'Really?'

'Um, yes, I think so. For the best. Don't you? Need-to-know basis, all that?'

'It was monstrous!' said Vanessa ignoring audience preference in favour of closely following the script. Her voice had dropped an octave, effectively underlining her case that Jacko's behaviour, whatever that was, was not only monstrous but *MONSTROUS*.

'Oh well, that's Dad, I guess,' said Derry. 'Personal or professional?' No sooner had Derry asked than she knew that curiosity had led her to a fatal mistake.

'The word professional does not apply to that man! The word honourable does not apply!' Vanessa's voice was quavering as a judge's voice might when recounting the villainies of a freshly convicted felon about to get his comeuppance.

'When you see your father—and note I do not say *if*—you might mention that *when* I find him, he will regret the day he tried to pull his Irish wool over my eyes. Tomorrow the court will issue an emergency injunction. To ensure I have his full attention, I will also be suing him for every penny down to his last pair of ridiculous cowboy boots. You may also tell him that although I will not get to Dublin for a couple more days when I do get there I will shove that injunction up his ass!'

'Ah,' said Derry. 'Business.' But Vanessa had already hung up.

'Alright,' Derry shouted down the stairwell.

Up trotted Jacko, cigar in his mouth, puffing anxiously.

'Out,' said Derry. She pushed Jacko to the window, opened it wide and supervised as he flicked the half-smoked object out into the Dublin sky.

'*That* was a Romeo and Juliet,' said Jacko, sadly. 'Rolled on the thighs of a comely Cuban maiden. You have forced me to perpetrate a cultural crime.'

'I don't care if it was the Complete Works,' said Derry, wearily. 'Mom isn't happy.'

'You didn't happen to mention my whereabouts, I trust?'

'I am no kind of quisling or betrayer of fathers. She says you did something awful.'

'Nonsense,' said Jacko with a sniff. 'A little business disagreement. Normal between colleagues and partners. No commercial relationship can be expected to run smoothly. Always the human dimension. She should know that, she claims to be in the Arts. Ha!'

'She said she was going to get an injunction and she'd be in Dublin in a couple of days and she was going to . . . um . . . take a hard line,' said Derry, paraphrasing. She thought it wisest not to spell out the details of the sentence her mother planned on handing down. 'Come on, Dad, you know what she's like! Can't you two just sort things out? This is ridiculous.'

Jacko wasn't listening. His expression was strangely vacant, as though he could hear mice behind the skirting board.

'Dad!'

'A couple of days, you say?'

'That's what she said. Why?'

'Oh my Lord, it's an ambush!' Jacko's face registered pure alarm. 'Oh the sly devil! She knew you'd tell me she was coming in a couple of days. False sense of security! She should have been a general, that woman!'

Jacko had already fished his holdall out from behind the couch and was standing by the door. 'I'm sorry, darlin', I've enjoyed spending time with you, and I know you'll be disappointed, but I really must move on. We should do this again some time.' He hugged Derry, kissed her on the cheek and was gone.

'Where are you going?' called Derry down the echoing stairwell.

'Best you don't know,' shouted Jacko. 'She has ways of making people talk.'

What was there to do now but worry? Derry was too anxious to read; her mind kept wandering with thoughts of Bella. And after yesterday's frantic pre-raid cleanup, she had no housework left to do. She tried to watch TV, but the news was the usual catalogue of disasters, while the national channel was showing a soap she had auditioned for and failed. She could hardly be bothered making tea. What was the point of drinking borage for courage when you didn't know what to do? She didn't need courage, she needed answers.

Derry sat at the table, took her laptop from its case and opened it up. The machine buzzed and clicked into life. Maybe writing down what she knew would help.

Where to start? A week ago, she had met Marlene and Peter Doyle for the first time. But no—that wasn't the real beginning. Everything had started with Bella and Madam Tulip. Strange to think Tulip was hardly more than a week old. Derry felt she had always been Madam Tulip, had always played the role of listener, had always tried to sense what a person wanted to know or wanted to be. Then the thought came. What would Tulip make of all this? What future would she see?

Derry jumped up, ran into her bedroom and pulled from the bottom of the closet her Madam Tulip bag. Less than a minute later, without conscious effort and hardly knowing how she got there, she found herself back at the table as if she had never moved. But now, beside her laptop was her pack of cards.

Derry cut the pack. She dealt a spread face down and sat hesitant, unwilling to turn the cards. Her heart was beating hard in a way she had never experienced reading for someone else. She was reaching out to lift the first card when her phone rang. The interruption should have been deeply unwelcome but instead felt like a reprieve. Until she saw the caller ID.

'Derry!' said Doyle, his voice cheerful, friendly. 'I was hoping you were going to get back to me.' He paused, leaving an opening for the expected apology.

'I'm sorry, said Derry. 'Really, I am. I . . . had something come up. Can I confirm with you tomorrow?'

She heard Doyle exhale, the way a person breathes through their nose when they're irritated but unwilling to show it.

'I'm sorry, I *do* need to know,' said Doyle. 'Our evening is planned for Tuesday. Look, if money is the issue, we could make it two thousand, how does that sound?'

Derry couldn't have answered if she'd wanted to.

'If transport is a problem, I can have Paulo pick you up.'

'No,' said Derry. 'Thank you. I'm sure that won't be necessary. What time is the event?'

'Eight o'clock, but you'd need to be here for six. It's important that you're punctual.'

'Of course,' said Derry. 'I'm sorry about this, but there may be something I have to do. Can I call you tomorrow? I promise I will. Before teatime? I'll let you know for definite then.'

Doyle hesitated. 'Derry, this does mean rather a lot to me. I'd appreciate it if you'd do your best.'

'I will,' said Derry. 'I promise. Thank you.'

Doyle hung up. For a full minute Derry stared at her phone. Something was so wrong and so obvious that she couldn't see it, probably hadn't a hope of seeing it. She contemplated the backs of the cards spread out in front of her. In a single sweeping motion she gathered them into a pile, shuffling for good measure. Searching her own future was out of the question. That way was the road to paranoia, an infinite spiral of cause and effect. Derry didn't know how she knew, but instinctively she saw the impossible knots that fate would have to untie if she knew her destiny. She could almost hear her grandfathers say in chorus, 'Don't go there! Child, don't do that!'

Was it because she had renounced the wish to peek behind the future's curtain that the veil was briefly drawn back? Or was it the way she was staring at the neatly stacked cards on the table in front of her? Perhaps it was the screen saver on her open laptop. She had chosen the image because it fascinated her—a strange pattern of rolling swirls and spirals carved thousands of years ago on a gigantic burial mound. The spirals seemed to revolve of their own accord, making you think of whirlpools and black holes.

And now Derry did see a whirlpool, a swirling vortex of water, lethargic, but irresistibly powerful, a lazy spiral that would effortlessly engulf any swimmer, sucking them down into the darkness.

In an instant, the perspective changed. She was no longer looking down into the maelstrom but upwards, and the rippling fractured image of the disappearing sky through the darkening water was over her head. She gasped, knowing she was drowning, certain it was the end. One intake of breath, involuntary but inevitable, and death would come.

Was it her own shout that woke her from her dream? Perhaps some external change, a sound in the street, had brought her back. Whatever the cause, when Derry opened her eyes she was unable to move, pinned in her chair as if by gravitational force. Sweat was streaming down her face, and she knew then that the nightmare sensation of watery blackness closing over her head would never leave her.

18

Monday, and Derry woke at nine a.m. Unaccountably, she had slept well. Why hadn't she spent the night tossing and turning, waiting for her front door to be smashed in? She supposed that eventually the brain got tired of being afraid, shrugged its shoulders and said *what the heck*.

Right after breakfast, Derry phoned Bella's lawyer. Bella hadn't been charged with a crime yet, she said, but the police had applied to the District Court to hold her for another three days. If they applied again, they could hold her another two days after that. They hadn't pressed charges because they didn't want her sent to a remand prison where she might be able to communicate with accomplices. Did that mean Bella couldn't have visitors? 'Exactly,' said the lawyer. Phone calls? 'No.'

Derry's laptop was still sitting on the table, lid raised, its screen black. She pulled the machine towards her and pressed the button. There, still open, was the document she had abandoned last night when Doyle had called. She began to type:

Doyle supplies his wife Marlene with coke.

Coke mistakenly ends up with Sonya.

Sonya's boyfriend, Mojo, takes coke and dies.

Mojo is found ill by Bella.

Bella's car planted with drugs and money.

Own apartment, ditto.

Doyle invites self to a party on Tuesday, i.e. the day after tomorrow (twice).

Fitz insists self doesn't go, to preserve his cover story (whatever that is).

The facts looked so simple when you laid them out. But they made no sense whatever. Derry was still staring hopelessly at her list, feeling stupid, then angry at feeling stupid, when Bruce rang. She was surprised. The time was only nine-forty, ludicrously early for an actor. Maybe no amount of acting could overwrite whatever the military had done to Bruce's body clock.

'Latte at Bosco's?' he said, his voice cheery.

'Done. Twenty minutes?'

'Cool,' said Bruce. 'No visitors?'

'None,' said Derry.

'Coolest,' said Bruce, and rang off.

Sitting in the morning sunshine at a pavement table in one of Dublin's bustling side streets should have been a guilty pleasure. Derry routinely met friends at this cafe, mostly actors, to chat and sip coffee more slowly than the waiters thought humanly possible. But never had she imagined she would be having the conversation she was now having with Bruce.

'They can keep her a few more days without charging her if they want,' said Derry. 'No visits allowed.'

'Tough,' said Bruce.

'I printed off a list.' Derry reached into her bag and pulled out a sheet of paper. 'All I can see is that Doyle is probably behind everything. But it still doesn't make any sense.'

Bruce took the page, studying it for a moment before shrugging helplessly. He looked up and down the street, as if the strolling window-shoppers with their designer bags held the answer.

'Bruce, why would Doyle set me up to be raided by the police then insist I come to a party? I don't get it.'

'Me neither. But what about Fitz?'

'What about him?' said Derry. 'This is about Doyle.'

'We know Fitz didn't want you around in case you busted him. He sees you at the Celebrity Bash. He gets a fright. So he sets you up to keep you out of the way. But then you tell him we've cleaned up the apartment, so he knows now there's no point arranging a raid. Who else, besides me and Fitz, knew a raid on your apartment would find nothing?'

Now it was Derry's turn to inspect the passers-by. She found no inspiration, nothing to justify a protest other than the empty feeling in her stomach. 'Nobody,' she admitted, quietly.

'So?' said Bruce, not letting go.

'So what!' At her outburst, customers at the other tables looked around but quickly lost interest. A lover's tiff.

'Derry, you have to work with the facts. Not what you want to believe.'

He was right. She didn't want to see it, but the question mark was staring her in the face.

'Okay,' she said, taking a deep breath. 'We only have his word for it that he's still a policeman investigating somebody. He could be up to anything.' *There. She'd said it.*

Derry was unprepared for the misery that swept over her as she put her doubts into words. The more she thought about Fitz' carefully contrived aura of mystery, the more certain she felt. Even the redhead's call supposedly checking out Bruce could have been an elaborate charade. Fitz must think her a fool, falling for the cloak-and-dagger act. Did they go home and laugh about it?

'Let's not jump to conclusions,' said Bruce gently. 'It's only one possibility, a hypothesis, okay? And it doesn't explain a bunch of stuff. It explains why you got framed, but not why Bella was set up, right?'

Derry nodded. Bruce was trying to soften the blow, and for that she was grateful. And what he had said was true. Why would Fitz frame Bella? The only possible reason for Bella being targeted was to protect Marlene, and only one man would want to do that. Everything came back to Doyle.

'Bruce, we need to know if Mojo's coke was bad.'

'What difference does it make?' said Bruce. 'Bella will be charged with possession for supply anyhow. Okay, supplying bad coke is worse, but how much worse than disastrous is, like, *really* disastrous? Anyway, what about Sonya?'

'What has Sonya got to do with anything? Isn't she just another victim?'

'In detective stories they always say look at the partner. Who says Sonya didn't find Mojo was a little less perfect than advertised? She was a lot more successful than him, right? A lot richer? Maybe he wanted more than his share. Maybe he was fooling around. So she feeds him bad coke. Or maybe Marlene tried to kill him? The drugs were hers. Who knows with these people?'

'Oh, come on, Bruce.' She couldn't even begin to imagine Sonya killing Mojo. Nobody, not even the best actress in the world, could fake the feelings Sonya had shown. As for Marlene, she couldn't have known Sonya would find the compact and couldn't have guessed that Mojo would take the coke.

'And who says anything was deliberate?' added Derry. 'If you wanted to kill somebody, you'd have to make the coke bad, right? You'd have to poison the stuff. And poison would show in tests. Like Fitz said.'

Bruce shrugged. 'Uh, yes and no. I told him. But he ain't much of a listener, your guy.'

Derry ignored the implication that Fitz was in any way *her guy*. She was too busy being irritated by how confusing everything was getting. 'What are you saying? You're saying you can poison coke and not get caught, right?'

'Yes, you can,' said Bruce. 'You'd need to know what you were at, but you could do it. Sure.'

'And what if you did know what you were at?'

'You'd know the labs test for the obvious toxins, but they won't test for obscure stuff like—I don't know—curare? Frog poison? Fungi? Hey, are you okay?'

Derry was mopping her spilt coffee from the table with a napkin.

'I'm fine. Honestly.' But her hands were shaking. At least clearing the spill had bought her time to pull her swirling thoughts into some kind of order.

A coincidence, that's all, Derry told herself. It had to be. Frog poison had nothing to do with anything. Especially nothing to do with the strange vision she had seen so long ago—the odd, almost funny image of a little frog sitting on a lily pad.

Under different, less frightening circumstances, Derry might have laughed. Surely nothing could be so obvious, so idiotically literal-minded, as an image of a frog. So unmetaphorical. But what did she expect? Poetry? Perhaps sometimes, even in premonitions, a spade is just a spade and a frog is just a slimy amphibian.

'You said frog poison. The frog—what colour?' Derry's mouth was dry.

'Uh, yellow, I think,' said Bruce. 'Black spots? Called the golden poison frog. Lives in the jungle. Can't say I ever saw the actual, like, frog.'

'Bruce, how do you know all this?'

Bruce hesitated, looking uneasy in a way Derry had never seen. 'Uh, let's say we . . . uh . . . got around some. We were down South on an extended vacation—let's say that. And we made the acquaintance of some bad people, though they didn't much like *our* company.' He smiled, but his eyes were not smiling. 'And those nice folks sometimes use frog poison to get rid of associates they don't like, mostly when they need something a bit more subtle than, say, a car bomb.'

'Car bomb? Bruce, what are you saying? Who are these people?'

'Oh, everybody knows about them now—drugs cartels. What you don't hear so much is that those drug barons like to kill each other whenever they can, and that's not so easy. So they get creative. One method they like is nasty frog poison. They mix it with something you ingest—some cocaine does nicely if the competition is in the habit. And hey presto, problem solved.'

'So . . . the poison. What does it do?'

'Bit like a heart attack. Breathing problems. Convulsions. Our instructor said only a couple of grains of this stuff will kill you, so the bad guys keep the frogs in cages for a while. The poison comes from the ants they eat, so if you starve the frogs for a couple of weeks the toxins get less crazy, easier to manage. These bad guys, they like doing things right.'

'You said . . . instructor? What instructor?'

Bruce laughed. 'Oh, we got classes on everything. The Navy loves to give you classes. Then when you screw up they can say, '*Not our fault, dude. You got the training, man.*' He grinned. 'I can make you a poison dart if you want. Like the Indians.'

'No,' said Derry. 'Thanks, really. What Indians? Like where, Bruce? I'm not going to report you the CIA for goodness' sake! South America?'

Bruce shrugged. 'Guess you're not. Okay. Colombia. Where your boyfriend comes from.'

At first, Derry didn't have the faintest idea what he was talking about. When he said boyfriend, she had automatically thought of Fitz. Ridiculous. But who else?

'Pablo, right?' said Bruce.

'Paulo. He's not my boyfriend. And he's Spanish.'

'That's what he said? Maybe he thought y'all would find it more romantic. Flamenco, clicking heels, smouldering passion? He's no more Spanish than I am. I heard him talk on the phone. I know a Colombian accent in English and in Spanish—spent long enough in the dump.'

'Colombian, Spanish, whatever. Maybe it's connected, maybe it's not. All that matters is that Mojo's coke might have been deliberately poisoned. Or at least, it's not impossible.'

'I guess. But, hey, I only said that 'cos your friend was being a pompous ass, like he knew it all when he didn't. And one Colombian, even acting like a Spaniard, doesn't make a murder. Anyhow, there's a million easier ways to stiff somebody.'

But not, thought Derry, many ways that depend on a yellow frog.

'And why would anyone want to kill Mojo?' said Bruce.

'Not Mojo,' said Derry. 'Marlene.'

19

The city was spread out below like a toy—miniature streets, miniature buildings, a miniature boat ploughing its way up the sluggish, green river. To the West, blue mountains ringed the horizon. To the East was the glistening turquoise of Dublin Bay, sliced by the wake of a superfast ferry racing for port as though pursued by sea monsters.

The panorama would have been glorious on any other day—any day when Derry wasn't trying to save someone's life. As it was, sitting on top of a giant Ferris wheel high above Dublin, while strapped into a perspex bubble, was the most frustrating and ridiculous piece of secondhand melodrama Derry could imagine. And whose role did Fitz think he was playing?

When Derry had called almost begging for another meeting, Fitz had refused to let her explain on the phone. Nor did he offer a car to pick her up. Instead, he claimed he had always promised himself a ride on the Dublin Ferris wheel. A strictly temporary attraction, he assured her, and not to be missed. Derry's protest that this was an emergency had no effect. Fitz talked right over her. 'That's where I'll be,' he said. 'At two.'

To Derry's surprise, while the wheel slowly swung skywards, Fitz listened attentively. This time, he didn't scoff at the idea that cocaine could indeed be poisoned with substances too obscure for a lab to detect in routine tests. He looked thoughtful when Derry described the poison of the little yellow frog and its use by drug barons but shrugged at the notion that Doyle's driver was Colombian. When Derry insisted everything pointed to Marlene being the intended victim of poisoned cocaine, Fitz didn't dismiss the theory out of hand. But nor did he rush to accept it.

'I agree, it's not impossible,' he said. 'Far-fetched, perhaps, but not impossible. One doesn't like to be pedantic, but there's always the little matter of proof.'

But Derry had no proof. Even Bruce had said she was way ahead of the facts. Unless, she thought, you counted dreams as facts. A falling horse, a frog on a lilypad—facts or delusions?

'Furthermore,' said Fitz, as though he were a barrister arguing for the defence, 'you have to explain why an intelligent and capable man like Peter Doyle would take such a risk. At the very least he would be implicated in supplying drugs. At worst, the poison would be discovered, and he would be the first suspect.'

'He's clever,' said Derry, relieved to be on ground more solid than dreams and hunches. 'He had it all worked out. He gave Marlene the coke then left the castle. He made sure not to be anywhere near. He came back only when he expected her to be dead. He tried to talk me into coming up to their room with him.'

Only as she described those events did Derry grasp the full meaning of the invitation from Doyle in the castle lobby, the offer of champagne in Marlene's suite. She felt nauseated, as if she too had been secretly administered some horrible poison. Doyle had meant her to be the witness. She was to discover Marlene slumped on her bed or gasping out her last breaths in agony, just as Bella had discovered Mojo.

'We were standing in the lobby about to go up to their room, and his phone rang. It was Marlene. He looked shaken—she was supposed to be dead. And like a complete fool, I mentioned Marlene had lost her compact and Sonya had found it. Straight away he said he had to rush back to the stud—some emergency with a horse.'

Fitz inspected the horizon as if he thought vastly more interesting events might be happening somewhere beyond the city limits, occurrences more fascinating by far than anything Derry might relate. But Derry was used to that of old. The less interested in something Fitz looked, and the more he seemed not to be listening, the more rapt was his attention.

'Did he know Marlene was going to divorce him?'

'She didn't think so. But maybe he did. Doyle could easily have had her watched, and she would have been seeing her lawyer in town. Divorce would give Marlene half the business. Wouldn't that be motive enough for Doyle?'

'Alright. But then you're saying he went on to concoct an elaborate plan to frame you and your friend as the drug dealers.' The way he said it, Derry had to admit the accusation sounded wildly over the top.

Derry turned to Fitz, waiting to speak until he was forced to wrench his gaze from the scenery and return her look. 'Fitz, tell me the truth. Knowing everything you know, do you believe Mojo's coke was poisoned? And that the poison was meant for Marlene?'

Fitz contemplated the city below. He made the clucking sound she remembered he always made when he was thinking something through. 'Could be something in what you say. You've proposed a method, and we have a possible motive. Not that with husbands and wives we need much. Marriage often seems motive enough, don't you think?' He gave a grim smile that made Derry wonder whether he had married since their time together. Perhaps he had.

'Not marriage. Divorce,' said Derry.

Fitz smiled. 'Alright, divorce.' He paused, inspecting a seagull hanging almost motionless in the air. The bird seemed to be inspecting them back, questioning why the two humans had the temerity to leave their natural element and intrude into its rightful domain.

'Fitz, we have to warn her.'

Fitz spoke as though he hadn't heard a word she'd said. 'We need the toxicology. That's the main thing.'

'We can't wait for toxicology! Fitz, she's in real danger. I know it!'

'If you're right about poison, then . . . well, perhaps something can be done.'

'Perhaps? He tried to kill her! What's to say he won't try again?'

'We don't know he tried the first time,' said Fitz simply. 'A little premature to worry about a replay, don't you agree? And what would we warn her against?'

Derry was hideously aware that she was now living up to every man's idea of an hysterical female. But she couldn't help it. She was certain she was right, but she could hardly say her conviction was because of visions.

'We'd warn her against *him*! Alright, he won't try the same thing again, but what if he tries to arrange an accident? Isn't that how they do it? Mysterious fall down the stairs? The horse bolts? How about that?'

'She doesn't ride, I believe.'

'You know what I mean! How would I know what he is planning? If you don't tell her, I'll tell her!'

Fitz leaned back in his seat and addressed the sky. ' "Hi Marlene, I've no proof your husband tried to kill you with an obscure South American frog poison, but in case he tries to push you down the stairs, you'd better move out right now." Naturally, Marlene replies, "I believe you because you are, after all, my fortune-teller." Is that how it's supposed to go?'

'No need for that,' said Derry, quietly. There was no reason the fortune-teller jibe should have hurt—nothing was shameful about fortune-telling. But Fitz meant it to hurt, so it did.

'I'm sorry,' he said. 'Not fair. But we need proof. I'll see if the tests can be speeded up. We can't go marching in there, and that's all there is to it; there's too much at stake.'

Proof? By the time they had proof, it could be too late. And what did he mean by *too much at stake*? He was talking like a businessman worried about his investment.

'I'm going to tell her.'

'I forbid you to do that!'

'You can't forbid anything. Like you said, you have no powers in Ireland.'

~

'Make you some lunch?' asked Bruce.

While Derry was with Fitz, Bruce had waited patiently in his van near the entrance to the Ferris wheel. As Derry climbed into the cab, she was still in a fury. She had come close to telling Fitz exactly what she thought of his callousness. If they hadn't spent the last revolution of the wheel doggedly ignoring each other, she might even have said he wasn't the Fitz that she knew, that she didn't recognise this man he had become. But she hadn't said any of that. The only bright spot in the whole wretched business was that she no longer suspected Fitz of anything wrong. Doyle was behind it all; she was sure of that now.

Bruce said little as they drove across the city. He asked no questions, made no small talk, instead tactfully leaving her to her thoughts. For that, Derry was grateful. Almost before she realised, they had arrived at their destination and Bruce was showing her into his apartment.

The surprise was more than enough to jolt Derry out of her reverie. If she had thought about it at all, she would have guessed that Bruce lived in a place rather like hers, lots of character but low-rent. Instead, he had a basement apartment in a beautiful Georgian terrace on the prosperous side of the city. His sitting room was spacious and tastefully furnished. As Derry slid gratefully into a vast leather couch, she wondered how he could afford such a place but couldn't think of a civilised way of asking the question.

That Bruce was good in the kitchen was less surprising. She watched him efficiently selecting ingredients and warming the oven while simultaneously making coffee, and reflected that a remarkable proportion of gay men could cook. Derry was fully aware she was committing the grievous sin of stereotyping, but couldn't help wondering if the cooking skills were because gay men were more caring, and cooking for someone was a caring thing to do. Then she remembered that Bruce had been some kind of he-man in the jungle or desert or wherever, and the things he might have done didn't bear thinking about. Not too much caring, she imagined. Perhaps not much cooking either.

'I'm calling Marlene,' said Derry. She hadn't yet worked out what she was going to say, but one thing was for sure, she would explain nothing on the phone. This would have to be face to face. Otherwise, Marlene might think she was crazy. She might even mention the call to Doyle, and that would be disastrous.

'Hello?' said Marlene. 'Derry?'

Relief flooded through Derry. She had feared that Marlene wouldn't take the call. Last time they had seen each other she had been distant.

'Hi, Marlene. Sorry to bother you. I wondered if maybe you could spare me a few minutes, meet me in town? There's something I need to talk to you about. Say tonight? It's important.'

Derry hoped she had struck the right tone, urgent but not hysterical. Perhaps curiosity would get the better of Marlene and she'd agree just to find out what the mystery was all about.

'I'm sorry, Derry, I need to be at home right now.'

'How about tomorrow?' asked Derry, trying to sound casual.

'I don't think so. I have to . . . I should really be here. I'm sorry.'

'Couldn't you . . . Marlene, this is important. I wouldn't ask if it weren't.'

'No!'

Derry was shocked by the vehemence. She could hear Marlene breathing heavily but had to press her harder. 'Can I ask . . .' She got no further.

'Guess!' shouted Marlene. 'What do *you* think?' She must have been as shocked by her own outburst as Derry was. Perhaps realising how brutal she had been, Marlene made an effort to speak normally. 'I'm sorry. I'm not going anywhere just now, okay? I'm sorry.' Was that the sound of weeping?

Marlene hung up. Immediately, Derry called back. The call was rejected. She sank back in the couch, her eyes closed, aware of the most awful foreboding. Why couldn't Marlene leave home? Had Doyle restrained her in some way? But Doyle wouldn't need to restrain her. All he'd have to do was promise her the coke she must desperately want, for today, tomorrow or the next day.

'I guess that was a no,' said Bruce. He put plates in front of them laid out with delicately arranged salads, cold meats, a jar of olives, cheeses and a warm loaf of what looked like home-baked bread.

'Eat up,' he said. 'You'll think better after you eat.'

So Derry ate. After a while, she even stopped feeling guilty that she was enjoying the food while Marlene was in such trouble.

'You're an angel, Bruce,' she said, her mouth full. And she meant it. No one would be able to deal with this alone. Maybe no one could deal with it however many Bruces they had. The little girl inside her was whining, *why did this happen to me?* but Derry slapped her down. It *wasn't* happening to her. It was happening to Marlene. And Bella. And for poor Mojo and Sonya, it had already happened.

Derry was on her third piece of cheese and her umpteenth olive when her phone rang, almost sliding off the shiny tabletop as it vibrated. Her heart gave a jump, and her hand shot out of its own accord to catch the handset. Marlene! But it wasn't Marlene.

'Still at large!' boomed Jacko. 'Evasive manoeuvres completed, sir!' He guffawed.

'Dad!'

'Pumpkin! Star of my firmament!'

'Dad, make up your mind. Pumpkin *or* star.'

'Guess where I am!'

'Go on. You want to.'

'Peter Doyle's place! Living like the other half. I just dropped in, dontcha know, and he said stay a few days. And he's going to buy another picture or two. Says he enjoyed meeting you at the castle.'

Never had Derry understood that when people said their blood ran cold, they meant it literally. She felt as though all the warmth in her body were draining away.

'He says you're coming down for the surprise party tomorrow. Couldn't be better. We'll have a ball. He says can you confirm—he expected you to call. You need to be here for six. You do your thing with Marlene, predicting a golden future and a fun night for all, then we proceed in an orderly convoy to the restaurant. Can a place have six stars? I think this one has. Doyle says he'll have his driver pick you up at four.'

Derry had been unable to get a word in, so strong was the torrent, but this couldn't go on.

'No! I'm sorry. Tell him I—'

'But you have to come!' said Jacko. Derry could hear his astonishment. That anyone could refuse a party, much less refuse to be paid to go to a party, defied belief.

Derry's mind was racing. 'Okay. Yes I'll come,' she said. 'I'll come, but I don't need a lift. I don't want to be picked up, okay?'

Out of the corner of her eye Derry saw Bruce gesticulating wildly, pointing to himself and miming steering motions.

'I have transport.'

'Top class!' said Jacko. 'The Ackree Stud, off the N69, you can't miss it. Heard anything from herself?'

Derry could answer truthfully that she had heard nothing from Vanessa.

'Doesn't sound right,' said Jacko, after a moment's thought. 'You should have had a surprise visit by now. This is not like your mother. Should I be concerned?'

Whether he meant concerned for himself or Vanessa, Derry couldn't tell. 'Honestly,' she said. 'You two need to talk.'

'You're going to enjoy the party. Six stars—did I mention that?'

'Bye Dad,' said Derry.

Bruce put the coffeepot in front of them and laid out proper cups and saucers rather than mugs. Delicate china, Derry noticed. Nice.

'We going to a party?' he said, sitting down and pouring.

'Can't think of anything else. At least I get to talk to Marlene privately. That's one good thing about telling fortunes.'

Bruce sucked his teeth. 'If you're right about any of this, you're walking straight into the lion's den. Just be sure you don't end up in some sorta accident.'

'Nothing can happen with loads of people around. I'm glad you're coming down. But you don't have to, really. I can arrange something.'

'Like what?' said Bruce. 'Your other driver is in jail. And I'm guessing you're not keen on a nice drive in the country with Mr. Colombia? Guess we need a tacplan.'

'A what?'

'A tactical plan. Tells you what to do, so you don't have to think while you're getting shot at.'

'Ah,' said Derry. 'Sorry I asked.'

'You're going to talk to her, right? Next problem is getting her out of there. We've got to exfiltrate.'

'What? Never mind.'

'I'll come with you as your driver. I can be your boyfriend again, if you like. I think I've got it down now. Not so demonstrative this time.'

'Bruce, if you'll come down and help me, you can be my mother. But you might not be tough enough.'

At Derry's feeble attempt at a joke, Bruce looked puzzled. He hadn't met her mother.

'The van is the extraction vehicle. I sit ready; you talk to Marlene. You have to persuade her to up and leave with you, just like that. No packing, no favourite pets, no goodbyes. Talk, walk. Okay? Think you can do that?'

'I can try.'

'So where do we take her? She needs a safe house, somewhere she can lie low.'

'She'll have a lawyer. We could take her there.'

'Perfect,' said Bruce. 'I do love a plan.'

'Bruce, what if she doesn't believe me and refuses to leave?'

'Sometimes you have to accept failure, that's all.' He shrugged.

'Then what about Marlene? What about Bella?'

'You'd better hope your friend Fitz can help.' He hesitated. 'And don't forget, you might be totally wrong about everything.'

'I'm not,' said Derry, but she sounded more confident than she felt. One thing she was sure of—right or wrong, she couldn't sit tight and do nothing. If her dreams made a fool of her, so what? She'd live. And so would everybody else.

'And another thing,' said Bruce. 'Remember what we say, "No plan survives contact with the enemy." We may have to improvise.'

'Oh, great,' said Derry. This wasn't the kind of improvisation her drama tutors had in mind.

'Maybe, you should give me Fitz's number.'

'Why? I'm not telling him anything about this.'

'Backup,' said Bruce. 'Just in case.' He didn't say in case of what.

'I hope that's not because you think I won't be able to call him myself if I need to.'

'Naw!' said Bruce, smiling. 'Maybe I got the hots for Englishmen.'

20

The Tuesday afternoon traffic was light. Bruce and Derry left Dublin city centre just before four o'clock and were soon bowling along the near-empty motorway towards the river city of Limerick.

For the third time that day, Derry tried to get Bella's lawyer on the phone. This time she succeeded. Yes, Bella would stay in custody for several days at least. Then she would almost certainly be charged. She was still in a police cell but seemed to be bearing up well. Still no calls or visits allowed. Derry thanked her, saying she'd call again tomorrow for an update. The lawyer agreed without enthusiasm that she could do that if she really felt she must. 'Must,' said Derry, and rang off.

With Limerick still half an hour away, they swung off the main road and along the left bank of the River Shannon. Except for the freshly painted white lines, the road looked much as it might have done forty years earlier—dense green hedgerows on both sides, an overgrown grass verge, and now and then a sudden glimpse of the slowly rolling river, its far bank a good half-mile off. Every few hundred yards the hedge to their right was broken by an opening, a tree-lined lane bounded by ancient stone walls. Every road and track appeared to lead down to the great river, as if all life would sooner or later end there.

They were headed for Peter Doyle's stud farm, a three-hundred acre ranch bounded by a smaller watercourse, a tributary of the Shannon. Derry had Bruce's laptop open on her knee, and Google Earth showed the property well off the main road, at the end of a long winding lane. The only other road was an even narrower lane leading down from the complex to the small river. One way in and one way out.

'Not ideal,' said Bruce. 'But what the heck. We ain't gonna be shooting our way out.'

'I should hope not!' said Derry. An awful thought struck her. 'Please tell me you haven't—'

'What do you take me for?' protested Bruce.

Derry wasn't sure how to answer that. The correct response should probably have been *some kind of action-man soldier who can probably make a bomb out of a pack of soft tissues and a Q-tip*. But Bruce would probably retort that he wasn't a soldier, he was Navy. In fact, If Bruce had shown up with a machine gun and a couple of rocket launchers, Derry wouldn't have been surprised. Shocked yes; surprised not at all.

'And stop worrying,' said Bruce. 'This isn't the States. Nobody is going to be shooting at anybody. Relax.'

'What if they try to block us? I don't mean shooting, but they could try stopping us getting away with Marlene.'

'We'll just have to deal with that if it happens. Honestly, even if Doyle is the bad guy you think he is, he's still not going to forcibly prevent his wife leaving with friends right there in front of every-body. There'll be plenty people around. It's a dinner party, right?'

'I guess,' said Derry, unconvinced. Something about Doyle said that anyone interfering with his plans would be made to suffer, din-ner party or not.

'Anyhow,' said Bruce, complacently. 'I'm an actor; I have my props.' He reached down into the side pocket of the door beside him and pulled out an iron crowbar, waving it dangerously close to the windshield. He returned the implement to its hiding place before this time fumbling under his seat, causing the van to lurch drunkenly. He pulled out a baseball bat and sat it across his knee. 'Patriotic, right? I never felt cricket was a real game. Check your side.'

Derry fished in the door pocket by her seat. A hammer.

'Never be without ya tools,' said Bruce, grinning manically.

Bruce, Derry realised, was enjoying himself, and she had no idea whether that was a good thing or one more random factor in a lengthening list of random factors. *Please let nobody get hit with a baseball bat!* And what was she supposed to do with a hammer?

'Check behind you,' said Bruce, looking smug.

Derry turned around in her seat to inspect the rear of the van. She'd paid no attention before, but now she noted the neatly folded array of belts, clamps, harnesses and boots, all arranged on home-made shelving.

'Isn't that climbing stuff?'

'Gotta be prepared,' said Bruce.

'There isn't a mountain for thirty miles. So where's your parachute?'

'Huh?'

'The parachute you're going to strap onto Marlene so she can jump from the chopper onto the mountain where you're going to be waiting to escort her to the armoured car.'

'No need to be sarcastic,' said Bruce, with a hurt expression. 'You know we don't have a chopper.'

For the next several miles, Bruce sulked, refusing to say anything even when Derry tried to make it up by asking him whether he had ever really jumped into the sea from a helicopter. But Bruce wasn't to be charmed.

Great, thought Derry. I'm going to steal a millionaire's wife away, evading his drug-dealing gangster bodyguards, and my driver and associate is too busy having a strop to talk to me.

As the road veered inland, the views of the Shannon came less often. They crossed a bridge over a small river, passing a straggle of old-world whitewashed houses, two pubs and a couple of modern bungalows. The countryside was flat, empty and beautiful.

'Next right!' said Derry, watching the laptop map. 'Down here.' She pointed to a lane so narrow that two cars couldn't pass side by side. A tasteful sign in stained woodwork announced that ahead was the Ackree Stud. As they swung into the opening, Derry was surprised to find that instead of lurching over ruts and potholes, the van glided on fresh, smooth tarmac. On both sides the hedges were thick and overgrown, host to overhanging trees and thickets of hawthorn. Every so often the lush vegetation opened into a gateway revealing a grassy field. Derry saw no grazing animals but did see an ancient church, covered in ivy and long abandoned. Magical, she thought. For a moment, she almost forgot to be afraid.

'The Eagle Has Landed,' muttered Bruce.

Directly ahead was an impressive gateway, far more stately than anything you might expect at the end of such a humble lane. Two monumental whitewashed pillars were each topped with a ferocious stone griffin. The tall wrought-iron gates were closed.

Derry jumped down from the van, stepped up to the gate and pressed the buzzer on an entryphone. Only then did she notice the camera mounted on a tall pole overlooking the entranceway.

'Yes?' The voice that crackled through the entryphone speaker didn't sound especially welcoming.

'Derry O'Donnell. Mr. Doyle invited me.'

'Moment.'

Was the accent foreign? Derry thought it was. She climbed back into the van. For several minutes they waited, then a black SUV pulled up inside the gates. Oddly, though the gates opened automatically, the SUV stayed blocking the way ahead. A man carrying a clipboard climbed out and approached the van. He was dressed casually, no uniform or any sign that he was from a security company. The driver stayed where he was.

'Miss O'Donnell, sign please?'

'That's me,' said Derry, winding down her window, taking the clipboard and signing opposite the name she saw was ready printed. She was disappointed to see the page was a fresh sheet, showing no details of other visitors. Deliberate or accidental?

'You too, please,' said the man. 'Please print name, put time and sign. And open back of vehicle, please.'

Bruce, signed, jumped out and slid open the side door of the van. He stood, relaxed and smiling as the guard stuck his head inside and looked around. Whatever he was looking for, he obviously thought climbing equipment no great threat to a stud farm. Derry wondered what he would have made of the baseball bat, crowbar and hammer if he'd looked more closely.

The SUV reversed onto the verge, and the guard waved the van through the gates. When they were through, the SUV tucked in close behind them.

Inside the gates, the whole scene changed as though Derry and Bruce had crossed from one universe into another. The riot of vegetation on either side of the road was replaced by neatly trimmed rhododendron and azalea. Hedges and stone walls gave way to pristine white fencing. Beyond the fencing was a patchwork of neat, clearly defined paddocks, some with sleek horses grazing contentedly. Turning a final bend, the vista opened up to reveal an imposing Georgian house and an extensive complex of gleaming white outbuildings.

The mansion captured the eye. The house was graceful and stately, but Derry was equally fascinated by the rest. She had never before seen a stud farm, and *ranch* didn't seem the right word to describe something far more like a gentleman's estate. A restrained air of quiet industry pervaded the place. And behind the elegant exterior, Derry guessed she was looking at a hugely valuable business selling top quality thoroughbreds to the world's billionaires.

As Bruce swept the van around a gravel parking area to one side of the mansion, Derry saw a tall modern building, probably an indoor ring or training facility, and a stable block with an enclosed yard. In the yard were three horse transporters, one with its ramp down. A group of four or five men was standing watching as a magnificent horse was gently led out. The waiting men were transfixed, all eyes on the beast, as though royalty were arriving in state. The animal was led prancing towards its stable, and the ramp was slammed shut.

The small carpark was crammed with vehicles, mostly SUVs and pickup-trucks. Bruce swung the van around and found a space— right beside a bright red sports car. Derry sighed. What was it about her father that meant chaos followed him wherever he went? The uncharitable thought evaporated almost at once, as Derry realised she was being unfair.

This time, she was the one bringing the chaos.

∿

What do you say when you arrive at a millionaire's house meaning to steal his wife? Derry had asked herself the question a thousand times on the journey down and saw no sensible answer. As she and Bruce crunched their way across the pristine gravel to the ornate front doorway of Doyle's mansion, she got no further than imagining she should probably start with something like, 'Hello, Mr. Doyle.'

The doorbell was operated by an antique sliding brass contraption. Derry gave it an experimental pull, expecting no effect. She was surprised to hear the clang deep inside the hall. Only moments later, the heavy door swung open. Doyle himself stood smiling benevolently.

Lately, Derry had made an unwelcome but accurate observation about herself and her brain. The more troubling, difficult and dangerous real life became, the more she found herself thinking pointless, trivial and altogether unhelpful thoughts. Her mind would say something like, *Here we are, tied to the railroad tracks waiting for the train, so why not spend our last few minutes trying to remember whether those fluffy clouds are called cumulo-nimbus or alto-cumulus?'* This time, the thought that nudged its way into her head was, *What is the point of being a millionaire if you have to open your own door?'*

Doyle's greeting was warm. Derry might almost have imagined from his smile that he was genuinely pleased to see her. But his expression darkened as his eyes took in Bruce standing tactfully behind as befitted Madam Tulip's driver and factotum.

'My um . . . fiancée,' said Derry. She spoke before she had even thought about what she was saying. Lately, her mouth seemed to want to charge off on solo runs, leaving out the brain part altogether.

'Haven't we met?' said Doyle to Bruce, his urbane smile restored.

'He's an actor,' said Derry, quickly. Sometimes, thought Derry, leaving out the brain part worked. The merest delay might have given Doyle time to remember Bruce from the castle. Not that he was likely to recall a security man—did the rich even notice that hotel staff were people?

'Ah,' said Doyle, as if being an actor could explain pretty well everything about a person, from their haircuts to their preferences in fiancées and supermarkets. 'Come in, come in. Thank you for coming. Derry, I'll explain what I have in mind.'

They stepped into a spacious hall. As Doyle led them towards a reception room, Derry noticed that amongst the several paintings hanging on the walls were two almost certainly by her father, although she didn't remember having seen them before and couldn't linger to inspect them more closely. In the drawing room, she and Bruce were invited to sit on embroidered antique chairs. Interspersed between enormous gilt mirrors were more paintings, carefully positioned and individually lit. These weren't the old masters you might have expected from the style of the house and its furnishings but modern works collected with the eye of a connoisseur. Derry spotted three more of Jacko's pictures. No wonder Jacko called Doyle his good friend.

'I see you've noticed I am a collector of your father's work,' said Doyle, smiling. 'I believe one day he will rank with Richter or Koons. I have a couple of Koons in the dining room. Perhaps you'd like to look at them later.'

The prospect of touring the valuable possessions of P. Doyle Esq. didn't appeal to Derry one little bit. All she could think of was Marlene. Not quite true; all she could think of was Marlene and getting out of here.

'Is Marlene around?' she asked, as casually as she could. 'If she'd like, we can start any time.'

'Let me explain my little surprise,' said Doyle. 'You will spend perhaps an hour with Marlene—gaze into your crystal ball or whatever it is that you do.' He smiled indulgently. 'I hope you might see your way to predicting a surprise.'

Derry felt a trickle of sweat run down between her shoulder blades. Was this talk of surprises Doyle's twisted sense of humour? Or was his very normality, his casual ease, a sign she had imagined everything?

'After your session with Marlene, we will all meet up at a wonderful restaurant in Limerick. We will of course have the place to ourselves. It will be a small gathering, but you'll find some of our guests interesting company, I assure you.' He turned to Bruce. 'Unfortunately, we weren't expecting . . .' He opened his arms in a gesture of polite helplessness.

'No problem at all,' said Derry, forestalling the elegant speech he was certain to make. 'It's I who should apologise.' She wondered whether she should have said 'me' rather than 'I', but that was what talking to Doyle did to you. 'I didn't realise I'd be invited to the actual party. In fact, I have to be home rather early.'

'Impossible! Your father will be there. He's riding one of my horses right now, but when he returns I'm sure he'll persuade you himself. I'm sure we can make an extra place for your fiancée.' He stood. 'Why don't we see if we can find Jacko right now? Then I'll show you where you will be doing your readings for Marlene. Alright?'

Doyle led them out of the room, standing aside and holding the door as they stepped into the hall. Derry slowed as she passed the paintings she was now sure were Jacko's. Something was odd about them, something not quite right, but she couldn't think what.

Doyle opened the massive front door and shepherded them across the broad swathe of gravel in front of the house, avoiding a horse transporter being gingerly reversed through an archway into the stable yard.

'I'm sorry you won't be here later. We'll be bringing out Prince of Arran and loading him up for England. A marvellous animal, but sensitive—a million guineas worth of nerves. Always a worry these journeys. Can you imagine the consequences of an accident? Even an undue delay in a car ferry? You can see why we breeders are sometimes less than relaxed.' He waved an encouraging hand to a man supervising three others busily lowering the ramp of an empty transporter. Two other men stood watching. Derry recognised one as the security guard who had met them at the gates and inspected their van.

'Howdy, pardners!'

Jacko's voice boomed out from the yard. He sat high on a quarter horse, the type you saw in cowboy films, although his green coat and riding boots were more Dick Turpin than Jessie James. He slapped the horses flank, threw one leg over the saddle and slid to the ground gracefully. 'Beautiful animal!' he announced to the world at large, ensuring that if the animal wasn't beautiful before, with Jacko's endorsement it was now officially so.

Doyle smiled, either pleased at someone praising his property or amused at Jacko's style. He gestured to a groom who instantly ran to take the horse from Jacko and lead it away.

'Jacko, my friend' said Doyle. 'I was explaining to your delightful daughter that we will all meet at the restaurant for our little party after she and my wife have finished their business.' He turned to Derry. 'I have some matters to attend to, and Marlene is not quite ready.' He smiled wryly in Jacko's direction, inviting male sympathy at the lateness of wives. Jacko grinned back. Derry tried not to scowl.

'While we're waiting,' said Doyle, 'I'll have one of the men give you a little tour of the house and the stud. I'm sure you'll find it fascinating.' He turned to Derry. 'Then Paulo will drive you to my wife.'

Drive? All along, Derry had presumed she'd be reading for Marlene in the main house. Now it was to be someplace else. Wherever the reading was to be, she had to have Bruce and the van nearby or she and Marlene would never be able to get away. Perhaps Marlene would have her own car wherever she was? But maybe not. Derry had the uncomfortable sense of a neat scheme unravelling strand by strand. What was it Bruce had said about no plan surviving contact with the enemy?

'I won't need a lift,' said Derry. 'No need. Bruce can drive me.'

'Not at all,' said Doyle. 'It's a maze of country lanes around here. People get hopelessly lost all the time. Paulo knows where he is going.'

Courtesy of her laptop and the all-seeing eye of Google Earth, Derry knew the layout of the roads around Doyle's farm. One lane led in from the main road; one road led down towards the river. Nothing like a maze. Nothing at all like.

Doyle turned to Jacko. 'I've just had the pleasure of meeting your daughter's fiancée. He will be joining us for the party, delighted to have him.'

Jacko's eyes popped. He fixed Derry with a frown. He drew himself up as if he had an elbow planted squarely on the mantelpiece of an imaginary drawing room in an imagined Castle O'Donnell and, as paterfamilias, was preparing to lay down the law. Derry easily read his thoughts—in a shocking breach of protocol, Bruce had not formally asked Jacko for her hand.

'Derry and my wife will be proceeding separately to the restaurant,' said Doyle, 'so you will need to make your own ways into Limerick. I'll give you directions; it's quite straightforward.'

Jacko turned to Bruce. 'Why don't you come with me . . . er . . . my boy. We need to have a little talk.'

Bruce looked panic-stricken. His face was a mute plea to Derry to be rescued, quickly disguised as a fit of coughing.

'We'll take the Jag,' said Jacko, his good humour returning at the thought of showing off his beloved machine to a captive audience, even if in this case the captive had shown a sorry lack of respect for the rights of fathers. 'Wind in our hair!' he announced. 'Frighten the sheep!' Derry wondered whether he meant woolly animals on four legs, other road users or prospective sons-in-law.

'We're agreed then,' said Doyle. 'Dinner is at eight. That gives us a comfortable two hours.' He took out his phone and hit a speed dial. 'Paulo! Could you join us please.'

Derry followed Doyle's gaze. Paulo emerged from the stable yard and ambled towards them, in no particular hurry.

'Paulo,' said Doyle. 'I'll need you and the car for half an hour. After that would you take Miss O'Donnell to her meeting with my wife? You know where to go.'

Paulo smiled broadly. 'A pleasure,' he said. Was that a smirk or was tension making Derry imagine malice where there was none?

Again, Doyle made a call on his phone. This time to summon a man Derry hadn't seen before, introducing him as the stud's resident expert on local history. While the man led the little group back towards the house, insisting they would find the story of the estate fascinating, Doyle and Paulo boarded a white Range Rover. The engine roared. The powerful SUV sped away in a cloud of sandy gravel, negotiated its way through a gateway and disappeared down the leafy lane that led towards the river.

∼

The stud farm and its history might have fascinated someone who liked old houses, horses, the racing business and the smell of money. None of those subjects held much appeal for Derry at the best of times, but now her nerves made the delay almost unbearable. At least half an hour passed before their guide took a call on his phone and obediently ushered them back outside to stand at the front of the house. Paulo was waiting.

'Come with me,' he said, addressing Derry and ignoring the others. His tone was peremptory as though he were giving an order to his horse or dog. Derry wouldn't have been surprised if he had clicked his fingers. He turned on his heel, striding away to the white Range Rover, not bothering to look behind to see if she were following.

'I'll need my bag,' called Derry after him.

To her immense relief, Bruce was on cue. 'I'll help you with that,' he said loudly.

They left Jacko talking history with their guide and hurried to the van. Bruce opened the door, leaned in behind the passenger seat and reached for Derry's bag. 'You want me to follow?' he said, under his breath.

'I don't see how you can,' whispered Derry. 'You're supposed to be going with Jacko.'

'We could still follow you.'

'No use. You can't get more than two people in his stupid car.

We need the van. Tell Dad I won't be staying late at the restaurant; I'll want to go home early, so you want to bring the van to the party rather than go with him. That should do it.'

'Okay. I'll try to follow you. There must be other buildings somewhere around. I wish I had the faintest idea where he was taking you.'

'Not as much as I do,' said Derry.

She took her bag from Bruce and crunched over the gravel towards Paulo and the Range Rover, her heart thumping in her chest. She turned to wave to her father, but he was still deep in conversation with the guide and failed to notice. She thought of her grandfathers, the conduits for the strange gift she shared with Jacko. *Please Grandads*, she whispered to herself. *Please don't let me down. Anything you can do, okay?'*

Oddly, her little prayer, if that's what it was, made her feel better. She clambered into the Range Rover with more confidence. Marlene would either believe her story or not, leave with her or not. The important thing was that she would have a choice. Derry would have played her part. And if all Derry's suspicions and visions were shown to be the deranged products of an overactive imagination, so what? Nobody would die. Or at least, thought Derry, remembering Mojo, nobody *else* would die.

Paulo gunned the motor to a roar. As the Range Rover shot forward, throwing Derry back into her seat, he grinned a wide-eyed manic grin. He turned to look at her, holding the smile fixed on his face as if he were wearing a mask at some weird festival. Even as the Range Rover sped across the gravel, he kept his gaze locked unmoving on Derry. Only then did the horrific realisation dawn on her. Paulo had no intention of looking where they were going. The gateway was rushing towards them, but still Paulo stared at Derry with that crazy grin. Barely a second before they would plough through one of the heavy stone gateposts, Derry closed her eyes.

Paulo hooted the wildest laugh Derry had ever heard. And then they were through the gate, bouncing in the ruts of the lane, the trees on either side brushing the doors of the Range Rover. 'You like that?' shouted Paulo over the din. 'You like a little excitement?' He laughed again, as though it mattered not at all what Derry, or any woman, liked or didn't like.

21

Intercostal diaphragmatic breathing sounds a lot more impressive, creative and scientific than belly breathing, but belly breathing it is. Instead of inhaling and exhaling with the chest, the idea is that the stomach should rise and fall. Every student actor is taught the technique in their first year of training as the passport to calm, mental clarity and a lowered heartbeat.

Derry doubted that her drama tutors had in mind the need to act cool when driven at stone gateposts by possible Colombian drug-dealers and madmen. But the technique worked regardless. Her breathing was deep and steady, and her eyes were open as the Range Rover swung and lurched down the overgrown lane. Beyond that brief moment of terror, she betrayed no further symptoms of panic or even distress. Instead, she sat ignoring Paulo as though the vehicle were driving itself. As she breathed, she told herself to observe as much as she could. This lane might well prove her and Marlene's only exit.

Compared to the road that led to the stud's main gate, the track was potholed and neglected. No million-dollar thoroughbreds were driven down here. Behind, the stud had disappeared from view. Ahead, the lane twisted and turned, the tall hedgerows making it impossible to see far or guess at their destination. They passed no intersections or crossroads, nor did Derry expect any—the satellite view had shown only a straight track to the river below. Nor had it shown buildings of any kind. Then again, those pictures could be years out of date.

The Range Rover slowed, then stopped. The silence was shocking as the swishing of vegetation brushing its sides trailed away. All you could hear was the engine ticking. Derry could see no sign of a building, though just in front and off to the left was an unpainted metal farm gate. Derry was peering through the dense hedge trying to make out if that was their destination, when a hand brushed her cheek making her gasp.

Derry told herself to stay calm, but her body wasn't listening. She felt herself go rigid. All she could think was, *Not good. This is not good.* Paulo leaned over, ran his fingers through her hair and stroked the side of her face. Without warning, he pinched the lobe of her ear, making her gasp.

'Stop that,' said Derry, struggling to keep her voice level.

'I like a woman of spirit,' said Paulo. 'You are an actress, I hear. Perhaps you are acting now.'

'I am not acting. Stop. Can we drive on, please.'

'Don't you like the beautiful Irish scenery? I thought artists love beautiful scenery. It is spring. All the animals are . . . doing like us.'

'It is not spring. It is summer. Nearly. We are not doing anything. I am asking you to drive on. Mr. Doyle has made the arrangement.'

If Derry hoped that the name of his employer would have some magically deterrent effect on Paulo, she was mistaken.

'You think I am afraid of *Mister* Doyle?' He laughed, quietly now, as if the full humour of the situation could never be understood by anyone but himself. 'I am so terrified—sure, yes.' He leaned towards Derry, gazing into her eyes with a calm frankness she found utterly chilling. 'Peter Doyle is a fool. He is a fool who should choose his friends more carefully.'

He leaned back in his seat, smiling, as though teasing an unco-operative pet. 'Maybe you want money. Is that what you want? Fifty dollars? Euros?' He pulled out his wallet from his back pocket, wriggling in his seat as he did so. His shirt fell open. Tucked into his waistband was a dark metallic something. A phone? A pager? Derry's brain flatly refused to accept that the object it saw was a gun. But it *was* a gun. To Derry it seemed that breathing—breathing of any kind, diaphragmatic or otherwise—was an ability she had long since lost.

Paulo opened his wallet, taking out a fifty-euro note. Casually, he threw the note into Derry's lap. 'Keep the change,' he said. He leaned over to take her head in his hands.

An image materialised in Derry's mind like an apparition. Where had it come from? The effect was like a thousand different parts of her brain had caught fire all at once as her terrified grey matter blazed out a storm of random thoughts. And out of the chaos, in a slow-motion explosion of colour, emerged a man on a throne, the man with the magnificent headdress, the man with a severed head in his lap.

As Paulo's face closed on hers, Derry had no clue why she shouted so wildly and in such an odd way. Not the shout of a woman in desperate straits, but a shout like she was heralding with the utmost fanfare the arrival of a god, a ruler, a power in the land.

'The King!' she proclaimed. 'The King!'

Paulo froze as if struck by a beam from some alien ray gun, his power of movement seemingly suspended.

'The King,' said Derry quietly. She could hear her own breathing. 'The King says no.'

Paulo's mouth fell open. His hands relinquished his grip on her face. He shrank back into his seat, his eyes wide, staring.

'What do you know about such things?' he breathed, his lips scarcely moving, as though saying the very words could bring down on his head some awful retribution.

Many times in the past, when she had read the cards or gazed into a crystal ball for the amusement of her friends, Derry had asked herself where her real gift ended and her love of acting took over. She had answered her question with another one—how boring would it be to have your fortune told by someone in a business suit speaking like a newsreader? So Derry had always allowed herself the indulgence of hamming it up a little. Harmless fun. But now, not fun at all. A gamble. A dangerous last throw.

'You know what I do,' said Derry, piercing Paulo with what she hoped was a profoundly mystical look. She modulated her voice—deeper and slower, hypnotic, speaking as she might when reading the Tarot for maximum effect. 'You have heard of me?'

As all actors know, contrast is everything. *Dynamics, my girl,* said Derry to herself. Matter-of-factly, she turned to look out the window as if bored. 'I know many things,' she said. Her tone was offhand, casual. 'Please, drive on.'

Paulo said nothing. He clicked the Range Rover into drive, and they moved off, bumping down the lane in silence. Once, Derry caught him sneaking a sideways glance at her face, but when he saw her watching, he quickly looked away.

Should she tell Doyle what Paulo had done? Derry wrestled with the question as the Range Rover nudged its way down the leafy lane towards who knew what. If she did tell his boss, would Paulo take revenge? And what good would it do to tell Doyle his employee was a dangerous man if Doyle was even more dangerous?

Derry's imagination was running riot. Perhaps Marlene wasn't down here at all. Or perhaps she was at their destination, wherever that was, but was already dead. The sudden fear that she was too late gripped Derry's heart. Once before, she was certain, Doyle had set her up to witness the dead body of his wife. Fitz and Bruce might have perfectly justified doubts, but Derry was sure she was right. Derry O'Donnell, aka Madam Tulip—alibi for hire.

The Range Rover swept down into a dip in the lane then nosed upwards climbing a shallow ridge. As they crested the height, the hedgerows gave way to a clear vista of open fields, low stone walls and, directly below them, the muddy tributary of the River Shannon. On the riverbank was laid out a small gravelled parking space. A crude wooden jetty jutted into the river. Moored to the jetty was a sleek, white motor cruiser.

The boat was big, an elegant luxury craft built for speed and comfort, a millionaire's plaything. The vessel was ultramodern, the main cabin sporting a swept-back, streamlined windscreen. Above the cabin was a high, open bridge festooned with aerials. On the bridge stood a burly man in sunglasses, baseball cap and windcheater. He waved and shouted a greeting. Paulo didn't reply. Instead, he brought the Range Rover to a crunching halt by the jetty and turned to Derry. He wasn't smiling. 'I too can tell the future,' he said quietly. 'And I foresee you will soon change your mind.'

Paulo swung his door open and jumped down. All Derry wanted to do was sit exactly where she was. If she couldn't rewind the clock to before any of this happened, she would like time to stop, right there, even if that meant staying immobile forever like a statue in a fairy tale.

Paulo opened Derry's door and stood waiting impatiently. Derry grabbed her bag from the floor by her feet and reluctantly stepped down. Paulo nodded towards the boat. Derry's legs didn't want to move, but what choice did she have?

Down the wall of the vessel's main cabin was a row of long windows obviously designed to give a broad view of the water. She could see nobody inside. Below was a small line of narrower windows, presumably the sleeping cabins. Was Marlene down there? Was Doyle?

From the stern of the cruiser a low platform projected over the water. Most of the space was taken up by a rigid inflatable speedboat with a powerful outboard engine, sitting poised as if ready to be launched over the side at any moment. Barely enough room was left on the deck for Derry to jump down onto the platform, and she had to leave her bag on the jetty for Paulo to throw after her. He threw casually, with no regard whatever for the contents, like he was saying *you won't be needing these anyhow, so why worry?*

From the cramped afterdeck, Derry saw only two possible routes. She could step up a shining chrome ladder leading forward to the flying bridge or go straight ahead to where smoked glass panels and a sliding door led directly into the main saloon.

'In,' said Paulo, jumping down from the jetty onto the stern platform behind her. Derry slid the panel open and stepped inside.

The saloon was spacious and airy, opulent with leather and mahogany. The space was flooded with light from the picture windows. On Derry's left was a curving seat bound in luxurious cream leather and served by a circular table, its surface gleaming glass. Opposite was a shining wooden partition, waist high, separating off a kitchenette and bar. Ahead was the panoramic front windscreen, sweeping the full width of the boat, and two pilot's chairs facing a complicated dashboard of controls, dials and levers. Beside the chairs, a stairway spiralled to the bridge above, where Derry knew the man in sunglasses was stationed. Another staircase descended from near the kitchenette into the depths of the boat and presumably to the cabins. Were Marlene and Doyle aboard at all? Or was Derry alone with Paulo and his friend?

Derry sensed Paulo standing close behind her. 'You like? Boats make for good parties. The cabins are spacious. Very comfortable.' His smile made Derry's flesh crawl.

'Marlene—is she here?'

'You will see her soon. Meanwhile, you sit and wait.' He indicated the leather seats.

Derry sat. As she primly set her bag on her knee, Paulo's grin grew even wider. He turned away, strode the length of the saloon towards the pilots' seats and skipped lightly up the stairway to the bridge above. Derry could hear low murmurings as he spoke with his companion but could make out nothing.

With Paulo gone, Derry could at last think clearly. The main thing was to remember why she was here. She had come to tell Marlene her suspicions and give her the choice of leaving. All else was secondary. Okay, the plan had passed its sell-by date, but it was the only plan she had. Luckily, Derry hadn't dressed as Madam Tulip. Padding, jewellery and feathers meant Tulip was hardly built for speed. Instead, Derry had worn jeans and her sneakers—far more suitable for a quick getaway. If she were to get away at all.

What if Marlene were still unharmed? What would she expect Derry to do? Was Derry meant to tell Marlene's fortune right here at this table? If so, she might as well lay out the cards and the crystal ball right now. That done, she sat back on the leather seat.

Often, if Derry were forced to endure a long wait, she would deal herself a hand of Patience. She found the game calmed her nerves and passed the time. She dealt and the minutes went by. The only sound was a murmuring from the bridge where Paulo and his companion were exchanging muted remarks in Spanish. Derry felt a soft jolt as the boat bumped gently against the wooden jetty and rocked slowly, perhaps caught by a sudden breeze.

'Ah! You are here. Excellent.'

Doyle's head appeared, rising from the deck below as he climbed the stairway. In three strides, he stood towering over her, beaming. Something about his face and the way he held himself suggested a state of barely suppressed excitement.

'And what do you think of my little barge,' he asked, waving expansively.

Strange, thought Derry. he was asking as though her opinion mattered. Perhaps everyone's opinion mattered to Doyle.

'Very nice,' she answered, politely. Maybe too politely. Doyle's brow furrowed, as if he were marking her two out of ten for appreciation.

His gaze fell on the cards spread out on the table in front of her. 'I have always wondered what the cards might hold for me. Ever since my wife took an interest. But I confess, like most men I see fortune-telling as let's say . . . a female preoccupation. You won't be offended if I say that?'

Derry shrugged.

'I have concluded that in this world it may be best not to know too much,' said Doyle. 'Do you agree?'

Doyle was good at asking questions you weren't supposed to answer, or at least not truthfully.

'I wonder . . . I wonder do you ever see your own future?' he said.

Another question Derry wasn't supposed to answer. Doyle was grandstanding, Derry was sure, acting some role he had written for himself. The question was, what part did he think he was playing? And what role did he have in mind for her?

'Come with me,' said Doyle brusquely. 'My wife is below. I'll show you down.'

He stood, waiting impatiently at the head of the stairway, allowing Derry time only to gather her cards and tuck the pack into the pocket of her jeans. She slipped her phone into her other pocket. As she moved to repack her crystal ball in her bag, he waved impatiently.

'Leave those things; we can get them shortly. Please, after you,' said Doyle, insisting she lead the way down the stairs into the narrow, windowless passage below. Derry wondered how hard getting back up those stairs would be, with or without Marlene.

On both sides of the passage, mahogany doors glowed richly in the soft lighting from tastefully concealed lamps. Doyle seemed to be leading her to the door that lay straight ahead, right at the end of the passage. Instead he stopped, opening one to his left. Without entering, he reached inside to switch on the light. Ever the gent, thought Derry. *After you. Thanks a bunch.*

'Please,' said Doyle, indicating she should step inside.

The cabin was of modest size, not by any means cramped but still somehow claustrophobic. Perhaps it was the dark wood of the panelling lining the walls that created an oppressive effect. The room was empty except for twin beds, one each side of the cabin, separated by no more than a couple of feet. A window ran almost the full length of one wall, but the venetian blinds were closed and Derry could see nothing of the world outside.

Doyle closed the door behind him with a click. He stood, his arms folded, striking a pose as if on stage. Now he was truly in character, thought Derry, alarm rising in her chest.

'I am distraught,' said Doyle, his face a mask of contrived regret. 'That you should have come to this is beyond my comprehension. I feel sorry for your father.'

Of the countless possible scenarios Derry had run through her head in the previous hours, nothing remotely resembled this.

'My wife is seriously ill. She is in the cabin next door. I am extremely concerned for her. A doctor will be summoned, but I fear it may be too late.' He extended his arms in theatrical pleading. 'How could you sell drugs you knew were contaminated? And not for the first time.'

Derry found some kind of voice. The words formed but emerged as a rasping whisper. 'You know that's not true!'

'That poor musician. My wife told me you supplied him. I imagine the police will find ample proof at your flat. You and your accomplice have so much for which to answer. Your phone please.'

Could Derry have refused? Could she have snatched out the handset, hit a speed dial before he could stop her? Then what? She handed over the phone. Doyle slipped it in his pocket and opened the door.

'Don't try to escape. These cabins are built to be secure when the boat is unoccupied, and you will not be able to force the door. I would appreciate it if you do not damage the woodwork trying.'

'I know what you tried to do,' said Derry quietly. 'I know how you did it. Poison. She's dead isn't she? And I'm not the only one who knows.' A reasoned, calculated gamble or the hysterical product of sheer terror? Whichever it was, Doyle seemed unperturbed.

'You, and you alone, will be responsible for . . . whatever happens.' He shook his head in sorrow as if the wickedness of the world were beyond comprehension. 'Using the facade of the fortune-teller to cover your drug-dealing business was clever. Who would have guessed?'

'Don't be ridiculous! *You'll* be the main suspect, you know that. The husband always is!'

'But I won't be here,' said Doyle, as if explaining to a child. 'And neither will Paulo. We will shortly disembark, and the boat will proceed to Limerick driven by an employee who is being well-rewarded. Miraculously, he has no criminal record. On docking, he will discover the . . . crime and secure the culprit. The police will discover the evidence in your possession—here and in your flat.'

Too late Derry realised the significance of Doyle insisting she leave her bag behind in the saloon. In that bag, she had no doubt, the police would find a small package of white powder and a wad of cash.

The door closed behind Doyle. The key rattled in the lock.

In films, when the villain is gone, leaving the victim locked in a room, the victim concerned will always rush to the door and jiggle the handle pointlessly. This was exactly what Derry found herself doing seconds after the door clicked shut and the key turned.

She put her ear to the door, again as the script demanded, again pointlessly. She felt the gentle bumping of the boat against the jetty and the suggestion of footsteps or some activity on the deck above, but nothing that made sense. Did the sounds mean Doyle and Paulo were leaving the boat in the charge of their colleague for the fatal journey to Limerick?

The boat's engines roared into sudden life. The craft trembled and vibrated. Derry raced to the cabin window, pulled up the venetian blinds and pressed her face to the glass. Outside, the jetty and the car park were deserted. Paulo's Range Rover sat mutely. Now, the cruiser was swinging away from the jetty with muffled rumbles and gurgles as it manoeuvred into the stream. Then a gradual but remorseless acceleration as the vessel forged purposefully downriver.

The sense of desperation was overwhelming. Surely Bruce must have followed her by now? He would have seen the direction Paulo had gone. How long could it have taken for him to make some excuse and follow in the van? If he left the stud farm by the back gate, he couldn't end up anywhere but at the jetty. But then what?

How much time to get to Limerick by river? Derry had no idea how fast a cruiser like this could go but guessed twenty or thirty miles an hour. If the city were half an hour or so by car, that would make it—what? An hour and a half by boat? Two hours? Two hours until they arrived at a marina to be met by police cars and handcuffs. And an ambulance for Marlene that she surely wouldn't need.

Just as Derry was about to drop the blinds and cut off the horrid sight of the empty shore, Bruce's van emerged from the leafy lane. It raced down the hill to the jetty, pulling up haphazardly beside Paulo's Range Rover.

Derry knew the feeling was ridiculous, but a blaze of hope she couldn't suppress sprang up in her heart. At almost the same time, the voice of reason in her head asked what she expected Bruce to do now—leap out of the van equipped for a daring rescue, wielding his baseball bat? Swim after the boat with a knife between his teeth?

Proof that reason was right came when Bruce didn't get out at all. No one got out. The van sat motionless until, finally, a door did open. But it was the passenger door, and the person who got out was wearing a flowing green coat. Jacko strolled to the end of the jetty, now receding fast from Derry's view, and waved.

Derry let the blinds fall back over the window.

∼

The cruiser picked up speed in a surge that tilted the whole cabin backwards, making Derry stumble. She guessed the narrow tributary had opened out into the wide expanse of the Shannon, allowing the boat's engines to be used at near full power. Soon the vessel steadied itself on the placid water, and Derry could walk around her little cell without falling over.

First she checked the closet—empty, not so much as a hanger inside. A door opened into an en suite bathroom, but none of its fittings or furnishings were of the remotest use for breaking down a door or incapacitating a grown man. She opened the little cabinets that ran head high around the bathroom walls. Empty—not so much as a nailfile.

Derry left the bathroom, returning to slump on a bed. She had to think positive. What was it Bella used to say? No to Negativity. When Derry thought of her friend she felt tears well up—whether for Bella or herself she didn't know.

Alright, thought Derry. What was good about this situation? There had to be something good. She was unharmed—positive and, remembering Paulo, by no means inevitable. The Range Rover was still parked by the jetty. Did that mean Doyle hadn't left the boat? If he hadn't, perhaps he and Paulo planned to get off somewhere else. If they were going to stop, would she have a chance then? She had to believe so. A chance to do what, she had no idea.

22

All her life Derry had been amazed by the ridiculous thoughts her brain came up with uninvited. Not always ludicrous in themselves—some of those ideas were perfectly rational observations. The problem was the context. Like now, here she was, lying on a bed in a locked cabin on a boat taking her to prison, and her brain told her that the bed was remarkably comfortable.

If Derry had been scoring herself in some contest, she would right away have to mark herself down on two counts. Firstly, irrelevance—the comfort or otherwise of the bed was immaterial given that her journey would be over in two hours or less. Secondly, as any sensible person would remark, what did she expect of a couple of million dollars' worth of luxury cruiser? Hard bunks like a prison cell? *Ah,* thought Derry. Whatever meandering route her brain was taking, it had made its point. She wondered would she wind up in the same prison as Bella.

She got up, went to the window and opened the blinds wide. The shoreline was creeping past, deceptively slowly but a long way off, meaning they were now in the wide reaches of the Shannon and motoring fast. The move away from the bed helped a little, in that her brain stopped thinking about jail. Instead it busied itself focusing on the horrors of her arrest and public trial, the flashing cameras and the television news. Why did that seem worse than a prison cell? Actresses were supposed to like publicity, weren't they?

'Ha!' said Derry out loud. 'Fame at last! Oh, well done!' She heard herself laughing.

This was not good. This was panic, and panic was bad, bad, bad. Derry tried to banish all images of her future. Instead, she tried to think of the Granddads, wherever they were. She focused hard, working to conjure up an image of men only one of whom she remembered, while the other she knew only from an ancient photograph. But the more she said *help me!* the more they seemed to shrug and say, *Hey, it's a tough old world, right? You're a big girl now.* Or perhaps they hadn't answered at all. For the first time in her life, Derry wondered if anybody was really there.

She thumped her clenched fists on the cabin window as though she could punch a way through and fly to freedom. If only, instead of wild imaginings, she could truly see ahead to where all this was going.

'Oh,' said Derry. She hardly heard herself say it. She mightn't have said it at all—perhaps she had only thought it. 'Oh, oh, oh,' she said, this time aloud for sure. She stared through the cabin window. She scanned the shore to the left and right, upstream and down. But she couldn't dismiss the logic. She was looking out the left side of the boat, whatever that was called. And they were travelling downstream—you could see the rolling motion of the river clearly. The boat must have wheeled left as it swept out of the tributary river and into the Shannon. Limerick was to the right.

Derry felt a knot tighten in the pit of her stomach. *Not Limerick!* Then where? She remembered that Doyle and Paulo had to get off the boat somewhere. Could it be that the only suitable place was downstream? Whatever their plan, they wouldn't be arriving in Limerick for eight o'clock. Not now. And surely, if Doyle's story was to stand up with the police, the boat would have to arrive as if the passengers expected to get to their party more or less on time.

Derry's head hurt. She lay back on the bed. To her surprise, the motion of the boat and the thrum of the engines was soothing. Hypnotic. As if whatever was going on outside her head was the dream, and only her imagination mattered.

Derry didn't know how long she lay with her head propped up against the cabin bulkhead, eyes closed. But she knew what would happen next, and she had to have some sort of plan. The boat would slow down and pull into some landing place, perhaps obscure like the one they had left, but perhaps not. If it were a more public jetty, she might have some chance of attracting attention. She racked her brains trying to remember the Google satellite views she had studied and the shoreline of the Shannon downstream but could picture nothing; all her research had concentrated on the stud farm and its access road. She got up and peered out the window. The boat was moving closer to shore, but she could see nothing like a suitable place to land. She was still staring out when a sound made her heart stop. Someone was turning the key in the cabin door.

Derry sprang backwards onto the bed in shock, retreating against the headrest like she wanted to back through the wall and out into the open water. The door was flung roughly open. Derry's only thought was, *Please, not Paulo. Anything but that.* But it wasn't Paulo. Or at least, it wasn't Paulo who entered first.

Peter Doyle almost fell into the cabin. He stumbled before landing in a heap on the floor and lying motionless, curled into the foetal position, his hands tied behind his back. Paulo stood over him, gun in hand. On his face was a grin like it was Christmas and he was going to a party.

'Later, the company will be better,' he said. 'For now, you must make do with an idiot and a loser.' He prodded Doyle in the stomach with his foot making him curl up even more tightly. Paulo laughed. 'Look at him. How do you say it, Lord of the Manor.'

Doyle groaned. Paulo beckoned to Derry with the gun. 'Come here. Turn around. Hands behind your back.'

Never before had Derry known what it was to have a gun pointed at her. Nothing she had ever read or heard prepared her for the sheer terror instantly created by that black, staring muzzle. Slowly, very slowly, she did as she was told.

Paulo pushed the gun into his belt and from his jacket pocket took a roll of heavy tape. Derry could feel the tape wind tightly around her wrists again and again. 'Please, not so tight!'

'Quiet,' said Paulo. 'Be thankful I'm not taping your pretty mouth. Don't worry. It won't be for long.'

The door slammed shut behind Paulo. The key turned in the lock. The bundle on the floor that was Doyle groaned.

'Are you alright?' asked Derry, some reflex forming the words before her mind could cut them off. Why should she care how he was?

Doyle sat up, leaning his back against the foot of the bed. 'Never better,' he said.

Derry stood over him, awkward with her hands tied behind. 'You don't look to me like someone in a position to be sarcastic,' she said. 'You killed Marlene.'

Doyle shuffled around on the floor trying to make himself comfortable. 'I didn't kill anyone.' He looked away as he spoke.

'You're lying.'

'Why would I lie? What would be the point? So I can impress a cute little actress before we die?'

At some other time and in some other place, Derry might have appreciated being called cute. Even being called little could be construed as a compliment. But not from a probable murderer. And not when he had mentioned *dying* and *we* in the same sentence.

'What are they going to do with us?'

'I thought you were the psychic,' said Doyle. He turned away as if bored.

'It's Paulo, isn't it? Paulo who's behind all this?'

'Congratulations.'

'Stop that!' Derry kicked him ineffectually in the side.

'Ow!' protested Doyle.

'You're being stupid,' said Derry. 'We need to think. We have to be positive!'

'I don't believe it,' said Doyle rolling his eyes. 'A motivational speech. Don't tell me, you've got a PowerPoint presentation lined up and a booking for a weekend of paintball!' The last words he shouted as if all his shock and frustration were bursting out of him at once.

'We have to work together,' repeated Derry calmly. 'What choice do we have?'

Derry could almost see Doyle's mind weighing up the pros and cons of playing along. He sighed. 'You are concerned for Marlene. Of course you are. I assure you, I had no intention of doing what you suspect. Have you any idea how difficult it would be to murder your spouse and evade justice?'

'You won't evade it,' said Derry simply. 'Whichever way this goes.'

If Derry's pronouncement stung Doyle he didn't show it.

'Paulo is behind everything,' he said. 'He was planning to frame me as a murderer and a drug smuggler. He sedated Marlene and locked her in the master cabin. I had to do what he asked, say everything he told me to say. I pray she is still sleeping. Otherwise she might panic and endanger herself. And us.'

'That,' said Derry, 'is the biggest pile of crap I've heard in all my life.'

Doyle shrugged as if neither he nor anyone else could care whether Derry believed him or not.

'And Paulo?' asked Derry. 'Why is he doing this?'

'I suppose if I said disgruntled employee, that wouldn't satisfy you? Let's just say I hope it's all a misunderstanding. But I doubt it.'

'What does he mean to do? Now. With us.'

Doyle gave a rueful snort. 'Kill us, of course. Dump us overboard. Shortly, if I'm not mistaken, they will load ten million Euros worth of cocaine onto this boat.'

Derry was aware she looked foolish standing with her mouth open. She didn't have to do the mental arithmetic to know that ten million euros was eleven million dollars in real money. Eleven million dollars was plenty motivation to kill any number of people.

'This is a small country with a huge coastline,' said Doyle. 'Smuggling drugs into Ireland from South America is easy, but moving them on is hard. Paulo was using my horse transporters to ship the drugs out of Ireland and get them through customs into Britain and the continent. What customs officer would dare use sniffer dogs or in any way disturb a highly strung racehorse known to be worth a million dollars?'

'Where is Paulo going? Why is he running away?'

'I don't know where. He's running because a certain acquaintance of mine, an English gentleman of impeccable credentials, turns out to be a policeman. Or something like a policeman.' He closed his eyes and sank back.

Derry tried to control her breathing, to give nothing away. He meant Fitz. Of course he did. She wondered why she was bothering to hide her reaction. Soon it wouldn't matter what Doyle knew or didn't know. But she hid it anyway.

'Who *is* Paulo?' she asked.

'Let's say his uncle is a business associate of mine. Was. If you ever find yourself in Bogota, I advise you to reject any opportunities for advancement from a certain Carlos Rey. I wish I had, I assure you. His name means the King. He certainly acts like one.'

At some other time, Derry might have felt some small satisfaction, tinged with awe, as the pieces of the puzzle went click. She might have felt wonder at the strange gift she had been given for no reason other than being the daughter of a seventh son of a seventh son. But this wasn't the time or the place. And Doyle was still talking, as if telling his story was a relief now it was of no possible consequence.

'In Bogota, Paulo messed with the wrong man's daughter. So the King brought him to London. And I did the King a favour. I brought Paulo here.' He closed his eyes. 'I thought I was giving him a job.' He gave a hollow laugh.

Without warning, the boat changed course, banking hard to the left. Derry felt the force of the turn push her backwards into the cabin wall. She struggled to her feet. With no free hands to help keep her balance, she was in danger of falling over but managed to navigate her way around Doyle to the cabin window. She pushed the blinds aside with her head.

'What do you see?' asked Doyle. He was trying to get up, but with his feet and hands bound he was struggling.

'A jetty. A proper concrete one. With some small buildings. It's like at the bottom of a steep hill. I can see a town behind, higher. Up a narrow winding road.'

'Who's there? Is anybody waiting?' Doyle had gotten to his feet by pushing his back against the wall and pushing. He hopped over to the window, swaying and looking as if he might fall every time the speeding boat bumped or surged.

'Yes,' said Derry, hearing the despair creep into her voice. She didn't have to describe what she saw—Doyle could see for himself. He swore. A big black SUV sat parked at the end of the jetty. Two men stood beside its open doors. One Derry recognised immediately—the security guard from the stud. On the ground beside them, but hidden by the bulk of the SUV from anyone casually observing from the town above, Derry could see a pile of five large suitcases. The sight was bizarre as though the men were about to set off on vacation. But remembering what Doyle had said about eleven million dollars' worth of drugs, Derry doubted the cases would hold much in the way of suntan lotion or shirts in poor taste.

The boat levelled off as its engines cut back to a gurgle. The craft slid smoothly alongside the concrete jetty, the bump muffled by hanging tyres. It rode high—the river must be tidal here, thought Derry—but at least that meant her window was above the level of the jetty by a foot and she had a clear view. Even before the boat slid to a halt, Paulo leapt ashore, landing light-footed on the dusty concrete right in front of Derry's window. He walked towards the waiting men, his arms outstretched in greeting. The men grinned. Paulo hugged each in turn.

It was like watching a mime show. The boat's engines were still throbbing as if eager to be on their way. Derry couldn't hear a word the men were saying, but she didn't need to hear. Paulo, on his knees, quickly snapped open each of the cases, inspected the contents and closed it again. So much for trust and group hugs; Paulo was not about to sail away with four suitcases full of someone's dirty laundry.

So engrossed were the men in their business, and so confident they could not be observed from the road, that what happened next must have come as a profound shock. Down the curving road from the town high above screeched a purple van. It swept onto the jetty, skidding to a stop no more than twenty yards away. The three froze, gaping in disbelief but otherwise making no move.

Paulo was first to react. Slowly, almost imperceptibly, his right hand snaked under his jacket. The hope that had surged through Derry died instantly. What could Bruce do? Nothing, except get himself shot. Paulo was armed and perhaps so too was his accomplice on the boat's bridge. Derry had never thought of herself as a telepath—if she had abilities, they lay in a different direction—but now she was concentrating her thoughts so hard her head hurt. *Turn around now, Bruce. Go away! Don't get out of the van!*

The door of the van swung open. Out stepped Jacko.

With a single glance behind, Jacko marched purposefully towards the three men standing transfixed on the jetty. Could he see her through the tinted glass of the cabin window and the tangle of blinds? Probably not. In fact, far better if he didn't. Further up the road behind the van, beyond the small buildings at the jetty's far end, a white car was creeping down the hill. An innocent tourist or someone else? Derry thought of Fitz, and her heart leapt. Then Jacko made her forget how to breathe.

Jacko was striding towards the men on the jetty. His face bore an expression of lordly command as if obedience were a mere technicality. Only then did Derry understand what Jacko was doing. With a last glance backwards to the van and the road behind, he powered straight past the men, ignoring them, waving his arms and pointing at the boat. He was only yards away when Paulo and his henchmen woke up. Derry closed her eyes.

When Derry dared open her eyes again, Jacko was pinned to the ground by two of the men, wriggling and protesting his outrage. Beyond them, halfway between the van and the fracas, stood Bruce, his hands in the air. Derry closed her eyes once more. This time she kept them closed until she heard scuffling feet on the deck. The commotion was unmistakable—Jacko and Bruce were being bundled down the stairs and along the corridor outside to be locked into a cabin. Now came the sounds of far off grunting and thumps as heavy men's bodies crashed to the floor. Silence for several minutes, then footsteps once again passing by their own cabin door but this time confident and moving quickly, job done.

Doyle hopped backwards and lay on one of the beds. 'Bloody amateurs,' he said.

Beneath their feet, the deck rocked and bucked. Derry felt the sliding motion as the craft edged back from the jetty. Without warning, the engines screamed. The boat abruptly leaned over as the craft swept around in a high-speed turn that threw Derry and Doyle clean across the cabin.

The floor sloped at a crazy angle. The hull reverberated with rhythmic crashes. The boat leapt on the mighty river as if alive and racing for some glorious prize.

23

Derry sat on the bed, watching Doyle through the open bathroom door. He was leaning back awkwardly against the mirror above the sink, almost sitting in the washbasin. He was trying to use the corner of the mirror frame to saw though the tape around his wrists but was getting nowhere. Doyle slid down from his perch and hopped around the bathroom testing anything he could find resembling an edge. Nothing was remotely capable of cutting heavy tape. Every time the boat bounced on a wave in its headlong race, Doyle lost his footing. Still he wouldn't quit.

'Help me!' he ordered Derry. 'We have to break a shower screen.'

Around the shower was a gleaming glass stall, heavy and of the highest quality. What chance did anyone have of smashing such a thing? Derry scanned the cabin and bathroom looking for anything they could use as a battering ram or hammer. No chairs or stools. No lamp-stands. Nothing.

'You'll need to use your feet,' said Doyle impatiently, as if the required method for breaking a glass door should be obvious to the meanest intelligence. How they would afterwards get past a locked cabin door and two armed men, he wasn't saying. Then again, if Doyle were to be believed, their destination if they did nothing was the bottom of the river.

Doyle hopped out of the bathroom to make way for Derry. Derry positioned herself carefully, stood well back and prepared to kick.

Although Derry was female and, as a result, had failed to spend her school lunchtimes kicking vehicles or classmates, she *had* studied as an actress. In the cause of Art, she had taken intensive fight-training classes. Martial skills were important in case she should be required to play an FBI detective who single-handedly tracks down and arrests serial killers. At significant personal cost in bruises and sprains, Derry had learned karate chops, body rolls, somersaults and sword fighting. However, her instructor had taken pains to point out to the class that these particular karate chops were not in fact true karate chops, and the kicks, though impressive, had been devised for dramatic effect. He added the friendly recommendation that if members of the class were stopped in the street by a mugger they should immediately give him the money.

Although Derry had yet to audition for the role of a female FBI detective pursuing serial killers, she had learned an important fact from her classes. When you wish to kick something other than a football, you kick with a sideways motion, turning and shooting out the leg horizontally so the flat of the foot contacts the target. The result, hopefully, is more damage to the target than the foot.

Derry sighed. She carefully adjusted her balance, a challenge with hands tied behind her back, stood sideways-on to the glass door of the shower stall, and kicked as hard as she could.

For every action there is an equal and opposite reaction. So Mr. Newton had long ago insisted from under his apple tree. Now Derry discovered that Mr. Newton was spot-on. She shot backwards, colliding with Doyle who in turn stumbled and fell. Both lay entangled, breathing heavily. The shower door stayed where it was.

'Let me try again,' Derry gasped. She lined herself up for another kick, this time trying to keep Newton in mind. She was balancing herself, ready to launch a thrust she hoped would be simultaneously mighty but cautious, when the cabin door rattled and was roughly flung open.

If anyone had been standing behind they would have been slammed against the wall, but nobody was standing behind. Derry was poised on one leg in the bathroom. Doyle was lying on the floor just beyond the door's travel by inches. In the corridor, his gun in his hand, stood Paulo.

Paulo prodded Doyle in the ribs with his foot, ignoring Derry. 'Up,' he said.

Doyle obediently struggled to rise, pushing himself back onto the bed and to his feet. Paulo stepped back to stand in the cabin doorway out of reach. Obviously he had no intention of taking chances or of underestimating his enemy. A pity, thought Derry. The serial killers in FBI films always underestimate the female detective because she is a female, even though she can keep her makeup intact and her hair in perfect order. Disappointingly, Paulo wasn't underestimating Derry; he wasn't estimating her at all.

'What have you done with my father?' said Derry.

Paulo seemed to notice her presence for the first time. He cocked his head to one side and smiled.

'What have you done to Bruce?' asked Derry.

'Is he the gorilla who sniffs around after you like a little dog? If he is your lover, you must wish you had already said goodbye.'

'He is not my lover!'

Would it have been better to let Paulo believe Bruce was indeed her fiancée? Instinct told Derry no. Paulo might then hurt Bruce out of sheer spite.

'And your father is a pompous idiot,' said Paulo.

Why this should have outraged Derry the way it did, when she had known for most of her adult life that her father was indeed a pompous idiot, was a mystery. But Derry had never felt so angry. Her father had walked straight past armed men—seasoned criminals and thugs—to rescue his daughter. When Derry thought about that she felt a lump in her throat.

'My father,' said Derry, with as much dignity as she could summon, 'is a man.'

Paulo smiled tightly. 'You will see who is a man.' He turned to Doyle 'Out!'

Doyle obediently hopped from the cabin as Paulo stood well back.

'*You* will stay here,' Paulo ordered Derry. 'I may want my fortune told.' He grinned. 'I feel my future is good.' He slammed the door in Derry's face. The lock rattled.

Five minutes earlier, if anyone had said to Derry that she would miss Doyle's company, she would have laughed in their faces. Doyle was a man capable of anything. Most likely every word that came out of his mouth was a lie. But Derry had never in her life missed anybody as much as she now missed Peter Doyle.

Derry sat on the end of the bed. Her hands behind her back had lost almost all feeling. Could you get gangrene if the circulation was cut off for too long? Probably, thought Derry, then realised it took time to get gangrene—time she was unlikely to have.

Every fibre of Derry's being told her the same thing. Every cell in her body screamed, *Panic!* In her mind's eye she imagined throwing herself at the cabin door, kicking, yelling and sobbing. Why didn't she do just that? Perhaps because her father was somewhere close. Bruce too. Derry knew without a shadow of doubt that if they heard her scream they would be distraught, despairing at their inability to help. So she didn't panic, and she didn't scream and shout or throw herself at the door. But she couldn't bear to look at it either.

Overwhelmed by hopelessness, Derry let her gaze settle on the blue carpet of the cabin floor. The carpet was expensive but had no pattern, unless you counted a scatter of playing cards. Laying randomly at Derry's feet were the cards she had tucked into her jeans pocket when she had followed Doyle down the stairs. Oddly, they were mostly face down. What were the chances of that? Only six showed face up—two by the bathroom, the rest between the cabin door and her feet.

As Derry contemplated the upturned cards, her eyes drifting aimlessly, she was thinking of nothing at all. What was the point thinking anything?

If you stare at any image long enough, the picture will blur, drifting in and out of focus. The cards on the floor in front of Derry were now doing exactly that. As she looked, the pattern shimmered and floated as if the cards lay not on a deck covered in carpet but on the placid surface of a sheet of water.

A lake? A river? The sea? Whatever the glistening surface on which the cards lazily floated, the clear water beneath was deep and thick, like liquid crystal. The bottom was a blazing white carpet of smooth sand, the snowy floor empty of life. No fish swam; no crabs scuttled away; no fronds waved in whatever current there might have been.

The door rattled and swung open. Paulo stepped into the cabin.

'Stop!' said Derry, appalled. The upturned cards and the billion grains of sand at the bottom of the water were now rippling and fractured as though someone had stepped into a clear motionless pool and wantonly vandalised its beauty, carelessly destroying its priceless magic.

Paulo jumped back, clear out of the cabin as if in danger of treading on a mine. 'What?' he said, panic in his voice. He was staring at the cards.

And Derry saw a way.

'Ooooh!' she moaned, closing her eyes and swaying back and forth. 'I see!' she breathed. 'I see!'

'Stop this!' protested Paulo, clearly shaken.

Derry looked up, gazing calmly into Paulo's eyes. 'Why don't you come in,' she said wearily. She spoke like she had just woken from a trance and was already bored with the world of ordinary things.

'What do you see?' whispered Paulo.

'Perhaps your future is not for you,' said Derry. 'Only the cards can tell.' She paused, as though considering. 'Do you truly wish to know what it is they say?'

Paulo peered at the cards warily, as if they might fly up and whizz around the cabin to circle his head like a swarm of bees. He nodded.

'I need my hands,' said Derry.

'I will come back,' said Paulo. He stepped out, closing the door behind him.

Derry was disappointed to hear the lock turn. But such an easy success was too much to hope for. She returned her gaze to the floor. The water was gone. The cards lay forlorn, abandoned on the blue carpet where they had fallen. She stood and stepped to the window, nudging the blind aside. Shockingly, the bank of the river seemed miles away as the Shannon opened out into its wide Atlantic estuary. The sky was cloudy and the daylight was fading. What time was it? Without her phone, Derry had no idea, but it was long past eight o'clock. Nine? Nine thirty?

The cruiser's rhythmic surge had changed to the choppier, fretful motion of a boat at sea.

~

Paulo couldn't have gone far. He was back in a couple of minutes carrying a half-full bottle of whiskey and two glasses. His gun was tucked into his waistband.

'You are going to tell me everything,' he said, standing in the doorway. 'And I will tell you some things also. Perhaps we will be friends.'

Derry had no desire to be friends with Paulo. But she gave him what she hoped was her most enigmatic smile. She thought how hard enigmatic was to pull off at any time. Perhaps thinking of the Mona Lisa might help? Anything to give her facial muscles precisely the right amount of noncommittal.

'It is a game; I know that,' said Paulo. 'A game for old women. But you are good.' He said it as if complimenting an equal. He stood, his pose like a bullfighter, demonstrating how he, for one, was not an old woman, or a woman of any kind. Even so, Derry saw that when he stepped across the threshold and into the cabin to place the whiskey bottle and glasses on a shelf, he was careful not to stand on the cards. Instead, he picked his way between them like a kid avoiding the lines on the pavement.

'My hands,' said Derry.

Paulo took out a pocket knife. Derry twisted around, thrusting her arms out behind. Paulo cut. Derry gasped as pain shot through her fingers with the returning circulation. She rubbed her wrists, almost saying thanks out of sheer habit but catching herself just in time.

Paulo sat on the bed, uncomfortably close, so the cards were at their feet.

'We are going to have a nice time,' he said as though settling the debate. He considered Derry carefully, pointing to the cards. 'You are going to tell me about . . . this. Maybe I will ask you something.'

Derry didn't respond or acknowledge his little speech in any way. She knelt and collected the cards before sitting back on the bed as far from Paulo as she could get. The most distance she could achieve was barely a foot.

Derry shuffled the cards idly—relaxed, casual, the fluid motions of her hands betraying long experience. The cards flowed as if they had life of their own, and she saw that Paulo couldn't take his eyes from the pack. She kept shuffling, keeping the movement going as though juggling a magic trick.

'Now,' she said.

'Okay. It is good.'

'There is one thing.'

'What is that?'

'The cards never lie, but one cannot always know at once what they mean. Many things are not what they seem.'

'That thing, I understand,' said Paulo. He turned aside, took the bottle from the shelf and held out a glass to Derry. 'You will drink. Like I said, we have little party.'

'I am afraid the vision would grow cloudy,' answered Derry. She spoke as if with mild but genuine regret. Unbidden, a slight Eastern European accent had entered her speech, a mannerism she had noticed Madam Tulip sometimes indulge. She would need to be careful. Paulo was foreign and unlikely to detect hamminess as quickly as a native, but even Paulo might suspect Madam Blavatsky played by Zsa-Zsa Gabor.

'Later?' asked Derry, as if the Fortune-tellers' Guild had no rules forbidding whiskey-drinking once the future was safely told.

'Sure,' said Paulo, smirking. 'Later.' Paulo poured whiskey into a glass, sipped and replaced it and the bottle on the shelf. 'Tell me,' he said, 'I am curious. Do you read the future for yourself?'

'No. It is not permitted to us.'

'I am impressed,' said Paulo. Was he being sarcastic? It seemed not. His expression was thoughtful. 'If you are afraid of what you might see, that is proof you believe.'

Paulo might have been handsome in a Latin toyboy kind of way, thought Derry, but he was no bimbo. What he said was true. Only your belief stopped you peeking at your fate like you were playing a party game.

Derry sat back on the bed, crossing her legs in the lotus position. She held out her hands, palms outstretched. She closed her eyes. She breathed deeply and noisily through her nose. In an unexpected tribute to the power of yoga, Derry felt calmer almost at once. She was acting and had neglected her yoga for years, but it seemed to be working regardless. Her fears melted away. A blithe confidence took its place. But not so much that she didn't simultaneously think, *this is nuts.*

She dealt a spread of cards, face down, onto the bedspread beside her.

'I will test you,' said Paulo. 'If you know the future, you should be able to tell me the past. Who am I?'

Derry turned a card. She studied its face, then slowly turned another. 'I see . . .' she intoned, her voice a throaty whisper, 'I see a green place and a city.'

Paulo laughed. 'My pretty, you will have to do better than that or I will get bored.' He made it sound as though him being bored was something nobody would wish to witness.

Derry's expression didn't change. She saw clean through this arrogant upstart, this handsome man with the heart of a teenage psychopath and the ego of a four-year-old who would stamp his feet and break things if he didn't get what he wanted. This *taker*.

'In Bogota,' said Madam Tulip, 'was a girl, beautiful, dark.'

Paulo froze. His eyes flicked from Tulip's face to the upturned cards and back.

'Go on,' he said, his voice barely audible.

Derry looked up from the cards. In her own voice, dropping the persona of the fortune-teller, she said, 'There are things here I don't want to see.' She turned the cards so all were face down.

'Continue!' Paulo shouted. 'Now. I warn you!'

His intensity was terrifying. Here was a man capable of anything. So violent was his outburst that Derry should have recoiled against the cabin wall cringing. But she didn't. Although Derry O'Donnell, actress, might cringe, Madam Tulip would not. To Madam Tulip, all events were equal. All happenings were to be met with equanimity.

Even when Paulo's distorted features were only inches from her face, Derry neither flinched nor blinked. She had seen this man for what he was and would feel no fear, no revulsion, nothing at all. Paulo's fate was nothing to do with her or with anybody. His fate was fixed and lived in his soul.

Paulo leaned back and swallowed a shot of whiskey. 'Continue,' he said. Once more he was icy calm, the relaxed playboy who took nothing seriously as long as he got his way.

Derry turned over a card, then another. 'For what you have done,' she said, matter-of-factly, 'he will pursue you to the ends of the earth. He is in London.'

Paulo's mouth fell open. He slugged back half his whiskey in one gulp. Beads of sweat formed on his forehead.

'He is with . . . the King,' said Derry.

Derry had expected some kind of reaction, like when she had before chanced mentioning the King. But nothing like this. Paulo stood, breathing heavily, his face pale. Sweat dripped from his nose.

'You . . . are . . . a witch—'

He swayed once, then again. The boat gave an especially violent judder as it crashed through a wave, flinging Derry backwards. Paulo went down like his limbs had melted beneath him. He collapsed in a crumpled heap onto the bed, his head lolling over the end. His eyes rolled back in his head, then closed. His breath came in grunts.

Derry had been dumped in the gap between the two beds. She picked herself up. Paulo weakly moved an arm then let it fall back over his chest. Derry saw the cards still on the bedspread where she had left them. Could they have done this? Was it possible that some power had acted through the cards? *Insane.* But insane or not, this was real. And no time for philosophy.

Derry jumped off the bed, threw herself at the door and wrenched it open. Only then did she remember Paulo's accomplice. Presumably he was up on the bridge driving the boat, but he could just as easily be at the controls in the main cabin. Derry clicked the door closed behind her, frantically turning the key in the lock. Opposite was an open, rectangular space, a utility room with a washing machine and fridge, fire extinguisher and storage cupboards. Past that was another door, presumably a cabin, and at the end of the corridor, straight ahead, a door with more elaborate panelling, more impressive than the others. It had to be the master cabin.

Derry tiptoed down the passageway. In the lock of the master cabin was a key. She turned the key quietly, pushed the handle down and swung the door open.

'Oh,' said Marlene. 'It's you.'

24

Before Derry opened the door to the master cabin, she had imagined many competing scenarios. She pictured Doyle on the floor, trussed hand and foot. She saw Jacko and Bruce similarly bound, perhaps gagged as well to stop Jacko making speeches. The worst dread was seeing Marlene's body laid out, cold and dead. Even if Marlene were alive, she too would be bound, wearing the defeated, hopeless look of someone who knew her fate and feared the end was almost upon her.

Derry couldn't guess which of those scenarios would in fact greet her when she pushed open the cabin door, but of one thing she was certain—the captive occupants would be astonished to see her. The light of hope would flare up in their eyes as they recognised, not their enemy bent on their destruction, but their rescuer.

What Derry actually saw was as close to indifference as the cabin's occupants could have displayed without yawning and shuffling their feet.

'Hi, said Bruce. 'Good. Save us coming to get you.'

'Nearly there,' said Jacko. 'Your fiancée here is a fine lad. He'll sort things out, don't you worry. We have a plan.'

Jacko was lying back on the bed, legs crossed, hands behind his head, his wrists obviously unbound. For that matter, none of them had taped wrists or feet except Doyle, and he was bent forward stretching his arms out behind him to Marlene who was cutting the tape with nail scissors.

'There,' she said. 'I'm only doing this because Bruce says we need you. I'd prefer to cut your balls off.'

'No need to get personal,' said Doyle, rubbing his wrists.

Derry couldn't help feel that under the circumstances a little more interest might have been shown in her achievement. 'Paulo is unconscious,' she explained. 'I don't know what happened. He fainted.'

'Some people can't take sea voyages at any price,' observed Jacko. 'You'll have noticed the sea is where we're headed?'

'Um, yes,' said Derry, although as an explanation for what had happened to Paulo she felt seasickness was on the weaker side of no explanation at all.

Marlene sat up, smoothing her dress and arranging herself with the maximum elegance possible under the circumstances. 'He didn't drink whiskey by any chance?'

Doyle sniffed and inspected the cabin wall as though people fainting all of their own accord was an everyday occurrence, too tedious to get excited about.

'Matter of fact, he did,' answered Derry, surprised. 'Doesn't it agree with him? Whiskey has a funny effect on me, too.'

'Funny is right,' snapped Marlene. 'Didn't agree with me either when this bastard fed it to me. I was out for half an hour.' She kicked Doyle in the shoulder.

'Ow,' he said, rubbing the injured part half-heartedly, as if being kicked was his designated role for the day and he just had to put up with it.

'I should have left him tied up to be thrown overboard. Son of a bitch!' said Marlene, kicking him again. 'Fiend!'

'He said Paulo drugged you,' said Derry.

'Paulo wasn't even on the boat then! "Why not have a nice drink while you're waiting for Madam Whatsit to come," that's what this monster said.'

'Tulip,' corrected Derry.

'Whatever. Next I wake up, the rat is gone, and your friend Paulo is pointing a gun and telling me—'

'He's *not* my friend,' corrected Derry. Correcting factual inaccuracies seemed to be her assigned part in this conversation.

'—that my husband was planning to kill me because his boss told him to. And he'd already made a mess of it once. The boss said I was a liability—can you believe that? Jeez! If he knew what some of my friends were like! And Bruce says it's all true, and the swine was going to try again.'

'Boss? Did you say his boss?'

'Carlos Rey. I met him once, the sleazebag. Some kind of South American billionaire. Paulo claims he's his uncle. At least Paulo is out of the way now. That guy always gave me the creeps.'

'No doubt about it, Derry.' said Bruce. 'Him drinking drugged whiskey like that; y'all sure had some luck there.'

'Not *all* luck,' Derry pointed out. 'Okay, *some* luck, but before that I had to lull him into a false sense of—'

'He drank my whiskey and fell down,' said Marlene.

'Well, yes, I suppose he did—'

'Like I said, lucky,' said Bruce. 'Now, sit down and we'll tell you the plan.'

Derry sat, perched on the bed in what she now saw was a luxurious and impressively spacious cabin. They were all seated together, back to back, shoulder to shoulder. It occurred to Derry that the bed bore a strong resemblance to a famous picture, *The Wreck Of The* . . . something—a raft in a storm with a jumbled heap of shipwrecked sailors all crammed together. She hoped the thought was free association and not a premonition.

'First,' said Bruce, 'we were going to come and rescue you, break down that flimsy door. Now we don't have to—thanks by the way.'

'Don't mention it,' said Derry, pleased that at least some part of her achievement had been recognised, although being pleased was admittedly pathetic.

'Plan A,' continued Bruce, 'calls for Doyle to rush the boat's cockpit. This craft has dual controls, one set mounted on the bridge where the enemy has taken up his driving position and the other in the cockpit of the main saloon. Doyle knows how to switch control to the cockpit and seize the helm.'

'Helm?' asked Derry.

'Steering,' said Bruce. 'This action will cause the enemy on the bridge to leave his post and descend to the saloon. Meanwhile, Jacko . . . if you don't mind me calling you that, sir—'

'Not at all, dear boy. Fire away,' said Jacko with a gracious wave of his arm.

'Dad!' said Derry. In the heat of events she had almost forgotten how Jacko came to be captive in the first place. 'I saw what you did. I can't tell you much I admire that.' Derry felt a lump rise in her throat as she pictured his brave and determined face as he strode into a line of hostile armed men.

'Not at all,' said Jacko modestly. 'I simply demanded to see my daughter, exercising my paternal rights. Nearly got away with it too.' He grinned, as though getting shot would be no more than a temporary inconvenience.

'I,' continued Bruce, 'will rush with Doyle to the saloon. I will immediately engage the enemy with a fire extinguisher, several of which are conveniently located around this area of the craft. At the same time, Jacko will climb through the escape hatch hidden behind that screen.' He pointed at the bulkhead above the bed, and what appeared to be a small window covered by a blind.

'Won't it be locked?' asked Derry.

'It may be locked from the outside but, as Doyle has told us, for safety reasons escape hatches will always open from the inside. Paulo may not know it exists or may not care, since anyone emerging could be shot from the bridge.'

'Ah,' said Derry, feeling that in the matter of tactical insights she had little to contribute beyond moral support and a general can-do attitude. So far though, she had not been included in the script, and it wasn't at all clear what she would need a can-do attitude to do.

'While the enemy is descending the ladder into the saloon, Jacko will emerge from the escape hatch and distract him from behind.'

'But he could shoot Dad!' said Derry, 'Or you,' she added democratically. As the realities of Bruce's plan crystallised in her mind, Derry saw that against an armed man even three unarmed opponents would have little chance.

'True,' said Bruce, 'But Doyle here has explained that Paulo is almost certainly planning to rendezvous at sea and would never leave us as witnesses. He means to escape with a large quantity of drugs and send this boat to the bottom and us with it.'

To hear their fate spelled out so clearly was deeply shocking. To the bottom. Locked in a cabin. Down to the bright, white sand far below.

'You can see why a desperate plan is better than no plan at all.'

Derry nodded unable to think of anything to say.

'However,' said Bruce, beaming as if announcing the arrival of Santa Claus at a Christmas Party, 'things looked far more difficult before you arrived.'

Bruce smiled at Derry. Derry smiled back.

'Now, we don't have to worry about Paulo, and we'll have Paulo's gun. I'd better take that from you—wouldn't want it going off.' He held out his hand for the gun, allowing himself a grin hovering on the limits of condescension. His lips gave a little twitch, as if he were thinking *it's not because you're a female or even a civilian—you're a New Yorker, practically a European. And they don't know diddly about guns.*

Ignoring the potentially controversial question of guns, Derry chose to focus instead on the other thing.

'Door. You mentioned the cabin door? Where I was? When you were thinking of rescuing me?' Her tone was casual, relaxed. After all, no need for panic. 'Did you say it was . . . flimsy?'

'Sure,' said Bruce. 'Matchwood.'

Derry was appalled, but she was also impressed. Impressed, because matchwood was just what the splintering sound from the passageway outside sounded like. Two seconds later came the crash of their own cabin door slamming inwards.

The door bounced against the wall and came to rest. Paulo stood on the threshold. Part of Derry's brain calmly observed the new arrival, noting with interest how Paulo seemed smaller than before. That was because the gun in his hand—black and bluntly uncompromising—appeared way bigger than it could possibly have been in real life. The other part of Derry's brain, the larger and arguably more useful part, felt compelled to add its own observation, pointing out that this *was* real life. It felt further obliged to mention that soon, perhaps very soon, they were all certain to die.

'Not one word,' breathed Paulo. 'Not one.' His face was expressionless. 'I am going to lock this door. If I hear the handle rattle or any other attempt to open it, I will shoot through the door first and ask questions afterwards. Do you understand?'

Five heads nodded. The door closed. The lock clicked. Paulo was gone.

Derry looked at her four fellow captives perched on the vast bed. They should by now be screaming and shouting at her, accusing her of all kinds of stupidity. How could she have forgotten to take Paulo's gun? But nobody said anything. Jacko gave a little cough. Marlene made a sympathetic face, as if to say 'you win some you lose some.' Or possibly, 'what did we expect, a genius?'

'Plan A,' said Bruce.

'That's the plan where you and Dad rush the bad guys, right?' said Derry.

Bruce shrugged. 'Can't just sit here and wait.'

To that, Derry had no reply. No one in the cabin said anything more. The only sounds were the muffled roar of the engines and the regular crash as the boat crested a wave larger than the rest and slammed down into the trough. Perhaps it was that very lack of distracting conversation that meant they heard another sound, a distant buzzing as if a giant bee flew somewhere high in the sky overhead. The unmistakable sound of an aeroplane.

Like one person, all five bounced off the bed and in seconds had their noses pressed against the windows on both sides of the cabin. The sky was darkening and the moon had disappeared behind heavy cloud, but Derry saw the glint of reflected light on white wings. 'There!' she exclaimed. Five heads jostled at the window beside her.

'At least it's not a seaplane,' said Bruce. 'That would mean an enemy rendezvous right now. It's circling, though. Could be the cops.'

The transformation that came over the little group at the word *cops* was miraculous. 'Oh thank you, God,' breathed Marlene. She had never before struck Derry as being especially religious, but giving thanks was, after all, the way humans tried to grab a piece of luck and persuade it to stay.

'Don't get your hopes up too high,' said Bruce. 'He can't do anything from up there. And it's getting dark fast. Unless he's got some hi-tech gear, he'll lose us soon. Chances are he's just searching for illegal fishing boats. Let's face it, nobody knows to look for us.'

Horribly true. No one knew they were in any trouble at all. Would the guests waiting at the restaurant think there was anything strange about a supermodel being late for a surprise party? The shock would be if she turned up on time. Would Fitz suspect? Even if he did, why would he think of searching at sea? And did he have the authority anyway? He was an outsider, a guest on another force's territory. Almost a bystander.

The plane gave up its circling and drifted away, heading back towards the coast and disappearing in the murk. No one said anything, but they didn't have to. Their faces, as they turned away from the window told of their bitter disappointment.

Derry felt sick. Not the nausea of seasickness—despite the swell and the constant heaving of the boat none of them had been sick. Perhaps stark fear trumped the more humdrum ailments. Now only Derry was left peering out the window. She stayed where she was not because she had more hope than the others—she hadn't—but because she didn't want her father to see her face.

In the gathering dusk and against the black backdrop of the distant headland, Derry found it hard to make out anything. She focused her gaze on the water rather than the cloudy, moonless sky. The estuary of the river had opened out so wide they were effectively at sea, and the choppy swell was confusing to the eyes. But was that something white? In the distance, in the seaward direction, some bright object appeared and disappeared, glinting as it rose and fell.

'A boat!' Derry whispered. 'A boat!'

One thing was certain, this boat was no fishing trawler. The vessel was white and a cruiser like theirs, but many times the size. As Derry watched, the vessel grew visibly as it forged towards them. The others clustered around, Doyle pushing his way to the front.

'Anyone we know?' asked Derry, hoping her voice betrayed nothing of the dread she felt.

'Bastard,' said Doyle, his expression one of pure disgust. He sat back on the bed, lay down and closed his eyes.

'Do you recognise it?' insisted Derry.

'Sure,' said Doyle, still with his eyes closed as though he felt the world could be imagined a friendlier place if you didn't have to look at it. 'I wish I didn't, but I do.'

'Who is it?' asked Bruce.

'Rey,' said Doyle.

'It's like a cruise ship,' said Jacko, peering into the gloom. 'There's a few quid floating there, and no mistake. Who's Rey?'

'Paulo's uncle. The boss Marlene was talking about. Bad guy,' said Derry. 'Very bad.'

'Ah,' said Jacko. 'I hear a clock ticking.'

'Bruce,' said Derry. 'I'd like to join your Plan A.'

'Sure,' said Bruce casually. 'Why not?' He didn't say, 'No you're just a girl and you will certainly be shot.' Why say it when it was obviously true? Why say it when they had no choices left?

Bruce was businesslike as though briefing his men. Good, thought Derry. Act the part. At least we can pretend that what we do matters. Better than whining.

'We can't wait for the other boat to get close,' Bruce was saying. 'If we're going to try to seize control, we have to do it now while there's still a chance we could motor out of range. We don't know what kind of hardware they're carrying.'

Doyle coughed. 'I could speculate,' he said, 'if that were helpful?'

'Be my guest,' said Bruce.

'Machine pistols, at least. Some sniper rifles, possibly.'

'Rocket launchers?'

'Maybe. Not sure. I'm only . . . er . . . guessing.'

'That's it then,' said Bruce. 'We can't wait.'

Derry peered out the window into the dark. She could see the white of the approaching motor yacht flicker as the huge craft surged through the waves. It was still a great way off, but she didn't need to stare for long to see the distance between the boats was closing fast.

From behind Derry came the sound of sobbing. Marlene was hunched over, rocking back and forth. Her hands covered her face. She was weeping quietly as though she would never be able to stop. Derry couldn't find it in herself to feel contempt—hadn't Marlene more right to weep than any of them? No one else had discovered on their last day on earth that their spouse had tried to kill them. Then again, thought Derry, perhaps we should all be weeping, instead of planning something crazy. Maybe Marlene was the only one in touch with reality.

Derry observed each in turn. Bruce looked grim but completely calm. Impossible to believe this was a man who had panic attacks at the prospect of a three-line walk-on part in a provincial town hall. Jacko too, you might be forced to admire. He was leaning with his back against the cabin wall as if to be interested in the doings of armed drug runners in their yachts was beyond vulgar. Jacko had been known to remind anyone who would listen that at least five O'Donnells had been hung, drawn and quartered for rebellion.

Some, he insisted, had even deserved it. He would go on to point out with absolute but impossible certainty that no O'Donnell had ever been perturbed in the slightest degree by the idea of being killed horribly. Derry wondered if her father, with a gift of foresight like hers, might not have seen this coming. If he had, he had betrayed nothing. As for Doyle, he looked resigned to whatever lay in store as though he held his own fate in utter contempt.

'Jacko,' said Bruce. 'You stand by the escape hatch. Derry, when I bust open this door, you run for the little open room on the left with the washing machine. Snatch the fire extinguisher you see there. Let me and Doyle by, then bring it back and hand it through the hatch to Jacko as he climbs up.'

Was Bruce saving her from certain death by keeping her longest out of the fight, safe down here while the others faced the bad guys and their guns, armed with nothing but a fire extinguisher? How sweet, thought Derry. But how pointless.

'No,' said Derry. 'Marlene can do that.' Bruce studied Marlene for a moment. 'Marlene, can you do that? Did you hear?'

'Yes,' said Marlene, sniffing but pulling herself together to nod with a vigour she must have worked hard to summon.

Good girl, thought Derry. To Bruce, she said, 'I'll follow you.'

Bruce nodded. 'Action stations, guys.'

25

Derry took a deep breath. She stole one more glance out the window at the approaching cruiser. The craft was a powerful greyhound of a boat, almost a ship, the kind of mega-yacht owned by Russian oligarchs. The night was too dark to make out figures on the deck, but she imagined them waiting, ready with their machine guns and rifles. Would jumping in the water and taking her chance in the sea be the smartest move? Maybe—if she could stay alive long enough to get to the deck.

Just as Derry was bracing herself to face the final action, vowing she wouldn't let herself down, no matter what, the white yacht grew suddenly whiter.

'Look!' she called out. 'Look! Something's happening!'

Bruce raced to the window. 'Flare!'

Like someone had turned on a light-switch, every detail of the great yacht's superstructure was illuminated. Its several decks, its high pointed prow and tall bridge blazed white as did a hundred yards of the sea around. Then Derry saw why. Overhead hung a new star in the sky, the brightest light she had ever seen.

'Why would they do that?' asked Marlene. 'Can't they see us?'

'Another!' cried Bruce. You could hear the tremble of excitement in his voice. 'Look! They're changing course!'

Derry saw the white cruiser was sweeping around in a tight curve, showing its towering flank, its double tier of portholes, the helipad on its stern. The churning foam in the boat's wake showed blazing fluorescence in the flare's light as the yacht furiously accelerated.

Then they heard it. Unmistakeable. A dull *boom*.

'Two-inch gun,' said Bruce automatically.

'Am I right,' asked Jacko, 'that the drug running fraternity don't stretch to naval artillery?' He spoke casually, but you could hear the barely repressed excitement in his voice.

'And another flare!' said Derry, caring not at all that she was stating the very, very obvious. This flare seemed to be aimed at lighting their own boat as well.

Again, *boom*.

Bruce skipped to the other side of the cabin and peered into the darkness towards the barely discernible coastline. 'I see it,' he said. 'Navy ship!' He turned to Jacko, 'You guys have a navy?'

Jacko put on his haughtiest face. 'It's a deterrent to prevent you Americans opening any more hamburger joints in our poor benighted land. Useless against television, alas.'

If Derry had been able to think calmly, she might have reflected that in a situation like this, sooner or later someone was bound to say, 'We're saved!' That she didn't say it herself wasn't because she was especially slow on the uptake, but because her recent experience had taught her that *good* had a nasty habit of turning without warning into *not so good*. Marlene showed herself made of sterner stuff.

'We're saved!' Marlene wore the expression you see in Renaissance paintings on the faces of bright and shining angels ascending into heaven. The bright and shining angel turned to Doyle and scowled. 'You, mister, are in the deepest shit!'

Derry was thinking only of the white cruiser, the vessel almost certainly carrying one Carlos Rey. Would the King give up so easily? Would he abandon his faithful nephew and a fortune in drugs to the tender mercies of a Navy gunboat?

'Will they catch them?' asked Derry.

'Depends on how fast that Navy ship is,' said Bruce. 'Looks like an old coastal patrol boat to me. They'd catch us alright, but I don't know about the big yacht. And they can't chase us both. This is going to get interesting.'

Interesting wasn't the first word that came to Derry's mind as she peered into the darkness trying to make out their rescuer. Then again, maybe things *were* getting interesting. The surging motion of their own boat as it drove through the swell had eased. The whole motion of the craft had changed. Now they wallowed in the troughs and peaks.

'Are we stopping? Are they giving up?' asked Derry of nobody in particular. Out of the corner of her eye she saw Doyle smile grimly and shake his head.

'The inflatable,' said Bruce, quietly. He was intent, concentrated. 'They're going to try and catch the yacht.'

'Can they do it?'

'Maybe. That's a big motor they've got. I remember thinking it was over the top for a river boat.'

'Oh no,' said Derry. 'Oh no!' The thought had barely formed but was inescapable. Premonition or logic? It hardly mattered. Derry knew with absolute certainty what was going to happen now.

'Paulo—he has to slow the Navy down. If he's to get away, catch that yacht, he has to stop the gunboat following.' Bruce's face mirrored her fears exactly. It was left to Derry to say it out loud. 'Paulo *has* to sink us. Right now.'

'Bruce, do you need two people to launch an inflatable?' Her question hung in the air. If Paulo and his henchman had to leave the bridge unoccupied, neither man would be able to watch the escape hatch. The answer came from far behind, faint but unmistakeable as the inflatable's powerful engine burst into life, roaring and gurgling. At least one man was tending that engine. And the other? The answer came not as a sound, but as a smell—the acrid, eye-watering smell of gasoline. And it was coming from under their cabin door.

'Jacko, the hatch! Go!' shouted Bruce. 'Doyle, when the door goes down, stay right behind me.'

Doyle made no move to follow. He sat on the bed shaking his head.

'Coward!' screamed Marlene.

Jacko was shrugging off his long green coat, preparing to climb through the escape hatch. Derry moved quickly. She jumped on the bed, stood upright facing the wall above the headboard and ripped aside the blind to reveal the square steel hatch with its bright-red handle. She yanked on the lever and pushed, telling herself *go slow*.

'Hey!' Jacko was shouting and gesticulating, but Derry ignored him. She remembered to control her nerves, took a breath and eased the hatch slowly open. Her eyes took a moment to adjust to the eerie half-dark and the glow of the flares. The fresh, blustery wind was cold in her face, a shock after so many hours cooped up below. With the hatch open no more than six inches, Derry peered around the deck like a submarine captain in a movie scanning the horizon through his periscope. The huge bulk of the white yacht was powering away, racing for the open Atlantic. The grey hull of the naval vessel was nearer, its side high above the water but, as Bruce had guessed, it was a much smaller boat than Rey's mega-yacht. And although the Navy ship's gun was pointing at the gleaming hull of the cruiser, it didn't fire.

Derry had a clear view forward, but to see back to the stern of their own boat she would have to open the hatch all the way and push her head and shoulders through. If Paulo or his henchman were on the bridge above, she would invite being shot in the head. But how else was she to find out if the way was clear? She muttered a prayer, failing to address it to anyone in particular, and folded the hatch back onto the deck.

Nothing happened. No shot rang out. No one shouted a warning. The bridge was deserted. Both men must be at the stern, hidden by the superstructure, perhaps this very minute boarding the inflatable for their escape. Derry dropped back down through the hatch, bouncing on the bed.

'It's clear. Nobody up above! Dad, up you go. Be careful not to be seen just yet! Marlene, you go behind.'

'Derry!' shouted Bruce, 'Grab the fire extinguisher and follow me. If it goes bad, into the water everybody, okay? Whatever they're going to do, it's gonna be soon. Now . . . Go!'

Bruce's leg shot sideways in a mighty, explosive kick. His foot slammed into the door just below the lock. The effect was spectacular—as if Newton had stepped out for a coffee, suspending his famous law for the duration. The door splintered clean off its hinges, swinging drunkenly into the passageway. The reek of gasoline became an all-enveloping stench, making Derry's eyes water and her throat rasp. The taste was horrible.

As Bruce crept warily forward, Derry tucked in behind. Bruce signalled she should slip into the alcove as they went past. She did as she was told, grabbing the fire extinguisher from beside the washing machine. The idea had been to use it as a weapon, but with every inch of the carpet beneath their feet soaked in gasoline, Derry realised she might easily end up using the extinguisher the way its makers intended. Not too effective though when the slightest spark would turn the boat instantly into a fireball.

Cradling the extinguisher in her arms, Derry crept forward in Bruce's wake. As they reached the base of the stairs leading up to the saloon, Derry was close behind, so close she wondered was it wise. Hadn't she read somewhere how a single bullet could go clean through two people? Probably bad tactics. On the other hand, so much less lonely.

Bruce limbed the stair one step at a time. Derry handed up the extinguisher. Bruce took the canister, pointing it ahead of him like some weird red ray gun. The stairway was steep, and Derry was following so close on Bruce's heels that when he reached the top and stopped she could peer past his legs. Now she saw why he had so abruptly halted his climb and stood motionless. At the back of the saloon, in front of the open sliding doors leading onto the rear deck, was Paulo. His gun was pointed at Bruce's chest.

Behind Paulo, the afterdeck was empty—the space no longer occupied by the inflatable speedboat, which now rode the water behind. The craft bucked on the heavy swell, hard against the stern of the cruiser. Paulo's accomplice sat by the motor gunning the engine to keep the inflatable in position. In front of him sat a pile of suitcases held down by netting. He roared something unintelligible in Spanish, but his meaning was clear. Paulo was to quit stalling and do whatever he meant to do, right now.

Paulo ignored his companion's shouts. He raised his gun to aim squarely at Bruce's heart. Standing no more than twenty feet away, if he pulled the trigger he could hardly miss.

Bruce in turn raised the nozzle of the extinguisher, pointing it directly at Paulo's face.

Paulo smiled broadly as though he appreciated the boldness of the gesture. 'You can't be serious,' he said. He nodded towards Derry, 'And you, witch. You know what they do to witches.'

'Did,' said Derry. 'Out of fashion.'

'I had thought of reviving that fine tradition. But lucky for you, I gave up smoking. No matches.' Paulo laughed raucously as if this were the funniest thing that had ever happened to him.

'If you shoot, you'll blow us all up. You too,' said Bruce. His voice was relaxed, lazy, like he had all the time in the world.

'I am not stupid,' said Paulo. 'Perhaps you are not stupid either. If you stay where you are and do nothing foolish, I will leave you to your fiancée. And good luck with that.'

In three strides, Paulo was out through the double doors. He sprang from the afterdeck into the inflatable. As his feet hit the floor of the boat, his companion manning the engine was already powering the craft backwards. Now he held the inflatable in position no more than ten yards astern. Paulo stood, raising his right arm. He had something in his hand.

'No!' shouted Bruce. In one blindingly quick movement he flung the fire extinguisher aside and raced forward, diving across the saloon to the grab the door-handle with both hands. He hauled with all his weight.

Was it the sudden lurch as the crest of a wave lifted the boat higher? Or the speed and force with which Bruce slammed the sliding door across like a shot-putter heaving from the shoulder? Whatever the reason, as Paulo's hand vanished in a puff of white smoke, the flare slammed into the half-closed saloon door. The blazing projectile bounced back onto the stern deck, fizzing a blinding, flickering red.

The flare blazed, but only the flare. Paulo must have failed to pour his gasoline onto the outside deck, reserving it for the saloon and the passageway below. Derry's reaction was pure instinct—no reasoning, no planning, no thought for the consequences. She snatched up the discarded fire extinguisher and raced through the saloon, through the half-open doors and outside onto the deck, pulling the handle as she went. As she directed the stream of white powder at the sizzling, smoking object in front of her, the sound of the inflatable's engine screaming as it powered away made her look up.

At precisely that moment, Paulo turned back to stare. His eyes were locked on hers, his face a mask of anger, frustration and the purest, blazing hatred.

As the gloom and spray swallowed the speeding craft, Derry's whole body began to shake.

Sailors are cute. The thought came to Derry unbidden as she was helped into a wallowing rescue boat. The four sailors wore blue helmets and flak jackets. Two carried machine pistols. On their chests the legend 'Navy' was spelled out in bold letters—somewhat unnecessarily, Derry couldn't help thinking, as she was led to a low seat and a lifejacket was strapped around her.

The Navy ship was stationary, standing off at least fifty yards, its searchlights trained on the rescue boat and the silent cruiser. Paulo's fleeing speedboat and the big white yacht had disappeared into the gloom. Derry was puzzled to see the Navy making no attempt to pursue.

Bruce was standing on the cruiser's deck, handing Marlene over the side into the arms of beaming sailors more used to rescuing grizzled trawlermen than supermodels gushing their thanks and fluttering their eyelashes. Jacko was concentrating so hard on appearing nonchalant that he mistimed his jump, tripped and fell in a crumpled, swearing heap into the rescue boat, though still trying to look dignified.

'You say there's another?' shouted one of the sailors, clambering onto the deck beside Bruce. The door of the saloon slid fully open to reveal Doyle standing motionless. 'Hey, come on!' shouted the sailor as Doyle made no move to step out. Instead, he contemplated the rescue boat with its cargo of armed men and dishevelled passengers. His gaze lingered on Marlene as though he were about to speak but thought better of it. Instead, his eyes were fixed on Derry. He shrugged as if to say, *see how ridiculous fate can be.*

Marlene broke the spell.

'Come on, won't you! For goodness' sake!'

Doyle ignored her. He backed two steps into the saloon, all the while looking at Derry. He extended his right hand to point behind him into the blackness of the cabin. 'Go! Leave me!' His voice was a scream, as if a madness was emerging into the night.

Bruce was first to snap out of the trance. He grabbed the sailor beside him by the shoulders, heaving both of them bodily off the cruiser's deck and into the rescue boat.

'Cast off! Go! Go!'

The craft surged back in a mad gurgling roar, bow lifting crazily as it swung around, powering away from the yacht in an earsplitting torrent of sound.

So fast did everything happen—Doyle pointing his arm behind, Bruce and the sailor leaping from the cruiser's deck into the rescue boat, the craft twisting and surging away—that the explosion when it came seemed to happen in slow motion. Through the glass doors of the cruiser's saloon blossomed a bright-red glow. Against the hellish bloom of the magnesium flare stood silhouetted the motionless figure of Peter Doyle. Seconds later, slow seconds in which Derry's mind refused to contemplate the inevitable, the rolling crimson glare was laced with a creeping yellow so bright that the squinting eye could make out nothing beyond a racing, all-enveloping sheet of flame.

The explosion sent a wall of sound and a blast of hot air streaking across the water to their speeding boat. All around Derry, shocked faces were plainly visible in the fiery glow that lit the sea for a hundred yards. Even the sailors seemed stunned. Most horrifying of all was Marlene's scream, an unearthly howl, keening out over the water as though she were calling back the dead.

Derry screwed her eyes tightly shut. She felt herself give way to violent tremors she had no hope of controlling. But then, out of the darkness, came an arm around her shoulder and the unmistakable, priceless feel of her father's bulk hugging her like he would never let her go.

26

The captain of the Navy ship was a friendly, efficient woman. She snapped out a stream of no-nonsense commands to her crew while clucking over her new charges, ordering them below decks to be checked by the medic. Marlene was dazed and silent. Bruce snapped a salute and said, 'Aye-aye, Ma'am,' before remembering he was a civilian. Even Jacko obeyed without question. But Derry lingered.

'Please don't think we're not grateful,' she began. 'But shouldn't we be chasing that yacht? Or the speedboat with the drugs?'

Derry and the captain stood side by side at the rail, peering into the dark. You could still make out the faint lights of the fleeing yacht. The Navy ship's searchlight illuminated the smouldering, still flickering area of sea where the cruiser or what remained of the cruiser listed, black and smoking in the swell. The rescue boat was already returning to the scene, and Derry didn't dare think about what it was they were hoping to find.

The captain shook her head. 'Our first responsibility is to search here in case Mr. Doyle survived. We can't leave while there's that chance. Anyhow, that big yacht can do twice our speed. They'd be out of territorial waters long before we could catch them.'

She saw Derry's look of intense frustration. 'Maybe if the powers-that-be had known it was a drugs bust they'd have sent a bigger, faster ship. But we were in the neighbourhood. Or would you have preferred to wait?' She smiled.

'No. You showing up was a miracle.'

'I agree,' she said, amused. 'I tend to think it's a miracle whenever our orders make any kind of sense whatsoever.' She paused, a twinkle in her eye. 'I never said that.'

'Can't you make them stop?' said Derry. She nodded towards the ship's big gun, impressive but mute. 'Those people are drug smugglers and kidnappers. They'd have killed us.'

'I'm sorry. This is the West of Ireland not the Wild West. We have no proof the yacht has done anything wrong except refuse to stop. They'd plead their radio broke down, and the drugs would go over the side long before we caught up with them. In this game you catch smugglers red-handed or you don't catch them.' She pointed to where the rescue boat wallowed stationary in the heaving water, its searchlight trained on something. 'Looks like they've found him.'

Derry was thankful for the darkness.

As the ship ploughed its way upriver to dock in Limerick city, Derry tried to grab some sleep on a narrow claustrophobic bunk. Her dreams were an insane montage of flames, frogs and the tumbling hooves of a lucky escape.

They docked at four a.m. by a deserted jetty deep inside a windswept harbour flanked by cranes and warehouses. The ship's arrival attracted little attention, but as Derry, Marlene, Jacko and Bruce stumbled down the gangway onto the eerily quiet quayside, a reception committee of sorts did await them. At the door to a shabby office block, a little group stood expectantly—two uniformed police officers and three civilians. One of the civilians, a man in an elegant tailored raincoat, was leaning casually against the wall, his hands in his pockets. He smiled at Derry, stood up straight and ambled towards her.

'I hear you've had a lively time,' said Fitz. 'Still, all's well that ends well. The good people here will need to talk to you all for a little while. Why don't we get that part over with?'

The little party of survivors was led inside to sit at scattered tables, each person facing an officer. Opposite Derry was a male detective, quietly spoken and polite. A voice recorder sat on the table between them, its light blinking red.

Fitz asked no questions. Derry couldn't make out what his role was or if he had any official role at all. But at least his presence meant she didn't have to tell her story from the beginning, only from when she had arrived at Peter Doyle's stud farm. She finished her account in fifteen minutes, hurried on by a pressing need to ask her own questions. A million *whys* and *hows* were queuing in her mind jostling to come out. One question trumped all the others.

'How did the Navy find us? How did they know where we were or that we were in trouble?'

The detective smiled broadly and looked over at Fitz, raising an eyebrow as if to say, *better you handle this one.* What was so amusing?

Fitz shifted uncomfortably in his seat. 'That,' he said, 'was your mother.'

If Fitz had said that the Navy had been alerted by a phone call from aliens hovering in a flying saucer over Dublin City Centre, Derry would have been less surprised. She opened her mouth and closed it again, unable to hide her astonishment.

'It seems your mother phoned the police in Limerick, and when she mentioned Doyle they automatically red-flagged that and called me. Why she phoned in the first place, I haven't the faintest. Nor do I know how she knew where you were. Perhaps you should ask her yourself when you see her. I'd rather leave that to you, if

282

you don't mind.' Was he remembering the two occasions, back when he and Derry were an item, when he had met her mother?

'What I *can* tell you,' continued Fitz, 'is what we believe was going on at Peter Doyle's stud farm and perhaps why things panned out as they did.' He turned to the detective. 'That alright with you?' The detective nodded.

Derry listened as Fitz, in his economical way, recounted what he knew.

'In London, amongst many other places, was a Colombian called Carlos Rey—'

'The King,' said Derry.

Fitz' surprise was obvious.

'A guess,' Derry added and shrugged

'Rey was bringing hundreds of millions of pounds worth of cocaine into Europe from Colombia. We suspected him of leading a ruthless and powerful cartel operating world-wide, but we had almost no evidence against him. After consignments of drugs were landed in Ireland, the next part was to get them into Britain and across Europe. Which is where Peter Doyle came in.'

'Nobody wants to distress a million pound horse with sniffer dogs and inspections,' said Derry.

Fitz looked put out, as though someone had taken away his soapbox just as he was about to make a speech. 'Look here,' he said, 'is there any point me going on? You seem to know everything already.'

'Sorry,' said Derry.

Fitz gave a sniff but continued. 'We believe they were transhipping massive quantities of drugs through Doyle's bloodstock exports. And they used the business to move large sums of money around the world without attracting attention. Who is to say what a horse is or isn't worth?'

'What about Paulo?'

'Paulo is Rey's nephew and probable heir in waiting. A dangerous man—perhaps a psychopath; perhaps just very, very bad.'

Derry shivered. She felt sweat break out on her palms at the memory.

'Indeed,' said Fitz quietly, as though he knew what she was thinking. Derry felt his sympathy like a warm overcoat softly draped over her shoulders. She remembered now how Fitz, beneath his casual exterior, could be truly perceptive.

'We think,' Fitz went on, 'that Paulo was forced on Doyle by Rey to keep an eye on his interests. He played the driver-bodyguard. In reality, he ran the show. Doyle's original business had run into big financial problems. Rey pumped in cash to put it back on its feet but without taking an official share. He was the real owner alright, we just couldn't prove it. Doyle did what he was told.

Derry thought about Doyle and his air of wealthy success. She had more than once been reminded of an actor playing a part. 'Why did they turn against him if his business was so valuable to them? I don't understand.'

'Neither do we. And to be honest, as the football fraternity might say, we're gutted. Rey was the one we were after. We thought we could get the evidence through Doyle. Until . . . everything went off the rails.'

Derry knew what Fitz meant—until she, some silly woman, had stuck her oar in uninvited. 'He was going to kill Marlene.'

Fitz sighed. 'I'm not sure I like to admit it, but in that you were correct.'

'Frog venom?'

'Yes. The lab would never have thought to test for such an obscure toxin if we hadn't asked.'

'Will Bella be alright now?'

'Of course. There's no doubt about what happened.'

Derry thought for a second. 'There's something else I don't understand. Doyle sedated Marlene so he could leave the boat and get out of the picture. But if she was unconscious, how was she supposed to take the poisoned coke?'

'We think he meant to make her inhale the powder from a plastic bag held over her face. She would have had no choice but to breathe in. The autopsy would then show the required traces of cocaine.'

Derry fought hard not to picture the terrible scene Fitz had described. 'How do you know . . . about the plastic bag?' Derry needed the answer or images of the ghastly death planned for Marlene would torment her in her sleep as her unconscious mind tried to piece together the puzzle.

'Perhaps we can come back to that later?' said Fitz, looking evasive. 'Do you mind awfully?'

'I do mind awfully. How do you know? They found him, I saw that.'

'Yes . . . Most of him. Just the torso, I'm afraid.' He looked away. 'They didn't manage to find the . . . other part. But it's him alright.'

The other part. That other part Derry had seen so long ago. Doyle's disembodied head in the lap of the King. Horrible.

'Are you quite alright?' asked Fitz, alarmed.

Derry gripped the edge of the table to steady herself. 'I'm fine, thank you.' She forced her thoughts back into order. 'The plastic bag. How did you know?'

'In his jacket pocket we found a sealed packet of cocaine. I'm guessing toxicology will confirm it was poisoned. And two large, unused plastic bags.'

The detective sitting beside Fitz shook his head mournfully as if to ask was there no limit to human wickedness.

'As you discovered, Marlene was about to divorce Doyle. He must have gotten wind of her plan. In Ireland, a judge would award her half the business. Worst of all for Doyle, his assets would come under the microscope of a legal battle.'

'And the assets belonged to Rey.'

'Precisely. From what we know of Rey, it's easy to imagine him insisting Doyle deal with his wife or suffer the consequences. Rey would happily provide the means.'

Derry thought about the picture Fitz had painted—Doyle dominated by a ruthless and powerful boss with the ability to enforce his will anywhere, at any time. 'It's not enough,' she said. 'There's more.'

'Not sure we need any more,' said Fitz. 'Motive. Opportunity. Means.'

'I don't mean a court case. All you've said isn't enough reason for a man to kill his wife. Or himself.'

'I disagree. All it takes for a man to kill himself is that he fears living more than he fears death. To a man like Rey, failure is unforgiveable. Doyle wouldn't have survived a month in prison. Rey's revenge would reach him in any jail in Europe.'

Derry thought about that. 'More than fear made him want to kill his wife,' she said quietly. 'She embarrassed him.'

Fitz gave a sharp bark of a laugh, making every head in the room turn. 'Imagine if every husband or wife killed their embarrassing spouse. We'd have a massacre.'

'I saw it,' insisted Derry. 'He found her coke habit and her drinking intolerable. And other things. The way she manipulated him. Used him. He found the sight of her revolting.'

Fitz wasn't convinced. Or perhaps he wasn't interested. 'Be that as it may, the really big question is why Paulo made his move when he did? Why not let things play out? My guess is that Doyle, by trying to kill his wife a second time after botching the job first time out, risked making the whole situation worse. What if he got caught? Attract undue attention and you might as well shut up shop.'

'And something else,' said Derry, her voice low.

'And what might that be?' asked Fitz, seemingly unconvinced that much more could be deduced, and certainly not by an amateur.

'Excuse me,' said Derry to the detective. 'Would you mind if I had a word alone with . . . Mr. Gilbey-Jones. Just for a minute. Thank you.'

Graciously enough, the detective stood, leaving them alone.

'I'm sure nothing is so private that you can't share it with my colleague,' said Fitz, frowning. Was he afraid of reviving their old intimacy? *To hell with him if he was*, thought Derry. She knew she was right to want to say this privately.

'So?' asked Fitz.

'You wondered why Paulo made his move, why he grabbed the cocaine and ran? I think I know.'

'Why is that?' asked Fitz. He spoke coolly now, formally.

'They knew about you.'

Fitz' face turned chalky white. He swallowed, then took a deep breath as if he had only just remembered how. He collected himself, feigning a relaxed pose, crossing his arms and leaning back. Derry knew he was faking. Overacting was always the giveaway.

'Paulo said Doyle was a fool who should have chosen his friends more carefully,' continued Derry. 'Doyle said an acquaintance of his, an English gentleman, had turned out to be some kind of policeman.'

Only after she said it out loud did Derry grasp the full meaning of her own deduction. If she hadn't appeared on the scene as Madam Tulip, disrupting Doyle's neat plan to kill Marlene at the castle, how long before Fitz was found buried in a bog? Perhaps he would never have been found.

'I'll admit I didn't exactly welcome your intervention,' said Fitz.

'I did it for Marlene.'

'I may be in your debt,' said Fitz. 'Thank you.'

For a long moment they sat facing each other in silence.

'Don't mention it,' said Derry.

The police interviews over, they gathered in the reception area. Quite a crowd—Derry, Jacko, Marlene, Fitz, the police—even the sailor from the rescue boat, now deep in conversation with Bruce. Derry smiled to herself. Mutual interest in military matters or something more social?

They were to be ferried in police cars to a good hotel outside the city where they would stay overnight to recuperate. They needed time to absorb what had happened, to get used to the idea they were still alive. To get used to the idea that one of their number was dead.

Derry watched as Fitz took command of the transport arrangements while cleverly seeming not to. Ever the diplomat. Ever the one in control. Or at least he *was* in control until the front door burst open and the policemen, Fitz, Bruce and his new friend were all swept aside with the force of a tsunami.

'Darling!' wailed Vanessa. 'Oh my poor sweet!' She rushed across the hall arms outstretched, designer bag flailing. Behind her, standing awkwardly as if some things were just not worth the pay packet, was Mr. Sideburns. With a jolt, Derry recognised the red-faced man from the parking fracas outside her flat. She had no time to wonder what he was doing here as she was swept up into the irresistible embrace of her mother.

'Who would have thought that an ordinary girl could have inspired such passion!' demanded Vanessa of the room at large, 'Kidnapped! Carried off to sea!'

She stepped back, inspecting Derry closely. 'Was it too, too awful?'

'I'm fine, Mom,' said Derry. 'Honest. All okay now.'

Vanessa looked her daughter up and down, as if taking in Derry's chain store jeans and top, her wildly disarranged hair and the four or five pounds recently returned in spite of Derry's best attempts to avoid the cookie jar. Derry was acutely aware that the whole room was staring in bemused fascination. 'I will never, ever, understand men,' said Vanessa.

Her gaze alighted on Jacko. 'Jack!'

Jacko stood, sheltering as best he could behind the towering bulk of Bruce and his friend. But evasion was impossible; this time there could be no escape. Bruce and friend treacherously parted like the waters of the proverbial Red Sea, leaving Jacko to his fate.

'A hero!' announced Vanessa in the dramatic voice she deployed when hosting awards for lifetime achievement in the Arts. She gazed soulfully into Jacko's astonished eyes. 'I saw what you did! Down below us, too far for Mr. Wallis to intervene, we watched as you faced those men in defence of our darling daughter. You didn't see us, but I saw what they did to you. Monstrous!'

Vanessa seized Jacko's arm, beckoning to Derry to join them. Flanked by heroic daughter and even more heroic ex-husband,

Vanessa offered her best profile, adopting for the camera her most entrepreneurial expression. The flash of a camera illuminated the tableau as Mr. Sideburns took the picture. As if on cue, the whole room burst into spontaneous applause. More flashes, and Derry had no doubt that within an hour her mother's Twitter and Facebook accounts would throb with an epic story of survival against the odds. Her heart sank as it dawned on her that those same photos, liberally sprinkled all over cyberspace, would follow her around for the rest of her life.

27

That every one of the rescued party woke in their luxury hotel room to a full change of clothes and a range of expensive toiletries was a tribute to Vanessa's impressive powers of organisation and the pedigree of her Platinum Amex. Who knew how Vanessa had discovered everybody's size? But she had. And who knew how she had contrived to keep the press away, at least for the time being? But she had managed that too.

Fresh clothes weren't the only surprise to greet Derry. At noon, she was awakened by the ringing of the phone beside her bed. She had to take a moment to gather her wits and work out where she was.

'Hello. Derry.'

'It's me! Bella!'

'Bella! Where are you? How are you?'

'I'm home. They let me out! They said it was all sorted or would be. Janice turned up to collect me. Get this—she drove me home in a limo and she's taking me for a posh lunch later! Says she's a friend of a friend of yours.'

Derry had to take a breath before she spoke. Friend? Not exactly. 'That's terrific. She's . . . nice.'

'She says you've had adventures.'

'I'll tell you everything when I see you.'

'Well it won't be tonight,' said Bella. 'Tonight, I am eating the biggest pizza I can find, and I am doing it in my own bed. I am watching TV. I am drinking alcohol. I may or may not be alone.'

Derry laughed. 'Hey, I've lost my phone, I'll get sorted tomorrow and call you, okay?'

'Say No to Negativity,' said Bella, and she rang off.

Late in the afternoon Derry got her first chance to speak to her father alone. Vanessa was still in bed in the hotel's finest suite. Derry was sitting by herself in the deserted dining-room nursing a coffee and thinking nothing at all when Jacko stuck his head around the door and joined her. He looked sheepish but pleased with himself. Lunches had long since ended, but Jacko ordered most of whatever the chef had left and sat ladling beef into his mouth with infinite satisfaction. Derry felt unaccountably peaceful as if time had expanded until the requirement to do anything whatsoever had shrunk to a tiny speck and vanished. Her gaze lingered on the groomed hedges and ornamental trees beyond the hotel's French windows. A male pheasant glistening in full colour strutted across the lawn.

'Dad,' said Derry.

'Apple of my eye?' said Jacko.

'How come you followed me to the boat in Bruce's van? You were supposed to be taking the Jag to Limerick.'

Jacko shifted uneasily in his seat. 'A little mechanical bother,' he admitted. 'Car wouldn't start. No idea why. Then that fiancée of yours says get in, and away we go chasing down the lane after you.' He sighed. 'Reminds me, I need to organise a tow.'

'He is *not* my fiancée.'

'Oh,' said Jacko. 'Never mind, you'll make it up. That English fellow, running interference is he? Can't advise you there. D'ye know he looks familiar? Can't place him for the life of me.'

'No and no,' said Derry. 'No fiancée. Never was.' After a moment, she added, 'No Englishman either.'

'Talking of the ties that bind,' said Jacko, 'I may have misjudged your mother.'

'I'm glad to hear that,' said Derry, surprised but willing to believe that perhaps the trauma of the last hours had caused Jacko to take a more balanced view. 'You two really should talk things over.'

'I had her down as uncompromising, legalistic, literal-minded, Machiavellian and shallow,' continued Jacko. 'I now add relentless to the point of obsession.'

So much for balance. 'Come on, Dad! How can someone be both Machiavellian and shallow?'

'Did I mention the little matter of the signatures?' Jacko studied the pheasant through the window as if he had just noticed a long extinct species of small dinosaur casually strolling across the lawn and found the sight fascinating, though not a surprise.

'As in writing one's name with a pen?' asked Derry.

'Not exactly,' answered Jacko, avoiding Derry's eye. 'D'ye see, the mere agent has no understanding of the concept of artistic freedom.'

The agent in question was Vanessa, and she had the exclusive rights to sell all Jacko's work.

'The *agent* talks brands, products, commodities,' said Jacko. He shook his head sorrowfully as if announcing the death of civilisation. 'But not the true *collector*. Oh no! The man or woman of culture cares not a whit how the artist signs his pictures.'

'You sold pictures on the side,' said Derry. 'Don't tell me, you signed as somebody else.' A moment's reflection told Derry her suggestion couldn't possibly be true. Jacko's ego could never be subsumed in an alias. She was correct.

'Certainly not!' said Jacko. 'My patrons have no doubt that in ten years' time, everybody will be fully aware who painted those pictures. Initials are perfectly valid as symbols or glyphs of identity.'

'Initials! Dad, you forged your own paintings!'

Jack returned to studying the dinosaur on the lawn. '*That* is an ontological impossibility,' he replied complacently. 'And hardly justifies your mother hiring a private detective to pursue me with legal injunctions. Sledgehammer. Nut.'

So that was Mr. Sideburns. And that was why he was hanging around outside her flat. He was dogging Jacko's every step.

'After you'd sailed off to who-knows-where, we drove back up to the stud and there was your mother in the car-park glaring at the Jag. All Bruce wanted was to chase your boat, so we did. Your mother and her bloodhound followed us.'

'Dad, if they hadn't followed you, with or without an injunction, we'd all be dead. It was they who called the police.'

'Just as well I did sell a few pictures then, even if they were initialled,' said Jacko, in one swoop taking full credit for their rescue. 'Imagine if I hadn't? No bloodhound, no Navy. D'ye know, I had a strange feeling selling those pictures was the right thing to do. Who knows what forces were at work?' He tapped the side of his nose significantly.

Derry had a sudden, shockingly clear view of precisely the forces at work. She kept her voice carefully neutral.

'I was touched by the way you tackled those men on the pier. The way you jumped out of the van and marched straight towards them. Not even waiting for Bruce.'

'Heat of the moment—think nothing of it. Anyone would do the same.' His expression was shifty. Derry knew that look of old. 'Don't you think that bird on the lawn reminds you of a—'

'I was so impressed,' insisted Derry. 'My father braving armed men like that. For me! I thought—the crazy fool, but what a hero. Mom thinks you're Superman and Batman rolled into one.'

Jacko's gaze took in the empty tables around, the chandelier, the third-rate landscapes on the walls.

'You spotted Mom and the detective following you onto the pier!'

Jacko made a squeaking sound through his teeth. If he had worn a watch he might have consulted its face and remarked how time was marching on. But Derry had no intention of leaving open even the narrowest of escape routes.

'You were running from Mom!'

The door of the dining room opened. 'Mind if I join you?' said Fitz.

'Dear boy!' said Jacko, rising with the most expansive of gestures as if he had waited all morning for the chance to welcome Fitz to his table.

Fitz wouldn't stay. He only wanted to ask if they were alright for transport back to wherever they wanted to go. Jacko insisted all was organised. He meant to stay to see to his ailing car. Vanessa was staying to keep him company. At that, Derry sighed and rolled her eyes. *Parents.*

'Perhaps I could run you back to Dublin?' said Fitz to Derry. 'If that suited?'

'Bella told me that . . . Janice was looking after her. Please thank her for that.'

'Of course. She's a good sort. In fact, I'm at a bit of a loose end; Janice is leaving tonight, due a spot of leave. Done a good job. Wants to get back to hubby and kids, and so forth.'

'Kids?' Derry hoped she sounded casual.

'Three, I believe.'

'Three is nice.'

'Quite. Not blessed that way myself. Hopeless bachelor, I'm afraid.' For the first time in Derry's memory, Fitz seemed at a loss.

'Uh, me too,' said Derry. 'Hopeless.'

'Perhaps I could take Madam Tulip to dinner somewhere?'

'She might like that. Can I come along?'

Fitz laughed. 'Delighted. But Madam Tulip will have to promise not to tell me my future. Prefer not to know, thanks very much.'

'Deal,' said Derry. 'She can eat cake.'

Fitz smiled. Derry smiled. Jacko looked on, benevolently smiling.

'Alright, splendid,' said Fitz. 'See you in half an hour?'

Derry agreed that half an hour would be fine. Fitz departed, giving Jacko the quick but correct bow normally associated with moustachioed cavalrymen.

Jacko nodded his acknowledgement. 'At least the English have manners,' he said. 'Not like our crowd of hooligans.'

Derry smiled. Was there anybody like Jacko?

'Dad.'

'Light of my eyes?'

'This . . . thing we have . . .' Derry didn't need to explain what the *thing* was. 'What use is it? It didn't stop bad stuff happening. So what's it *for*?'

'Does it have to be *for* anything at all?' asked Jacko, gently. 'Maybe it just *is*.'

'I don't want it any more,' said Derry.

Jacko waited.

'It frightens me, and it's no help. If it helped, maybe I'd feel differently.'

Jacko carefully considered Derry's words. 'And what makes you think it's optional? What makes you think it's a gift you can refuse?' A fleeting shadow flickered across his face. 'And if you fight it . . . I don't have to tell you, do I?' He left it there. No need to explain the danger of resisting a power so elemental, so mysterious—not just to the person gifted but a mystery to the doctors, the priests, the psychiatrists. How could you fight such a force and not lose your mind?

'So it's not a gift. It's a curse,' said Derry. She had never felt so hopeless in her life, as though she had been told she had a terrible illness for which there could be no cure.

'Let me ask you a question,' said Jacko. 'Do you believe in everything you see—all that's out there in the world, everything in front of your eyes? Do you believe it's all there is?' He opened his arms wide, taking in the table, the room, the garden, the hotel and the entire universe.

Derry shook her head. No. Of course not. How could she, when she saw the things she saw?

'And would you wish to live without that knowledge? The knowledge that there's more?' Jacko spoke so quietly Derry had to lean towards him, straining to hear.

'No. Of course not.' The answer had come straight away, no need to think at all.

'And how many people in this world know what you know, absolutely for certain, objectively, no faith required?' Jacko paused to let his meaning sink in. 'That's the gift. That's the gift that changes everything.'

Derry couldn't find words. She nodded dumbly. Tears came to her eyes.

'And for the privilege,' said Jacko, smiling, 'there's a price, that's all. You need to pay back. Up to you to work out how.'

Derry kissed her father on the forehead. 'I'll remember,' she said. 'Promise.'

The dining-room door opened. Fitz stuck his head around.

'Ready, old thing?'